Winter Downs

Jan Edwards is a Sussex-born writer of Celtic parentage, now living in the West Midlands. Her short fiction can be found in crime, horror and fantasy anthologies in UK, US and European anthologies – close to fifty stories in print – including *The Mammoth Book of Dracula; The Mammoth Book of Moriarty; Terror Tales of the Ocean* and the *MX New Sherlock Holmes Collections* volumes five and six.  She has also edited anthologies for The Alchemy Press and Fox Spirit Press. Jan has also written a script for a *Dr Who* spinoff for Reel Time Pictures.

As author

Sussex Tales (Penkhull Press, 2014)

Leinster Gardens and Other Subtleties (The Alchemy Press, 2015)

Fables and Fabrications (Penkhull Press, 2016)

As editor

The Alchemy Press Book of Ancient Wonders
(The Alchemy Press, 2012)

The Alchemy Press Book of Urban Mythic (The Alchemy Press, 2013)

The Alchemy Press Book of Urban Mythic 2
(The Alchemy Press, 2014)

Wicked Women (Fox Spirit Press, 2014)

For more information visit:
http://janedwardsblog.wordpress.com/

Winter Downs

Jan Edwards

To Andrecke
Happy Reregading!
Jan Edwards

PENKHULL PRESS

Published June 2017 by the Penkhull Press
by arrangement with the author.

FIRST EDITION

ISBN 978-0-9930008-6-7

Published by Penkhull Press
Staffordshire, UK
www.penkhullpress.co.uk
Email: penkhullpress@gmail.com

Acknowledgements

Writing is a lonely process but few of us work alone and I have a long list of folks to whom I owe thanks for their help in the writing of *Winter Downs*. The list, as I have said, is a long one but a few names deserve mentioning in despatches. Firstly and always my undying thanks to Peter Coleborn who nursed the process from inception to final edit with patience and wisdom; to Misha Herwin for the Trentham cafe brain–storming sessions and editorial comment; to Jem Shaw and Mike Chinn for technical expertise (World War Two guns, airplanes and assorted details); to long time friend, best critic and author Debbie Bennett for plotting tips and beta-reading; to crime writers Paul Finch and Rachel Amphlett for their advice and inspiration; to the staff at the Old Police Cells Museum in Brighton for their time and patience; and lastly to the Renegade Writers for their rigorous Wednesday night critiquing.

❧ONE❧

The first gunshot flushed a clamour of rooks into a yellowish sky to circle their tribal elms. Rose Courtney glanced at Daphne and wondered if she even noticed them. Since George's funeral it was so difficult to know whether her younger sibling was woolgathering or had sunk so deep into mourning she simply failed to acknowledge her surroundings.

Understandable, Rose thought, *but it's still frustrating.* She had intended this hack across the Downs to lift the spirits. It would be Rose and Daphne – or Bunch and Dodo as their family knew them – riding out just like old times. Except that it was anything but the old times, and even Bunch was beginning to concede that, on this occasion, horse riding might not provide the answer. She tucked rogue strands of dark hair beneath her hat, secured her plaid scarf, and thought how tempting it would be to return home. The sky had grown heavier in the half hour they had been out and fresh snow was beginning to fall in earnest.

The second blast was louder and deeper than the first, scattering rooks and pigeons in a fresh flurry, setting Dodo's horse into a fidget. Bunch waited without comment for her sister to bring the animal under control.

'Pigeons.' Dodo looked upwards, allowing snowflakes to flutter across her cheeks. 'Georgie loved them. Cook bakes them with pears and a little port.'

It was the first time Bunch had heard Dodo mention her husband without prompting, and without tears, since the funeral. *That's a good sign, surely?* 'They don't have a lot of meat on them,' she said aloud. 'Hardly worth the cartridge.' She slapped her Fell pony's neck, muttering, 'Easy Perry, steady lad,' though her mount had barely twitched so much as an ear. Her sister's mare sidled nervously again so that its hooves slithered on the snow-covered slope. 'Everything all right, Dodo?'

'The old girl's a bit fresh from the box but I won't let her get her head.' Dodo backed her horse a few paces to prove control. 'See? All tickety-boo.' A seedling smile touched her face as she adjusted immaculate gloves and cuffs.

Trust Dodo, Bunch thought. *Middle of a windblown Sussex hillside and she still thinks it's a fashion parade.* Her own passions had been fixated on horses since she could first reach a stirrup which, their mother maintained, was why her eldest daughter had descended into old maid-dom at the ripe age of thirty-two. Bunch had always considered her habit of speaking her mind had far more to do with it. 'You're looking chilled, old thing. Want to go back?'

'No, I'm happy to carry on.' Dodo resettled her tweed fedora over silk headscarf and waved toward the trees. 'Let's cut through Hascombe Wood. We'll be out of the wind.'

'Absolutely. After you.' Bunch allowed Dodo to take the lead and used the moment to stand in her stirrups to ease damaged joints. A few months on from the accident in France she still ached. She maintained that riding out every day would see it heal itself, and that Dodo would be fine if she would only follow suit. As this was Dodo's first real show of animation since George's death, Bunch was reluctant to squash that tiny spark by heading home.

'Heel, Roger. Come here, damn you!' She put two fingers in her mouth and whistled up her yellow Labrador. Roger snapped at the patch of snow as he ran, mouth wide in a canine grin, and in no special hurry to obey despite her cussing. He was getting on in years but allowing him to become victim to the pet culls of the previous year had been unthinkable for her boy.

A southerly gust, straight off the Channel, sliced across Bunch's forehead. She pulled her hat down and scarf up to lessen the expanse of skin open to the elements. 'Best keep moving,' she mumbled, 'before we freeze to death.'

They followed the wood's perimeter to the bridle path that cut through its centre. Hascombe Wood now covered around fifteen acres, a mere scrap of the ancient forest that had once carpeted both the Sussex Weald and the Downs in a single swathe of green.

The rooks had circled back to their roost and were calling to each other in more conversational tones, and somewhere in a nearby field the estate's David Brown tractor was being pushed to its limits; they were the only sounds to be heard as the women entered the wood.

They rode in near silence until they reached the first large clearing where several woodland giants had been felled and stacked to one side of the glade. Bunch pulled off her tweed hat and ruffled her wool-itched scalp. With her ears uncovered, the pitter-patter of gritty snow in the trees, the odd creak of branches, and the steady clumping of hooves on centuries of leaf litter were clearly audible. She breathed in the scents of sheer cold mixed with the rich tang of the old leaves stirred up beneath hoof. A peaceful moment until the dog cut across the stillness with a frantic barking.

'Roger, do shut up,' Bunch shouted. 'Be quiet!' The Labrador ceased his yammering but continued with something closer to a howl. His tail and hackles were up as he harried a stand of sweet chestnut that sprouted at drunken angles to each other. Bunch slid from the saddle and walked to the trees but stopped just short of them as she glimpsed a motionless figure seated between the trunks.

'Hey, you there.' Bunch edged forward. There had been many displaced people passing through in recent months, people who might take refuge in the wood, but it took a strange sort of person who did not to react to Roger's noise. 'Hello? Are you all right? Are you … oh, good heavens.' She caught hold of Roger's collar and tugged him into a sit as she realised what she was seeing. 'Dear God,' she muttered.

A man was slumped in the bowl of a split tree. His hands hung loosely along thighs, legs stretched out before him. His head lolled forward obscuring what was left of its features. The rear of his skull had been blown away and smears of dark pinkish brain matter had spattered across the bark immediately behind, dotted with shards of bone. Bunch flexed her fingers against the blood rush tingling through them and released one deep breath before taking another, and edged forward for a closer look. Though she could not see his face she knew this was not the corpse of someone unknown. This body had a name, and she would have known him anywhere. *Calm,* she told herself, *be calm.*

Bunch recognised the Westley Richards near the dead man's

feet and it left little doubt as to what had caused the massive damage to his skull. She clapped a hand across her mouth to stop her stomach adding more colour to the scene. She had seen a few corpses during her brief stint driving BEF staff cars in France. Many of the corpses had been far more mutilated than this one. Beside, they had been different. They had lacked identity but this corpse had a face and a name that Bunch had known all of her life. This body had not been slaughtered by a mindless steel capsule packed with explosives, dropped from far above. This corpse had come to be through a deliberate and very personal act of violence. This was Jonathan Frampton.

She wiped at her eyes and shuddered out another draconic steaming into the cold air. *Pull yourself together. Never waver. That's the Courtney way.*

'Oh Jonny,' she whispered, 'what in hell has been going on here?' Bracing herself for the routine she had last practised with the First Aid Nursing Yeomanry, Bunch crouched to feel beneath his collar for the carotid artery though she knew finding a pulse would be highly unlikely. His flesh was cold in the refrigerating winter wind and unyielding to her touch, but not yet fully stiffened in rigor. The red splattering all around was dulling to brown, telling her that the blood had ceased flowing several hours ago. *Long before those shots we'd heard just moments ago.*

'Bunch?' Dodo was dismounting and looping the reins of both horses over a fallen tree. 'What's going on?'

Bunch held her left hand, palm out, toward her sister as she pulled the excited dog away from the corpse with the other. 'Stay there, Dodo. Please. Just stay there.'

'What is it? Oh dear, is he dead?'

'Yes, he is.'

'Is it ... is it someone we know?' Dodo craned her neck to see around Bunch, taking another step forward.

'You don't need to see, truly. It's Jonny. Jonathan Frampton.'

'No, it can't be. Jonny's away up north for another month or more. He told me so himself.'

'It is him. Absolutely. No question.'

Dodo stared at the body, her features asserting the quiet control they had both been raised to practise. The trembling in her hands that she held close to her face was evidence to the contrary.

Best get her as far away from this as quickly as possible. Bunch slipped her hand beneath her sister's elbow and guided her back to the horses. 'There may be evidence here so we shouldn't trample around too much. Look Dodo, why don't you ride on home and telephone for PC Botting? I'll wait here. Somebody should.'

'Are you certain?'

'I am. Absolutely. Take Roger with you. He'll only be a bloody nuisance here.' She gave Dodo a boost into the saddle and watched her ride out of sight, with only a few words but a few dozen misgivings.

Perry nodded vigorously, snickering after his stable mate. Bunch worried that he would chill standing in the flow of the wind, and led him around to the far side of the log stack where there was some respite. She adjusted his quarter sheet to cover as much of his rump as possible and went to sit on the end of the log pile where she could watch over the body.

The trees towered around her; they felt not unlike a cathedral with the building's whispered sibilance echoed by the surrounding woodland. *Keeping vigil,* she thought and shivered, not entirely through the chill. She missed Roger's comforting presence. *Dodo will need it more though, silly old sausage.* She scrabbled through her inside pocket for the hip-flask and raised it toward the corpse. 'God speed,' she called, and took a small mouthful, swilling it around her gums and swallowing, feeling the warmth welling into her throat. She rattled the container and pulled a face. It was half empty and there was a good hour to wait before anyone came to help. *It's a long time cold.*

Bunch took another quick swig and swapped the flask for a cigarette case, taking her time in tapping the white cylinder on the silvered lid, glancing around the clearing, her gaze skating over the body. She struck a match, cupping her long hands to protect the flame, and once sure the tobacco glowed red leaned her head back to send the first lungful of smoke upwards into the falling snow. It was a ritual calming, a gathering of wits that came from habit. Even alone she would not willingly permit emotion to surface.

The horse muttered at the waft of sulphurous match and

tobacco smoke, which made her smile. 'Yes, Perry, I know. All the bloody vices. You're starting to sound like Mother.' She flicked the spent matchstick in his general direction and drew again on the tailor-made cigarette, expelling blue-grey mist at the trees. *There are matters that need to be addressed and I shall address them like a Courtney – once I've gathered a few wits about me.*

Bunch waited and smoked and gazed across the space between her and the lifeless body of her old friend. She had a clear view of Jonny's legs and torso but his face was obscured, and she was glad of that. She did not relish staring at what remained of it for however long it took Stan Botting to arrive.

Her attention began to wander over the surrounding terrain. Tracks in the snow were masked by dark slices of leaf mould, and she amused herself by guessing the cause of each line and heap. Her own boot prints were clearly discernible and Roger was the likely culprit for most of the rest. Other dips and furrows, however, had been made indistinct by fresh snow so that none could be read with any certainty. *They could have been made by deer or sheep – or by Jonny.*

She lit another cigarette and as she scuffed the cold match beneath her boot a metallic glint caught her attention. Bunch bent to retrieve a spent .22 cartridge and held it up at eye level. Its strong cordite odour cut through the tobacco smoke. This was a fresh firing, no question in her mind. The Westley Richards lying at Jonny's feet certainly posed another query.

There's every chance the .22 has been ejected from some poacher's rifle. The Jenner brothers are in these woods several times a week, she thought. *Yet, it was in the surface snow. It can't have been here much longer than poor Jonny has.*

She slipped the cartridge into her pocket and wandered across to stare at Jonny's remains. *He might be wearing his boots and a good wool suit but where's his coat and scarf? And gloves? Jonny is – was – a chilly morsel despite all those years in drafty farm houses and freezing school dorms.* 'What were you doing out here, dressed this way?' she said aloud.

Bunch rubbed at her arms, chilled now by more than the iced wind. 'I do not believe you would kill yourself. I don't believe it. I won't believe it.' Crouching down she stared long into his bloodied face. *What were you thinking, my darling boy? This is not who you are. You were in the choir. You talked about taking the cloth. You'd never kill yourself. So what is this about?* 'Oh, damn it all to hell. It makes no sense.'

She wheeled back to her log seat, scrubbing out the cigarette against the bark before lighting another within a minute. She knew what this looked like, what other people would see, yet she could not, would not, believe that Jonathan Frampton would take his own life. The image of his placing the Westley's barrel beneath his chin and pulling the trigger denied all he had ever believed in. What or who had brought her old friend to this secluded spot, surely it was not to kill himself. Of that she was utterly convinced.

~ ~ ~

Noises coming from beyond the trees drew Bunch to her feet and she took out the flask for one final nip. As she returned the empty container to her pocket her fingers brushed against the brass cartridge. She drew it out and turned it end over end just a few inches from her eyes, mesmerised by its brilliance.

'Whatever else happens, Jonny,' she murmured, 'I shall get to the truth.'

'Miss Rose.' PC Stan Botting scrunched along the woodland path with a steady tread that spoke of many nights on the beat. He was a tall man of even proportions, his most defining features being a neatly trimmed moustache and serious brown eyes, which took in the scene with a professional calm. 'This is a sorry thing, Miss Courtney.' He saluted Bunch gravely. 'Not what you might expect.'

'It certainly is not.' She watched him pick his way over to the corpse and go through the same pointless ritual of confirming death. 'Where is my sister?'

'Miss Daphne – beg pardon – Mrs Tinsley stayed at Perringham House, I imagine.' He picked up the shotgun, out of the deepening snow, and trudged back to her. 'A sorry day, indeed. He's dead of course. No question. And from the state of him it's the worst kind of passing.'

'What could possibly be worse than being killed?'

'Suicide, Miss. From what I can see here it's the most logical explanation. He took his own life. Sad thing for a young man to do.'

It was all Bunch could do not to shout at him. Botting was not a stupid man and this stating of the seemingly obvious was beneath him. 'Jonny would never do that,' she muttered.

'There's folks do it every week of the year. Always a tragedy,' Botting continued. 'We'll need the Coroner to confirm it, of course, but there's little doubt in my mind.'

'Is the Coroner coming now?'

'Eventually. But you don't need to stand around waitin' for him, Miss. No need for you to catch your death. You pop along home now.' He gestured at the path. 'Someone's coming now, so you cut along and I'll be down the house for your statement later.'

'No, I'll wait,' she said.

'If you're sure now?'

'I'm certain.' She had barely sat back on her tree trunk before Major Barty Tinsley stumbled into view, puffing steam far harder than Botting had with the exertion of the climb.

'Rose, good to see you. Or it would be if it wasn't in such sad circumstances.' Dodo's father-in-law swept off his European-styled fur hat and used it to beat snow from his coat before cramming it back on his balding head. Barty was a big boned man, shorter then Botting by half a head, yet muscular enough to fill any doorway. He went to examine the scene at closer quarters and rose within moments, shaking his head emphatically. 'Very sad. Suicide quite obviously. Is there a note?'

'I've looked,' Bunch replied, 'but nothing, so far as I can see.'

'That would be unusual. In my experience people are usually compelled to leave some final words. Perhaps it was blown away. Or he left it at the farm.' Tinsley looked around the clearing with obvious disgust. 'It hardly matters. The circumstances are clear enough.'

'I am not so sure about that,' said Bunch. 'Besides, it's not for you or me to say. It's up to the Coroner. What brings you here, in any case, Barty?'

'I was at lunch with Lewis when Botting called. I thought I should offer to assist.'

I bet you did, she thought. *Never miss a chance to play at Army with your bloody LDV.* 'Where is Doctor Lewis?' She looked past him. 'He must be here to pronounce death before the Coroner arrives, one would think.'

'He hoped to be along with the stretcher party but there was an emergency call. He thought the needs of the living were more urgent.'

'Of course. Anyway, the Coroner will be here soon.'

'Unlikely before the morning,' said Tinsley. 'I heard that snow has set in deeper along the coast road and if we have another fall tonight then he will be delayed further still. I am here as his proxy, in my official capacity as a magistrate, of course.' Tinsley raised his chin, challenging Bunch to disagree. 'Daphne told Botting it looked like suicide,' he added. 'She would appear to have been correct.' He nodded agreement with his own judgement. 'Jonathan was involved in some rather delicate war work, from what I gather. Pressure was too much for him, perhaps?' He glanced at Bunch and clamped his lips together in a white line. 'Saul Frampton told me the boy failed his RAF medical. Some chaps are just not up to the mark.'

There was an implication that Jonathan had somehow deliberately evaded service and it stung. Bunch had always recognised Jonny as a gentle man and it angered her that men like Tinsley mistook that for weakness. 'I don't think he did it. Jonny wasn't the sort. I can't quite see what's what as yet but something very wrong occurred up here.'

'Wrong? Of course there is something wrong. A young man takes his own life? There's nothing right in tha—' He shook his head. 'Not the time or place.'

'I concur, Barty. The Coroner will make a decision at the inquest, of course. I don't know what procedure is but shouldn't we make sure he views the scene intact?'

'There were two military incidents out at sea and the Coroner has a mortuary filled to the gunwales as a result. He can't get along before tomorrow, and if we are in for a heavy snow tonight we cannot leave the body where it is. It simply is not practical, especially when the circumstances are so clear. You get along home before the snow gets any worse, Rose. Leave all this to us. No need to bother your head about it in the least bit.'

Bunch breathed harshly through her nose, fighting her impulse to be unspeakably rude. *How dare he? The pompous arrogant old dinosaur.* The shock of finding her old friend dead in such a ghastly fashion was painful enough. She had been closer to Jonny than almost anyone she knew; she had known him in every sense possible. They had grown from childhood friends into fumbling lovers, exploring the secrets of each other's bodies in mutual wonder. To her lasting regret the affair had foundered though they had remained the best of friends. Being so comprehensively patronised by Barty Tinsley regarding somebody he barely knew, and who was so close to herself, was positively breath taking. She glanced at Botting, who looked away. Plainly he was not going to argue with the magistrate on her behalf. 'I think we should wait for Doctor Lewis to give us the benefit of his experience. We two can agree to differ another time.' She felt pleased at keeping so remarkably collected. *Mother would be proud.*

Tinsley regarded her coldly. 'What happened here is a terrible shame and totally obvious to everyone – except you, it seems. I realise you mean well, Rose, but you mustn't get yourself involved. It's not the right sort of thing for a young lady.'

'Jonathan was Georgie's best pal. They were at Harrow together, and Balliol. It can only help Dodo if we can say Jonny didn't do such an awful thing, surely?' She smiled, dropping her chin to come as close as possible to looking up at someone shorter than herself. She was not a flatterer or a flirt by nature but it seemed to work on Tinsley well enough.

'If speaking with Lewis will put your mind at rest then by all means,' he said. 'I've seen this sort of thing on the Bench, you know.' He shook his head. 'One has to feel sorry for the boy. He found himself unable to carry on with the responsibilities he had been given and shot himself. Some people are simply not cut out for times like these.'

'Times like what, exactly?' said Bunch.

'War, obviously.'

'Jonathan knew as much about war as any of us. Probably more. He was joining some new special Whitehall department,' she said.

'Look at him. Look at the shotgun,' Tinsley said. 'Stop digging around in things that don't concern you, Rose Courtney. Or must I speak to your father about it? What young Frampton was working on is not for discussion. Careless tongues, my dear. There's quite enough for you to worry about without making more.'

'I doubt we've got a Jerry spy hiding in the leaf mould. Oh, and I found this.' She scrabbled in her pocket and held out the cartridge casing. 'It was fired today. You can still smell it.'

'A .22 wouldn't make so much mess,' Tinsley said, 'not even at point blank. That, however, would be more than capable.' He pointed to the shotgun.

'The Major is right, Miss Courtney.' Botting hefted the Westley and frowned at her. 'It's not your place to interfere with the process of law. You cut along, Miss. You've had a shock.'

Bunch glanced down at Botting's other hand clamping her elbow and gently urging her toward the horse. She shook his hand free. She was cold and shocked, of course, but perfectly lucid and starting to realise she was getting nowhere. Tinsley was convinced he was right and Botting would agree out of deference to the magistrate, and because he had little choice.

She mounted Perry in silence, compliant only because she was outnumbered. She had no intention of letting it drop. Jonathan Frampton had more joie de vivre than anyone she knew. *You will not be remembered for blowing out your own brains, Jonny. I swear by all we held dear that I shall prove it.*

❧TWO❧

Bunch prodded at the aromatic fish on her plate feeling mildly annoyed at its mass of tiny bones. She had never like kippers very much but, with bacon on ration and Cook in a state over moving her domain to the Dower House, the usual breakfast sideboard was smaller than usual. Bunch focussed on that break in custom as the source of her own foul mood. It was easier to rail against small things than think about the steady and inexorable implosion of her world.

The very thought of Perringham House being stuffed to its eaves with strangers was anathema to her. The list of queries and demands made by the newcomers was already long and all but impossible to solve. Plumbing appeared to be a particular obsession, and one that she was certain would never be resolved in an ancient pile built piecemeal from the days of Henry Tudor to those of Queen Victoria. Despite her father's presence, Perringham had begun to feel like an alien space.

Her mother Theodora had executed a strategic withdrawal to the family's London house a week before, saying, 'You are always so good at dealing with these things, Rose darling. You always manage so wonderfully well and besides, a girl your age should be managing her own house by now.' The dig at her spinsterhood was something Bunch refused to be drawn on.

Her father, seated across the table from her, was the consummate diplomat. He had barely flicked an eyelash through that exchange, which Bunch had found infuriating since the handing over of Perringham was his doing in the first place.

A clatter of boots out in the corridor followed by a series of thumps brought her back to the present. 'I assume these people will pay for breakages,' she said. 'I saw a pair of cavemen in fatigues dropping a filing cabinet on the Minton floor. I know it's below stairs but Mummy will have a fit. Really, Daddy, I wish you had told us more about what to expect.'

'We all have to make sacrifices, Rose. I hope I've brought you up better than to balk at the first hurdle.'

Bunch glowered, feeling eleven years old once more when she argued against her first pony being given to Dodo, despite her having outgrown the Shetland by several inches. The pony had been important: it had been passed down to her and was a reminder of two older siblings, victims of the influenza pandemic in 1919. She had lost that battle and knew she was losing this one. The Honourable Edward Courtney was a skilled diplomat and hardened to blandishments of almost every kind, one of the few in the world impervious to her will.

'Can't we turn Perringham into a convalescence home? Granny did that in the last war.' She heard the child in her voice and sighed. 'You and Mummy are off to Singapore. Dodo is over at Banyards and I have to uproot to Granny's. It simply isn't fair. The Howards are going to stay on at Arundel Castle. I don't see why we need to move out.'

Courtney folded his paper and regarded her wearily. 'Please don't be tiresome, Rose. The Howards have an entire castle to share out and a completely different agreement for all their estates. No, my darling girl, you will move to the Dower House. At least then you shall have my mother to back you up. If she isn't a battalion all on her own I don't know who is.' He checked his watch and stood abruptly. 'Speaking of which, I must go and talk to that Colonel Kravitz chappie or he will think me unspeakably ill-mannered.' He raised a warning finger to her. 'Treat him and his people with respect. Is that clear?'

'I'm already running the estate single-handed while you are away. This bloody invasion of the house will make that ten times harder!'

'My dear child.' Courtney sighed. 'I am sorry. Sorry for landing this on you and sorry I can't be here to oversee it all. Finding a suitable base for Kravitz's project was necessary for the war effort. Once they are set up it will be fine. They will be hand-picked personnel, I can assure you. Breakages should be at a minimum once everything is stowed away.'

'Yes, Daddy.'

He stared at her for a moment and then shook his head. Her

easy capitulation plainly roused his suspicion. 'Behave yourself, Rose Courtney. With luck your mother and I shall be away for only a few months. When we return we shall all be jammed into the Dower together and then you really will have something to complain about.'

'Mummy won't slum it. Unless the town house takes a direct hit she'll dig in there for the duration.' Bunch shrugged 'We all know how she is.' She sighed. 'I would much rather stay here at Perringham.'

'Impossible,' he replied. 'This is an important project so you will watch from a distance, without fuss, and ask no questions. If you want something to occupy that restless spirit of yours, keep an eye on Dodo. She's a grown woman but young Frampton's demise coming so soon after George appears to have shaken her up. She will need you.' He grasped her shoulders and gave her a shake of encouragement. 'I have things to do so I shall see you for dinner.'

He strode away, leaving Bunch to her kipper for another ten minutes before she finally gave up on it. Dodo seemed to be sleeping the morning away and there was much work to be done. Bunch retreated to the estate office to continue sorting heaps of box files to be crated for transfer to the Dower House. Since she had volunteered to coordinate local Land Army placements the paperwork was always waiting, and a cold snowy day was the best time to do it.

Two deaths in almost as many months had unsettled her every bit as it had her sister. It irked her that her father didn't see that. She had been raised to hide her emotions and had learned the lesson rather well. George's death had been an act of war, which might be senseless but was understandable, perhaps even to be expected. Jonathan's death was vastly different and completely bewildering.

She lifted a stack of dusty boxes from a top shelf and peered inside the first one to cast a quick glance over a clutter of old rosettes from local agricultural shows and gymkhanas. 'Keep,' she muttered, replacing the lid and opening the next to reveal programmes and photographs neatly tied together. 'Definitely keep.' She took out the top bundle, slipping off the battered ribbon and leafing through them. More pictures of horses and cattle and sheep, with beaming estate staff standing beside them holding cups and shields of various sizes.

A slightly faded image of Jonny and herself in the owner's enclosure at the Brighton races made her pause. Their gamine younger selves smiled from the black and white image. He was stylish, as always, in a well-cut suit. She was gauche, her dress marking the years that had passed since the photograph had been taken, as changing women's fashion invariably did. She flipped it over and checked the date. 1928. *Has it really been twelve years? We weren't much more than bloody children.*

Bunch turned it back. Jonny was looking straight at the lens, his swagger cane resting on his shoulder. An unlit cigarette was clamped between lips curved in a disarming grin. She was clinging to his elbow in the throes of helpless laughter. She could not remember who had taken the snapshot; one of the usual crowd circulating for the Season, she supposed. Memories of the day itself came to her quite vividly. She and Jonny had paired up in self-defence, seeking refuge from the incessant hunting out of mates expected by family and friends. Their attachment had not been wholly fabricated; romance had budded though ultimately failed to bloom, and now never would.

A crash of something large and metallic being dropped in the yard broke her reverie. It sounded like gunfire, and the image of Jonny as she had last seen him crowded out all memory of a summer's day at the races. She was not sure if she were entitled to grieve when she was not blood kin.

Suicide. The word alone chilled her. Her every instinct fought against it. Once again the thought came to her that George's death was wrong because war was wrong, yet Jonathan's was wrong in every different manner possible; and she simply did not believe the conclusions that others had drawn.

She tossed the picture down and picked up the .22 cartridge from the pen tray, examining every scratch and dink, wondering what gun had fired it and why it was there, so close to the body of her friend. How she wished she had rammed it under Tinsley's nose with more conviction. She had a good idea he would not have listened but at least she would have felt she had tried.

Bunch swapped cartridge for pencil and pretended to mark up some papers. Try as she might, she could not prevent her mind from dwelling on recent events. It was obvious to her why the simple conclusions had been reached. The damage to Jonathan was plainly the result of a shotgun blast and there was a shotgun at the scene; ergo the shotgun had become the focus. It was a neat bundle of evidence, on the surface. *Yet that cartridge had so obviously been freshly fired. And I found it lying on top of the snow. That has to mean something. Doesn't it?*

Bunch frowned at the pencil thrumming on the blotting pad, forgetting for a moment that it was her right hand guiding its frenetic tap-tap-tapping. She threw the pencil into the ever-accommodating pen tray. If the weather had been good she'd have gone for a ride to tamp down her rising frustration. It wasn't just the prospect of a marauding tide of the military that had her distracted but a different frustration altogether.

Dodo had become distraught after her return to Perringham House. On Doctor Lewis's advice, Edward Courtney had slipped one of Theodora's sleeping powders into Dodo's hot drink and she had yet to wake, something Bunch found perversely annoying. She needed to talk over Jonathan's passing and Dodo was the only person in the house who would begin to understand.

Bunch stared at the discarded photo until her vision blurred. She and Jonny had shared the bond of first sex. *Had people known about it we would have been all but married in most eyes.* She shook her head and smiled. She had known far more expert lovers since then but she and Jonny would always share that tie.

He could not have become so desperately unhappy and not confided in her. Bunch was positive of that. The more she considered it the more she knew with every sinew that he had not taken his own life. She thought back to the injury Jonathan had sustained the previous summer and tried to recall what had been said at the time. In retrospect, she realised it had preceded a sustained war of attrition between the Frampton men. Yet, because father and son had been at daggers drawn since Jonny had hit puberty, there had seemed nothing new or unusual in their arguing.

The pencil had somehow crept back into her hand and continued its relentless syncopation in time with the dance tunes that drifted from elsewhere in the house. She slammed the pencil down, exasperated, just as a light rap on the door sounded a bare second before it opened.

'Miss Rose? There's a policeman waiting to speak with you.'

She smiled at her housekeeper, one of the few indoor staff remaining at the house. 'Oh, Knapp, I'm too tied up with paperwork to bother with PC bloody Botting right now. Isn't Daddy around to speak with him?'

'No, Miss, Mr Courtney went across to the farm.'

'Oh, all right. Did you take Dodo her lunch tray?'

'Yes, Miss, I took it in myself. She was still asleep and her breakfast tray was untouched. Should I wake her?'

'Sleep is probably the best thing for her. She's been running on scotch mist these past few weeks.'

'As you wish, Miss.' Knapp bustled around the desk tidying and straightening before gathering up the selection of cups and glasses Bunch had managed to acquire since breakfast. 'Chief Inspector Wright is waiting to see you.'

'Chief Inspector?'

'Yes, Miss. I did inform him you were busy but he's quite insistent. Should I show him through here or will you come into the house?'

Bunch looked around the tiny cluttered room with its single Spartan guest chair and grinned. 'Here will do. Morning room's too bare now for interviews.'

Knapp allowed a small frown to crease her brow. 'Yes, Miss, I'll show him straight in.'

'You do that, Knapp. Then go and see where that bloody music is coming from. I can't hear myself think.'

'Another car full of people arrived this morning. French this time, I think. Three men and a woman.' The housekeeper sniffed obvious disapproval. 'They have put a very large phonograph down in the ballroom.'

'Then take it off them.'

'I shall try.' She withdrew, returning a few minutes later to announce, 'Chief Inspector William Wright, Miss.'

The Chief Inspector took in everything around him in a few seconds before turning a quiet gaze on Bunch.

She assessed him every bit as carefully and decided he was not a spectacular specimen, so far as they went. He possessed that round-shouldered stoop of the very tall trying hard not to intimidate. *Which,* Bunch thought, *could never be easy in his chosen profession.* He had brown hair, grey-eyes, strong features, and a slim build bordering on gaunt. Bunch assumed he was somewhere around forty, and a civilian. *He probably served in the last lot. Perhaps he failed his medical. He does not look the kind of man to play for pity. Far too cocksure of himself.* She looked at him for a few moments and realised she was conducting a rapid tally of plusses and minuses, something she supposed most people did for any man out of uniform. It shocked her to imagine she was capable of being so judgemental on such slight evidence.

Roger rose from the depths of shadow beneath her chair to rumble at him like a yellow thunder cloud of hair. Bunch laid a hand on the dog's neck and he lay to attention.

'How do you do, Miss Courtney. I'm Chief Inspector Wright. Sussex Constabulary.' He turned to her with hand outstretched, a professional smile on his smooth features as he presented his warrant card. 'You're alone?' He took a notebook from his inside pocket and flipped it open. 'I was also expecting a Mrs Daphne Tinsley.'

'Good afternoon to you,' Bunch drawled. 'Chief Inspector is it? How frightfully grand. I was expecting PC Botting to take my statement, so we are both at a disadvantage.' She watched him carefully for any reaction and was surprised and impressed to see very little showing on the surface. 'You will have to make do with me, I'm afraid. My sister is sleeping off the sedative our doctor prescribed for her. She is terribly upset by what has happened. Thank you, Knapp. Perhaps some tea?'

She waited until Knapp had gone before continuing. Unlike many, Bunch never forgot that servants, very much like those walls of the propaganda posters, really did have ears. 'My sister lost her husband very recently and all of this has upset her greatly.' She tweaked a polite smile and leaned forward to adjust a pile of books on the edge of her desk to cover the possibility of a break in her own voice. 'I've no doubt Mr Frampton has told you that my brother-in-law, George Tinsley, and his son were old friends?'

Wright inclined his head. 'He did and I quite understand how distressing this must be for Mrs Tinsley, but time is pressing. Perhaps if you could send someone to fetch her?'

'I could but I'm not inclined to do so, however.'

'Miss Courtney, I really—'

Bunch held up both forefingers for hush. 'I *could* send someone to wake her but I very much doubt she would make a great deal of sense. On account of that sleeping powder.' She gestured toward the cane chair on the other side of the desk. 'Do sit down Inspector. It is me that you need to speak with. Dodo did not get within twenty feet of the body before I sent her to fetch help.'

'Then we can leave her statement for another day.' He rubbed his eyes and let out a long breath. 'I need a few details and I'm sure you can supply those. I'm told the deceased was a particular friend of yours.'

Before she could answer, the revving of engines made both turn to the window. 'We are being invaded,' she said. 'The official term is requisitioned, which makes us sound like some damnable box of paper clips. I'm afraid quiet is out of the question.' Bunch waited for him to carry on. His accent was plainly rooted in public school though he tried to hide it. 'You sound like a Londoner,' she said.

'I've been seconded from Scotland Yard.' He smiled, lines of fatigue appearing around his eyes and mouth.

'Really? How curious. I should have thought London was the place to be.'

Wright shook his head abruptly, his jaw whitening. Bunch recognised that raw-nerve look. 'I've spent twenty years at The Yard.' He pulled a face. 'I'm not sure why I am telling you that.'

'Call it friendly interest,' she replied. 'We country folk love to know all there is to know and I am frightfully good at wheedling things out of people. Plus, we don't see many younger chaps these days with the call up.' She smiled, waiting for him to take the lure and divulge his status.

'Hardly young. I've been recalled. The constabularies have suffered a severe loss of seasoned officers.'

'Retirement? You can't be old enough.'

'It wasn't my choice,' he replied. Bunch waited for further detail and was miffed that none came. Wright only met her imperious questioning with guarded calm. From someone else she might have thought it insolent. Wright, she sensed, was above baiting her with such nonsense.

'Yet here you are, investigating murder,' she said. 'I can't tell you much more about this murder than I've already told Botting.'

'We are not currently treating this as murder. Mr Frampton's death has been logged as a *probable suicide*.'

The words hit her full in the senses, rocking her back into the chair. Tinsley had declared it suicide but she had been willing to dismiss him in favour of a more professional view, one that tallied with her own. 'Oh.' She gazed at him in shock for a count of two. 'Are you telling me there won't be any sort of investigation?' She looked Wright straight in the eye and tapped the cartridge on the desk top. 'That is a mistake, if you don't mind my saying so. I knew Jonathan Frampton rather well and I can assure you that he would not take his own life.'

Wright met her stare with a sadness that took her by surprise. 'There are no plans to open any further investigations but please do tell me what you found at the scene.'

'I think Jonny deserves that courtesy.'

'It's why I am here. Before you do make a statement, I should warn you that the Doctor's medical opinion matches that of my own officer and of one Major Tinsley, who I understand is the local magistrate. The powers that be must have decided to act in accordance with their judgement.'

'Jonathan Frampton would not shoot himself, whatever they might say.'

'Your opinion weighted against that of three professional men?' Wright raised a hand to quell her objections. 'Miss Courtney, your statement will go before the Coroner's Court and it's his judgement that matters in the end.'

'Who has all but ordered the case closed, it appears.'

Wright shifted in his seat. 'Technically. Except those orders come from a little higher up the chain.' He tapped the notebook. 'I should not tell you this perhaps, but anything that concerns your family also concerns the Commissioner, and Mr Frampton's War Office status boosted his case up to the same desk.' He shrugged. 'This visit is by way of a courtesy.'

'Sir Walter sent you?' Bunch quirked one brow in query.

'Not directly. It trickled a long way back down the chain before it was dropped on me.'

'Dear Uncle Walter.' A brief wave of affection washed away a little of the cold fire at her core. 'Comes of being a policeman for so many years, I suppose, but you would know all about that of course. I do apologise if the Courtney tribe has been making more work for you.'

'No trouble, I assure you Miss Courtney. I thought it best that both you and your sister were informed in person. The Coroner's Court will conduct the inquest in due course but suicide is the expected outcome.'

'That is all I can expect?' Bunch asked. 'A good man died in the most awful way and he doesn't warrant a few questions? I had assumed the police would give the matter some semblance of investigation, whatever Barty Tinsley might say.' She glowered at him, her breeding and manners holding back the full force of her anger. It had not occurred to her that a death, any death, could be signed away so easily. She would not allow it. Jonathan was not going to be sidelined. 'I beg to differ,' she said at last.

Wright gazed at her, a small crease of query marring his forehead. 'I do understand that you may be upset. What you should know is that war can drive the best of people to do things totally out of character. I saw it often in the trenches. You have my sympathy but unless we have evidence to the contrary the investigation is closed.'

'He—' She stopped, hearing a sharp edge creeping into her tone. 'Suicide went against everything Jonny stood for. In his eyes it would condemn his immortal soul.'

'He was a Catholic?'

'Anglican High Church. He'd been intending to take the cloth before war broke out.' She leaned forward. 'Jonathan Frampton valued his immortal soul. For that reason alone he wouldn't take his own life.'

'I would bow to your superior personal knowledge under normal circumstances. On this occasion, however, it is out of my hands.'

'Surely if someone was working on anything as top shelf as Jonathan appeared to be, it would be an automatic priority. One would think they would want to know more. I mean if he's been killed because of his work, it—'

'Orders from far higher up the chain decided this matter is not open for discussion. You of all people should recognise the implications of that. There will be a public hearing, which you may attend of course, although I wouldn't recommend it. They are depressing affairs even when you don't know the deceased.'

'Was he killed by some fifth columnist? Shouldn't we be told that much, at least?'

'The area would be swarming with troops if there was even a hint of that.' Wright smiled ruefully and shook his head. He gazed around him as he spoke and she could see him assessing the room just as she had assessed him.

Bunch felt her hackles twitching. Perringham House was not what it had once been. Shabbiness had crept in around the edges over the years; like so many estates, the slow decline had begun after the Great War and hastened during the Great Slump. She supposed it was one reason for her father's alacrity in leasing Perringham to the War Department.

How dare he, she thought, *how dare this bloody copper judge us? Judge me? How...*

'Now, your sister,' he was saying. 'I understand her registered address is Bantard.' He checked his little black book.

'My sister lives at Banyard Manor.'

'Banyard? Excellent. If you could fill in a few details about her. How was she known to the deceased?'

'She came to see Daddy before he left on official business. You do know he is a diplomatic attaché? Dodo's husband George was Jonny's best pal, before he was killed in action last November. His plane went down over the channel. They were not married for long, you see and... Chief Inspector, if you are closing the case does it matter? The statements, I mean.' She smiled a bland smile and wondered why she was babbling like an idiot.

'No, I don't suppose we will need to bother her. More important that she tells the Ministry of food if she changes her accommodation,' he replied. 'These new ration books, and all that.'

There was a tap at the door and he leaned back in the chair, which creaked ominously under him. The maid scurried in with a tray of tea, giving Wright a wide-eyed stare and an even wider berth, before she scuttled out again.

Bunch watched Wright watching Sheila and wondered if he knew the girl came from a long line of poachers. He appeared the kind that would make it his business to know. She suppressed her own amusement. 'Milk?' She did not wait for a reply, pouring two cups and passing one across to her guest inquisitor. 'No sugar, I'm afraid. I might be able to sponge some from the Canadians fitting out the house. They are far less affected by rationing, I've heard.' She smiled politely and did not mention that the shortage was due to the kitchen contents being transferred to the Dower House.

'Without is fine.' He took the cup and saucer, which looked like a doll's service in his big hands, and took a cautious sip. His eyes closed for a moment as he savoured the beverage. 'Heaven. I'm certain our canteen in Brighton dries the leaves and uses them for a half-dozen brews. I dread to think what they will do if rationing gets any worse.' He smiled amiably and waved the cup at her in salute. 'First of the day. Tea is such a simple pleasure and so easily spoiled.'

'Indeed. You say you are no longer at Scotland Yard?'

'No, Miss Courtney, not anymore.' He shrugged. 'Perhaps we should get on with the statement? I'm led to understand from Mr Frampton's father that it was not his first attempt. If that's true he was fortunate not to be prosecuted.'

Bunch drew her lips into a tight line, unsure of herself in that moment. She had never heard mention of a previous attempt, and if it were gossip in the village it was almost certain she would have. 'That's because he didn't do anything. Not then and not now.'

'You seem very certain.'

'Because I am.'

Wright jotted a few notes. 'Once we have a clear picture of the day's events we can get statements drawn up for your signature. Then you and your sister can put it all behind you. To confirm Botting's report, I understand you heard the shot?'

'Shots. Plural. We wouldn't say either one of those killed Jonny. And he could hardly have fire them both.'

'Possibly he fired once as a test. People do strange things under duress.'

'Only one barrel was fired. I saw the gun, and all that aside, in my opinion he had been dead for several hours before the shots that we heard in those woods.'

There was a hesitation, his pen poised like Damocles' sword, before it moved on. 'That is for the Coroner to decide. Let's stick to the facts at hand. You say you found the deceased a short while later with the weapon at his feet?'

Bunch stared. *Is he deaf?* she thought. 'That weapon may have been fired, I agree. I still maintain—'

'Mr Frampton was shot in the head at very close range by that gun. Until we have positive proof to the contrary we will have to assume that was the cause of death.'

'I—'

'Facts. You found the deceased a short while after hearing gunshots, with a weapon at his feet.'

'Correct.'

'And you saw nobody at or near the scene in all the time you were in the woodland?'

'The weather was pretty grim so no, not near the woods. We heard the two shots. There was also a tractor somewhere close by.'

'A tractor? Don't most farms have them now? Did you see something that should not have been there?' Bunch shook her head. 'Then unless you have anything else to offer I am afraid the evidence would seem to bear out the suicide theory.'

'I disagree. Vehemently. Jonny had been dead for some while before we got there.' She glared at him, a steady gaze copied from her grandmother that was fully intended to intimidate. Her technique appeared to need work. Wright put the cup to his lips once more and took several slow sips, gazing back at her over the rim. To her annoyance there was a hint of amusement in his expression. She held up the cartridge casing, warm from contact with her hand. 'I found this at the scene,' she said. 'Close to a pile of cut timber. Roger had stirred up the snow and I very nearly missed it.'

'Roger?' Wright consulted his notes. 'There's a third witness?'

For a moment Bunch considered playing him along. *It would be too funny.* 'Roger is my dog,' she said.

Chief Inspector Wright gave the Labrador a brief glance and nodded before leaning forward to take the spent cartridge. 'A .22.

I imagine there must be more than a few dozen rifles capable of firing this, all within a mile radius of where we sit. Every farm-hand and poacher in these parts will own one.'

'They will also own shotguns, though few would fire them in Hascombe Wood. We all know Saul Frampton is perfectly rabid over trespassers.'

'Never the less, one discarded cartridge from a commonly available weapon proves nothing.' He stood the casing on the desk between them. 'Unless you saw something or someone at the scene that disagrees with the official view, there will be no further investigation.'

'You'd think somebody would give it some thought before we all sign away Jonny's death. He deserves a proper burial and he won't get one with a suicide note hanging around his neck.'

'Miss Courtney, we do not have the officers to investigate something that has already been ordered to be set aside. War is a greedy beast. The services are accepting any police officer under thirty-five and our lads are volunteering in droves, which leaves our station full of retirees and Specials. All of our clerks and most of our drivers are women, now. We've had rationing for less than a month and already we have black marketeers by the dozen, there's a half-baked saboteur cutting phone lines all across the Downs, five established murder cases between Worthing and Eastbourne, and once your house guests arrive we shall undoubtedly have more mayhem.' He waved his hands in exasperation. 'The Coroner says suicide. The WD concurs as does your GP and local magistrate.' He stared at her, breathing hard. 'We don't have the men to spare. I'm sorry. Truly I am.' He rubbed a hand over his mouth and gave an almost imperceptible shake of his head. 'I have no idea why I am telling you all of this. It isn't very professional.'

'Because there's a war on?' His distress was obvious and she felt a pang of pity for him. She also had an idea he was not entirely unsympathetic toward her case, which gave her some little hope. 'The estate has exactly the same problems. Well, perhaps not exactly the same. I am fairly sure we don't have a crime wave on our hands, except...' she reached across to tap the desk in front of him '...you have not had the chance to examine the crime scene, have you?'

'Not much point now under a foot of snow,' he said. 'There would be little to see.'

'Exactly. You can't form an opinion until you have all the facts. Am I right?' She was wheedling, sounding more like Dodo than herself. 'Jonathan Frampton would not take his own life. I know I can prove that given a little time. Please, can you delay things a little? At least wait until the snow clears and you can examine the scene properly. Surely you can do that much?'

'The case is as good as closed.'

'So it would seem. Except there are anomalies. For instance, he was cold when I reached him. Even allowing for the weather, he had been dead longer than the ten minutes that passed between those shots and our finding him.' She paused, her face pinching in concentration. 'Surely that is something? If I put all of that in my statement would it be enough evidence to call for a proper hearing? The Coroner has not done his post mortem so how can we be certain about anything? Humour me. I am positive Jonny did not kill himself. I don't say that just because he's a friend. Well, it has some bearing. I am convinced I can prove it though I can't think what I can do right now. Just give me some time. Please?'

She smiled at him, wishing she had more of her sister's winsome qualities, and wishing she hadn't been such a pill when he first arrived. Being the capable, horsey one did not lend itself to employing flattery and she was first to admit she had a bad record for making snap judgements. 'If you are that busy then surely you can let it wait for a week or two? A man's eternal rest depends on it.'

'All right.' He pulled a face. 'The post mortem will not be performed for a week, possibly longer. I can delay for a little while but not indefinitely. I can hold up my report until we have made a proper report on the scene, which we can't do until the weather improves. You have until the snow thaws.'

❧THREE❧

Dodo was bathed and dressed and looking better than she had the night before. *Or,* Bunch thought, *at any time in the past few weeks.* She glanced up from her scrutiny of the morning papers to watch her sister drift across the breakfast room to stare out at the winter world. Dodo was very nearly back to the coltish girl, barely out of her teens, who had married in the summer of the previous year. *Too young, but then so many are these days. War seems to add haste to every action in every part of life.* 'Good morning. Or rather, good afternoon. Trust you to smell out lunch,' Bunch observed. 'Are you feeling refreshed, old thing?'

Dodo scratched her scalp and yawned. 'You should never have let me sleep for so long. Hardly my fault if nobody wakes me.'

An engine was revved to its limits out near the stable yard, accompanied by many raised voices. The need for shouting was a mystery when both women knew the mechanics could not be standing more than ten feet from each other. It was a racket that had been going on most of the morning and Bunch found it desperately unnerving that these people, who did not answer to the Courtneys, would be here for the foreseeable future. Even more unnerving was knowing that this was just the vanguard.

It both amused and aggravated Bunch that Dodo had managed to sleep through it all. 'I was not going to wake you,' she said, 'and I doubt I could when not even the worthies of the War Department could manage it. You quite obviously needed the rest.'

'Did I miss Botting trotting up to take our statements? What a bore. I suppose he'll be tracking me down at the Manor.'

'It is where you live, darling.'

'Urgh! Don't remind me.'

The comment was emphatic, which caught Bunch unawares.

I suppose she's bound to be unhappy there because of George's death. Or maybe she misses Perringham House as much as I will when I'm forced to leave? Or is there something else? She pushed the various possibilities, especially the last one, aside. 'It wasn't Botting, as it happens. It was some inspector chappie from Brighton or Chichester or wherever it is detectives lurk these days.'

'Will he be back?'

'I should doubt it, not just to take your statement.' Bunch wondered if Dodo needed to hear the official line and changed the subject, just in case. 'Is it a bit brutal over at the in-laws? It must be difficult for them with the son and heir gone and all that.' She froze, aware that she was being her usual blundering and inappropriate self, putting her sensible size sevens straight into it. Mother frequently complained at how, despite all the money spent on her eldest daughter's boarding and finishing schools, she 'still possessed the social gifts of a chimp'. 'Sorry. We thought we'd let you sleep. You do look better for it.'

Dodo ran her tongue around the inside of her mouth and pulled a face. 'I have brushed my teeth and my tongue still feels like the bottom of a parrot's cage. Be a brick, Bunch, and pour me a cup of tea. I am absolutely parched.'

'You should eat. Nothing very special on offer, I'm afraid, though Cook has left us some Stilton. The kitchens are in an uproar with moving to the Dower House. Fortunately for us the stalwart Mrs Westgate hasn't managed a kitchen for all these years without knowing a few tricks. I gather she has dug out the churn to make butter off ration, as we speak. There's some cold pie from last night if you want it.' Bunch worried that her sister still looked so pale, so exhausted, despite her long sleep. She worried that Dodo had not slept properly at all despite the sleeping powder. And she worried about having responsibility for this wounded bird whilst their parents were away.

'Stilton will be splendid.' Dodo looked around her. 'Where's Daddy? Won't he be joining us for lunch?'

'He's eaten. Last minute rush with this and that. He slipped down to the farm to speak with Parsons on some estate business.'

'Oh, all right.' She crossed to the window and rubbed a little hole in the condensation. 'It's stopped snowing.'

'For now. I gather from Knapp it will hold off until tonight and then we could be in for a bit of a blizzard. I was going to trot out for an hour when we've finished lunch. Fancy blowing some cobwebs away?' Bunch waited, hands paused in mid-fold of the newspaper that she knew wouldn't be read before evening.

'You're not taking Perry out in this weather, surely?' Dodo said.

'You're thinking my poor old nag will break a leg?'

Dodo laughed. 'Perry has legs like an elephant and the feet to match. It would take more than a slip to damage that carthorse of yours. Actually, I don't know how you managed to keep hold of your trio. Emma was furious when she heard Bonny was taken away by the Min. Ag.'

Bunch gave her a curious glance. There had been a strong rumour that the Ministry was requisitioning horses as they had in the Great War, which she knew was largely nonsense. Many were going into the food chain because owners could no longer afford to feed them, or because old meadows and pastures had been ordered under the plough. She had a suspicion Barty Tinsley had merely seen Emma's ancient, sway-backed hunter as a waste of the feed that could go to his thoroughbred bloodstock, now that Emma had a lecturing post at Oxford. She decided her grieving sister did not need to hear that right now. *The girl*, she thought, *is fragile enough*. 'That sounds like Emma. She has a brilliant mind but she's a complete innocent when it comes to the big wide world.'

'Emma said you and she were close at school.'

'We were friends,' said Bunch. 'Even had a bit of a pash for about half a term when we were in the junior house. She was a swot and I preferred lacrosse.'

'I'd always assumed your only pash was horses.'

'Not quite but be glad I've kept our animals. So many people have got rid of theirs to save on feed. We need ours to get around with petrol coupons running low. I have started to get Perry trained to harness for the trap.' She gulped down her tea and threw her napkin onto her plate. 'I need some air and Perry needs riding out. Coming?'

'And I bet he needs to walk up Hascombe Hill again. Must you go there of all places? It's just too ghastly.'

'I know, but I want to have another poke around before it snows again and covers whatever there is to see.'

'Why? Come on Bunch. Out with it. You've always been a shocking liar.'

'Because the police have closed the case. In point of fact they don't believe there ever *was* a case.'

'They do *have* a point.'

'Oh, good heavens, not you as well,' Bunch snapped. 'Jonny would not shoot himself. You know that as well as I.' She smiled, with more than a hint of irony. 'I have talked the Chief Inspector into giving us until the snow clears to prove it.'

'It's not a game, Bunch. You should leave these things to the police.'

'If it were the police making the choices it might have been dealt with differently. I called Uncle Walter earlier to find out why it was being swept away and he was beastly about it. Apparently it's the WD who have closed it down.' She shrugged. 'Short and tall of it is if Jonathan had been involved in any secret stuff they would not want the press even acknowledging he existed. The police are happy to think he shoved a twelve bore in his mouth and pulled purely because it gives them one less thing to do.' She saw Dodo flinch and felt a tiny twinge of guilt. 'I won't let it drop.'

'If this is top secret perhaps you should.'

'Nonsense. Do you want him buried on some roadside at the dead of night?'

'That doesn't happen these days, does it? Not anymore. I mean, surely burial at a crossroads is a myth.'

'Perhaps. I don't know.' Bunch raised her hands in frustration. 'The point is, are you willing to risk it? I am absolutely certain that if his death is passed off as suicide he won't be permitted a proper Christian burial. An old school chum of mine took pills just last year. There was a hell of a stink when their vicar refused to allow her to be laid to rest within the walls.'

'How awful. What happened to her?'

'Her father pulled rank,' Bunch replied. 'I can't see old man Frampton bothering. Can you?'

Dodo picked up a knife and cut herself a sliver of Stilton. She bit into the crumbling cheese, savouring it, her eyes closed. 'This is awfully good. At least it hasn't been rationed yet.'

'Stop changing the subject.'

'I'm not... Yes I am, sorry. I liked Jonny, really I did, but getting involved in this sort of way, especially with the WD being involved. Is it wise?'

Bunch rubbed her bottom lip, biting back the things she wanted to say. In her opinion this was exactly what Dodo needed, mainly because she was a firm believer in the maxim of *getting back onto the horse*. Bunch was throwing herself headlong into the fray for that very same reason. It was how she coped, and though she knew there were many who would not agree with her, it was all she had to offer her baby sister by way of comfort. 'We need to do something,' she remarked, 'and I have no idea how I − we − are going to go about it. Let's pray we don't have a rapid thaw.'

Dodo dropped the Stilton back onto the plate. 'We can't,' she whispered. 'He's beyond anybody's help.'

Vivid memories of Jonny crowded into Bunch's memory. His wicked grin and fruity laugh; his tender kisses. Bunch felt a moment's anger at Dodo's display of anguish when her sister had hardly known him, not in the way that she had. Yet there was genuine sadness in Dodo's eyes, and watery guilt replaced momentary annoyance. 'I'm sorry. I'm a total clod. I didn't mean to set you off blubbing.'

'Cry?' Dodo rubbed her hand across her face. 'I don't think I can today. I've done nothing else of late. It's just that this thing with Jonny is not our job.'

'Perhaps not our job but I do believe this is our duty,' Bunch replied. 'We were close, Jonny and I. We even had a fling.'

'You? Don't talk such tosh.'

'Not tosh. It didn't last terribly long but you do get close to people you've shared a bed with.' She waved a hand impatiently. 'Oh, don't look at me like that. Half the county set are bed-hopping like crazy every chance they get. We were most awfully discreet. He was a darling. You can see why I have to do something, can't you? I was the only serious girlfriend he ever had.'

'I didn't know.' Dodo stared at her hands, which seemed to clasp and unclasp of their own volition. 'You're right. If we can get poor Jonny a proper burial then we should. At least I would have one grave that I could visit.'

Bunch decided to ignore Dodo making it about herself. The girl had been under a huge cloud and she could let her have this one. 'Are you in this with me?' she said. 'We either free Jonny from this ridiculous suicide thing or let it be a permanent part of how people remember him.'

'I suppose you're right.' Dodo looked around the room. 'Can I stay here with you for a bit? Olivia is being absolutely ghastly since Georgie— You know. Emma couldn't get back to her campus fast enough. She is always happiest with as much distance between her and the family as she can possibly make. I could do with getting away from Banyard Manor for a week or two, as well.'

'I can imagine.' Bunch played at slicing a wrinkled apple taken from the kitchen garden store, making a show of not meeting her sister in the eye, giving herself time to regain control. She had thought she might be brow-beating Dodo, as she had when they were young. It seemed she didn't need to and that made her feel better. If Dodo now felt it was time to escape from the black-edged sphere of her mother-in-law Olivia Tinsley, then she was beginning to come out of the mental funk that Georgie's death had thrown her into.

Olivia was a stickler for convention and what was to be expected of the well-bred, which Bunch felt was pretty rich from someone who had no discernible background. Olivia had, for instance, insisted on plunging the house into semidarkness and expected Dodo to join her in full seclusion like some Victorian Grande Dame. Bunch knew her little sister needed to grieve yet hiding in the shadows was not the Courtney way.

'You are welcome anytime. May not be *here* of course. What about that ride? We shall need to be quick. It's already gone one o'clock and it will be getting dusk by half past three.'

'I suppose I shall have no peace if I don't.'

'Absolutely not.'

'Then, *lay on Macduff*. I have a feeling we shall both *be damned*. Who isn't right at this particular moment?' Dodo grabbed a roll, stuffed it with the cheese, and drained her teacup. 'Shall we go?'

~~~

They were walking down to the stables when a second Army truck pulled into the yard. The back flap lifted and a dozen or more soldiers poured out onto the snowy cobbles. A barrage of shouts went up as they spotted the sisters. 'Hey there.' 'Haven't seen you around here.' 'Fancy a drink, honey?'

'Bunch?' Dodo stopped dead, easing herself behind her sister. 'Are these chaps always this forward? It is something of a liberty.'

'I haven't had a problem before today,' Bunch replied. 'These are Canadian from the camp down near Worthing. They aren't going to be living here though. They're just ferrying in the equipment.'

'Nationality makes a difference?'

'Not a clue. I suspect we are about to find out.' Bunch swung Dodo around to her left and glared at the gaggle of Canucks. She called Roger to heel and stood her ground as she always did. Their attitude was alien to her. It was not that of locals with their due deference, in full knowledge of her status and power. These were more like a pack of exuberant wolflings circling a brace of stray deer. She put an arm out protectively in front of her sister while Roger muttered at her feet.

'Fall in!' The voice piercing the cold air snapped the men to silence. ''Ten 'hut!' it continued.

The men formed a rapid line and stood to attention as a tall officer appeared on the far side of the yard. He marched across to them, tipping the women a salute as he passed.

He was followed, at a more leisurely pace, by an older man in leather flying jacket and officer's cap; a stocky figure with dark hair silvering at the temples and wide-set dark eyes. As he stalked toward the assembled men Bunch and Dodo could see how his demeanour was subduing them: sheer force of personality aided by the vast amount of hardware and braid pinned to his hat.

'Gentlemen.' He stalked along the line examining each man with deliberate care. 'We have not been introduced. I am Colonel Gabriel R Kravitz and I am the commander here. I realise I am Air Force and you are not, that this is not your station, but...' he stopped and took a step back to view them as a group '...when you are here on this base you will follow my orders. The first of which is that you will conduct yourselves in a proper manner. Is that clear?'

'Yes, sir,' was the ragged response.

'Is that clear!'

The line straightened as though jabbed with a very long stick. 'Yes, sir!'

Kravitz nodded. He pointed his swagger stick at Bunch and Dodo without looking at them. 'Now, these young ladies are the daughters of this house. They are not to be whistled at, yelled at, or otherwise addressed without a salute and a *Ma'am*. Do I make myself perfectly clear?'

'Sir, yes sir!'

He turned away from them, confident in his authority. 'Ladies, I apologise for this display. Not a great introduction to your new tenants. I can assure you we're not all bereft of good manners. It won't happen again.' He turned to glare at the Canucks. 'Will it, gentlemen?'

'Sir, no sir!'

'Good. Then fall out and get all of that equipment inside and installed. Then return to wherever you came from before dark! On the double!'

'Sir! Yes sir!'

They scrambled to carry out their orders and Colonel Kravitz glanced up at the windows before turning to salute the women again. 'I'm guessing one of you must be Miss Courtney?'

Bunch nodded. His smile was a lot more speculative than polite. His accent impeccable in that way only an expensively educated foreigner could be. His uniform, she noticed, was British yet he was plainly not. She appraised him in the same way she would a horse she was considering as a purchase, and what she saw made her uneasy. This was not a stolid nag. This was a continental thoroughbred that brooked no argument.

'And you are Mrs Tingley?'

'*Tinsley*', Dodo replied.

'Tinsley? Same as the magistrate?' He looked at them in much the same manner Bunch had done him, assessing them for worth and weaknesses. 'I am very pleased to make your acquaintance, ladies, and we shall have a more civilised conversation when time allows. Right now I'm in the middle of something, so if you'll excuse me…'

'I quite understand, Colonel.' Bunch nodded, smiled her gracious official smile, and waited to see if he offered a hand. He did so with a briefest tug of fingers. Not the hearty handclasp she had expected.

Kravitz looked keenly from her to Dodo. 'We will meet later, I hope, and under more civilised circumstances. I am sorry to run out on you but I really do have to go.'

He glanced up as he strode away and Bunch looked to see what caught his attention. Her father was at his study window, along with an older man in British Army uniform, whom she did not recognise. She waved and wondered what kind of politics was taking place behind that particular closed door.

'The elusive Colonel?' said Dodo. 'He sounds American with a twang. Free French do you think? Arrogant enough.'

'Not French,' Bunch replied. She was glad Dodo had reached the same conclusions she had. 'I think I recognised Polish ribbons. One can only surmise. I'd not clapped eyes on him until now. I thought Daddy was supposed to be down at the farm. I wonder why he told Knapp that?' She shrugged. 'Probably best not to enquire. I do wonder who the other chap was though.'

'You know how Daddy is with his meetings.' Dodo glanced at the squaddies scurrying about under the young officer's eagle eye. 'They are like excited puppies aren't they,' she said.

'Yes. Bull terrier pups.' Bunch was gratified to see her sister regain equilibrium so quickly. 'I've had some whistles from them down in the village. Anyone with bosoms and a pulse seems to be fair game to these people. For it to happen here … well, it's a bit forward, I agree, but I'm sure it will settle down. Daddy assures me the residents here will all be officers. I had assumed British.' She shrugged 'They seem to be all nationalities. I gather one or two have tried getting a little fresh with the Land Girls.' She sighed, tucking her arm more firmly into Dodo's. 'They probably thought we're Land Army.'

'Nylons and cigarettes are an awful temptation for those girls.'

'Don't be such an ass. Rationing goes across the board and it's only going to get worse, even with our estate produce to fall back on.'

'Barty and Olivia never seem to go without,' Dodo replied. 'Olivia ordered a sack of sugar from some London wholesaler just last week. I doubt she got that flirting with young officers.'

'Really? Tell Olivia she should be very careful about that. There was a piece in *The Times* only yesterday warning against stockpiling. The penalties will be punitive, just as they were in the Great War.'

Dodo drew her arm back. 'How could you even think that? Barty's a magistrate. I rather think it was a gift from grateful petitioners. You know what a terrible bore Olivia is; she would slaughter anyone who brought a whiff of scandal onto the estate. If she had an inkling that you were playing detective she'd bar you from her doorstep forever.' She pulled her scarf tighter round her neck and rubbed at her arms. 'God, it's cold out here. Why are we doing this?'

'Nanny would have called it bracing. You need to get out a bit more, Dodo, old thing. Good hack across the coombe will be just the thing.'

~~~

The mile across country from Perringham House to Hascombe Wood was largely deserted and their progress left twin trails across unsullied whiteness. A dark-grey blooming of cloud in the southern sky was made darker by the bright sun reflected off the snow.

Roger was floundering excitedly through the snow, biting mouthfuls of white and barking all the while. The sound of his excitement carried a long way across the empty landscape, sending the inevitable flurry of resident rooks out of the tree tops.

At the edge of the wood they reined in, glancing at each other without speaking, before they plunged into the trees. They trotted straight along the path to the clearing without all the detours of the previous trip. The snow was less thick than out in the fields and less arduous for the horses. What had fallen overnight was gathered in drifts around the trees. Here and there small hints of leaf litter were peeping through, exposed by the scouring wind.

As they neared the clearing they could see rope strung around the group of sweet chestnuts. It was hung with strips of cloth that swayed and twirled lazily. The rest of the space was a churned up mess.

'I don't know a huge amount about these things,' Bunch observed. 'Aren't the police supposed to go around on tippy-toes where there has been a crime? In case there are clues?'

'That sounds a bit Bulldog Drummond,' Dodo replied. 'Why would they be careful? So far as they are concerned there is no crime here to investigate.'

'Perhaps.' Bunch had thought Dodo would at least pretend to

be supportive. She slid from the saddle and walked around the edge of the roped area, craning her neck to see what little there was to see. Some of the new fall was already tinged a brownish-pink leaching from beneath and pinpointing the spot where Jonny had sat. She ducked under the rope and knelt to examine it more closely.

'You shouldn't, Bunch. They put the ropes up to stop people going in there.'

'For heaven's sake, Dodo, at times you can be so prissy. You just said yourself that they won't care. You said I'm the only lunatic who thinks there ever *was* a crime. Besides which, the Inspector said I could dig around until the thaw. We're practically sworn-in detectives.' She leaned across to brush snow from the trunk where Jonny's head had rested. She remembered from the day before that there seemed very little … *debris? Detritus? Viscera? I wonder what is the right word?* She took a stick poking up through the whiteness and scraped snow from around the tree bowl where his body had been. 'Whatever it's called there's not a trace of it there.'

'Trace of what?'

She swivelled on her heels to face Dodo. 'Blood. There really isn't very much of it and there should be.'

'Bunch. Must you?' Dodo slapped her gloved hand over her mouth.

'I think I probably should.' Bunch sighed, wondering yet again if bringing Dodo out here was such a good idea. 'There ought to be more blood than this. We've both been hunting often enough. Think how much mess there is when you finish off a deer at close range.'

'I'd rather not. And I think it's rather mean of you to compare the two.'

'I'm not saying Jonny is the same, you goose. I'm just saying I don't see how he could have died here. There is not enough of … of blood.' She looked into the surrounding trees as she digested the thought. 'If he did shoot himself, as everybody insists, then tell me this: how could he move his own corpse?'

'Does this mean you can prove to your Chief Inspector that he needs to do something?'

'That would be the ticket. I rather think it needs a little more than my opinion to sway the verdict. I need solid evidence.' She stood, dusting snow and wet leaves from her left knee as she looked around the dell. There seemed not to be any obvious bloody patches leeching through the snow cover. *But then*, she supposed, *it might have dried before it snowed.* The belief that Jonny had been murdered elsewhere and left here in a staged suicide was gaining momentum, but she had no idea how she could go about proving it.

'Think back, Dodo,' she said at last. 'Was the ground turned over when we came yesterday?'

'Not sure what you mean, darling.'

'Was the soil disturbed?'

'I really can't remember. I don't think so. Roger was doing his snow plough trick, churning up everything. I can't think of anything else. Frankly, once I'd spotted Jonny I wasn't seeing a great deal else.'

'Nor me, to be honest, although the snow is making the ground pretty soft, so I am fairly sure if there was any sign of anything being dragged it would have been quite obvious. He had to have been carried, yes?'

'How would I know?'

'I don't know, that is just it. If he was carried it would require more than just one person, don't you think?'

'Jonathan wasn't a beefy, rugger sort. I've seen gillies up in the Highlands carrying deer that would weigh a lot more than him, single handed,' Dodo replied. 'So not necessarily.'

'They don't carry the carcases far. No more than a few hundred yards. It would have to be a young and fit sort of fellow to haul a body any distance, and there's a distinct shortage of civilians around these parts answering that description.'

Dodo laughed aloud. 'You have a house absolutely bursting at the seams with them.'

'Are you saying it's a soldier?' Bunch demanded. 'You cannot point at them just because they're foreigners.'

'I'm doing nothing of the sort. I'm merely pointing out that there are dozens of chaps floating about who would be more than capable. There's the defence battery eight miles down the road with a platoon of home-grown squaddies, not to mention a whole camp full down near Storrington, and many more over toward

Eastbourne. Plus the train station is less than a mile away, giving access all across the country. Even assuming you are right, it doesn't narrow things down all that much. There are even a few of your Land Army girls who look more than capable. That Yorkshire girl in your dairy yard, for example. Annie is it? Came to help out when Barty's cowman was called up. She could lift full churns on her own. Jonny on the other hand was tall and a bit of a string-bean, in fact. It's probably why he failed his medical.'

'He didn't fail anything, trust me. He just got shanghaied into something off the usual track.' She frowned, staring into space for a moment. 'I don't know what to think, Dodo. There is something I saw here yesterday. If I could just remember exactly what.'

'Can't you think at home? I am positively freezing to death out here and the horses must be getting chilled.'

Bunch turned slowly to take in the clearing, wishing now she had brought her camera. There was little to observe that had not been seen by everyone with the slightest interest in examining these events. It was just a clearing in the woods covered with snow that, to a novice such as herself, had very little to show beyond the obvious.

Flurries of white were swirling around the space on the gathering icy wind, though whether it was loose grains sloughing from the trees or the start of a fresh fall she could not tell. She fumbled around her wrist for her watch. Two-thirty. They had an hour of daylight remaining, perhaps a bit more. 'Let's go and see Saul,' she said. 'Pay our respects.'

'Is that a good idea?' Dodo said.

'Poor chap won't know if he's coming or going. We should visit.' Bunch paused. 'Maybe we'll find something about what Jonny was doing.'

❧FOUR❧

Hascombe Farm was small when compared with Perringham House but substantial enough, nevertheless. The six-bedroom house owed most of its architecture to the late eighteenth century, though the rear of the building, complete with stables and courtyard garden, may have been a little older. Saul Frampton had taken to living in the old house after Jonathan had left for University a decade before. He had moved into what had been the butler's quarters and left the upper stories to descend into a drab twilight of dust and mould and closed shutters. It was no secret that he had not coped well after his wife's death. It was no secret that the adult Jonathan had rarely stayed there.

Bunch and Dodo found Saul Frampton in the below-stairs hall, sitting at the kitchen table before the ancient, black iron range. He was cleaning a shotgun, his movements slow, almost trancelike, and though he was looking down Bunch felt sure he was not seeing anything in the physical world. She recognised the weapon as the Westley Richards double-barrel shotgun. It seemed incongruous to Bunch, given the happenings of the previous day, that Frampton's idle hands should be so taken up with firearms. Even so, she knew dispassionately that the piece was worthy of the attention Saul was giving.

Why isn't that weapon in police hands? Any evidence it had has long gone, now. She wasn't sure what evidence but had read enough to consider fingerprints may not have been out of the question.

His actions were more than a little macabre and she was gripped by a moment's fear that he intended to mirror his son's supposed actions and take his own life. Frampton cracked it open and peered down one barrel. Satisfied with what he saw he carried on with his cleaning. He did not glance up from his task as they approached closer, merely continued polishing with an oil-stained cloth, up and down the barrel. Bunch had the impression they were being studiously ignored. His features held no hint of emotion as he worked on cleaning and oiling with a practised ease.

'Possibly the only clean thing in the room,' Bunch whispered.

Dodo dug her sister hard in the ribs. 'Bunch, shh...' and louder: 'Mr Frampton? We have come by to pay our respects. Mr Frampton?'

Bunch felt a sudden pity for the old man, who seemed to have aged fifteen years in a single day. She also wondered how long he had been sitting there giving the classic gun so much attention. 'Mr Frampton, Saul?' She walked softly across the room and reached out to take the gun from him. The iron barrel was warm in her grasp, despite the coldness of the room.

She looked at the Westley, trying to remember the last time she had seen it in Jonathan's genial *living* hands. Was it the shoot at the Nyman Estate at the latter end of last season? She doubted it was any later; Jonathan had hardly been home for months. She propped the Westley against the dresser and looked around the room. 'Tea,' she said. 'Shall we make you some?'

Frampton grunted, which Bunch took for a yes, and crossed to the range and was glad to find it was not totally cold. Beyond that she was not remotely familiar with its workings. Throwing a log on a drawing fire was wholly different to rekindling this beast.

Dodo appeared at her side and stared at the black iron monster with similar horror. 'Do you know how to fire that thing up?' she asked.

'I've stripped engines and set broken legs. This can't be so very difficult, can it?' Bunch grabbed a gnarled poker and teased the blanket of grey ash lining the grate and, when she saw a spiral of smoke emerge, picked a few small chunks of wood from the basket by the fire and tossed them in. They smouldered with little sense of urgency. *Clearly kitchen fire lighting is a singular gap in the Mont-Choisi Ladies Academy curriculum,* Bunch thought. She poked at the embers and scowled at her shortcomings. Smoke curled encouragingly from the ashes but it was quite apparent, even if she had been au-fait with the workings of the range, it could take a while to heat a kettle.

She looked around for some way of hurrying it on and noted a half-empty bottle of Scotch on the dresser and briefly considered a little liquid assistance. She noted that it was a cheap blended brand. Beside it stood a dimpled tot glass, sticky with residue. She could hardly blame Frampton for taking a few draws of whisky from the bottle and wondered about the wisdom of giving him more. *What the hell. Poor chap hasn't got a great deal else.* 'Perhaps a nip of something whilst it gets going?' she said.

'Aye.' Frampton waved at the dresser. 'Glasses.'

As she poured Bunch wondered what questions she should be asking. By her own admission she had no idea what she was looking for, and between shock and drink Frampton did not seem to be in any fit state to answer anything. She poured small measures and took them to the table. 'Water?' she asked.

'No.' Frampton knocked his dram back in one swallow and finally acknowledged the two women with direct eye contact. 'I'm not a child,' he rumbled. 'I can manage, girl.'

'Doubtless,' Bunch replied. 'We're just paying our respects.'

'Now you've paid them.' The unspoken order to leave was unmistakable.

Bunch opened her mouth to retort and subsided as Dodo said, 'I shall miss Jonny. He was such a good chum of George's.'

'He was that. They were such *very* good chums.' Frampton gazed blearily at the women, his eyes unfocussed and rheumy, his mood changed like a flipped switch. 'What happened? It is so damned unfair. He didn't get back for George's memorial and now he's going to need one of his own.' His moment of near-tenderness ended as abruptly as it had begun and his attention returned to the weapon. Expression changed from bewilderment to fervent concentration.

It seemed to Bunch that he was trying to rub it all away, as if by cleaning the means of his son's destruction he could erase the events of that day. *Was that the drink?* she wondered. *Guilt?* Grief, of that much she was certain. Strange when father and son had been at daggers drawn for so many years. Maybe it was all about blood, in the end. She watched him scrubbing at the stock with such intensity that she almost expected it to burst into flame, and gave herself a mental shake. His grief was intense and real, she was sure of that, but it was not more than her own. She had lost her best friend, her soul mate, or so she had thought. Saul's grief might be genuine, she believed; but it was, as his love for his son had been, totally misplaced.

'Is that why he was home,' she asked. 'He said he'd be away for another month, and he hadn't been to see us. Or called.'

Frampton half stood and reached across the table for the bottle and poured himself half a glass. 'He turned up out of the blue. Damned stupid boy. If he had stayed away, like he always did…'

'He didn't know we moved the memorial forward?'

'Seems not.' Frampton swilled back the raw spirit and poured another. 'I didn't tell him. Not spoken to him. If you didn't then I can't explain it.' He shook his head, his belligerence giving way to more bewilderment. 'He wasn't meant to be home,' he said. 'He was not meant to be here. He—'

'He took himself up the hill yesterday, in the snow? Why was that?' Bunch asked.

'I haven't the faintest idea,' he growled. 'He never told me anything. He just turned up. No message, nothing. I told him he should have called.'

'You had words?'

Frampton frowned. 'Yes. We had words. We were always having words. Every time we laid eyes on each other. Is that what you wanted to hear? That I drove him to it? Yes, we had a damned row. No louder and no longer than the usual, and then he scampered off up those woods, said he was looking for sheep. Sheep, dammit. In the middle of the bloody night.' The shot of whisky hit the back of his throat and was barely swallowed before he was reaching for the bottle once more. He poured a bare half tot and watched the last drips patter from the dry bottle.

Bunch was surprised he did not try wringing the bottle out. It was so typical of the man's condition. She had never seen him show his son affection, or even kindness. His current show of grief came was a bit of a shock to her. If she were being ungenerous she might suspect him of using the events as an excuse to allow him free rein with the liquor. 'Perhaps he imagined he saw something?' She spread her hands. 'You cannot possibly think he killed himself over a few sheep?'

Frampton laughed once more, a soft gurgling chuckle. 'I often wondered why he bothered coming here. He never gave a damn about me, taking off after those … secrets.' He held a finger to his lips and rose unsteadily to his feet. 'Not supposed to say. Did you know he was being stationed right on my doorstep? Right there in your yard? No?' He laughed sharply. 'He never cared about how it'd sit with me if he got himself killed. Ach!' He slapped the table top. 'I have work to do. Stock needs feeding.'

Bunch skimmed over Jonny's secret return. Surely he would not have done so without telling her. 'Your manager Pole will do that, or the Land Girls. That's what they're for.'

'Land Girls? Ha. They've all gone.'

'They can't possibly leave. They are allocated to this unit.'

'Unit? They're not soldiers. Nothing like. This is a damned farm, woman. Not a sewing circle.' He rose unsteadily and Bunch reached out to support him. He pulled away from her. 'They've gone because I bloody well told them to go. I'm telling you the same thing. Bloody clear out. Both of you.'

Dodo made to catch hold of his arm. 'Mr Frampton, Saul.'

'Are you deaf? I already know you're stupid; and apparently blind! Just clear out!' The glass was hurled to the floor, followed by the bottle. 'Get out of my house!'

'Come on Dodo.' Bunch glanced at the gun, gauging the possibility of sneaking it away.

Frampton swept it up and brought it to his shoulder. 'Bugger off.'

The gun was not loaded but a man like Frampton could have shells in the breech in seconds, drunk or sober, and he seemed sufficiently disturbed of mind not to care. 'Dodo, let's go.' Bunch hustled her out.

Dodo gazed back at the door in disbelief. 'Good God, the man has gone insane.'

'He's drunk and he's grieving.' Bunch grasped her arm and guided her away. 'I think he's more of a danger to himself than us. We should fetch his foreman. Pole will sort him, I'm sure. He's a good man.'

~ ~ ~

They found Len Pole in the barn loading bales onto a cart assisted by two Land Girls.

'Frampton said he had sacked them,' Bunch said. 'What happened, Pole?'

'He's drunk.' Pole dumped a bale onto the cart and turned to fetch another. 'Has been since before Master Jonathan was taken. Even before then he'd bin actin' up. Sacks us all every two days an' never remembers. We don't take no notice.'

'He seems to be in pieces about Jonny,' said Bunch. 'I thought they didn't get on. Just goes to show.'

'No more 'en they did,' Pole cut in. 'There were a lot more t'lose fer the old man than flesh.'

'Pardon?'

Pole dumped another bale in a flurry of dust and husks. 'Not my business no more 'en yours,' he replied.

'Isn't it?' Bunch said. 'Jonny was a good pal. Look, Pole, I'm only trying to understand what went on. I don't believe Jonathan shot himself.'

Pole frowned at her, opened his mouth and closed it again, returning to fetch more straw.

'Please?' she said. 'Saul says they had a bit of a ruck the night before.'

'They did. The old man was ranting like a good'n. Plastered of course. I steered him back home. Fer his own safety.'

'You thought Jonathan was in danger from him?'

Pole laughed sharply. 'No, the old man was more like to shoot hisself, he was that tight.' He fell silent, staring at the floor. 'Never imagined the young master'd do hisself in.'

'He didn't.' Bunch laid a hand on the older man's shoulder. 'He didn't. I know it.'

~~~

'I am surprised at you,' Courtney growled. 'Bad enough you go bothering a man in mourning. Messing around in police business is incomprehensible. I cannot imagine what you were thinking. Then to start telling him how to run his estate? It is simply not done.'

'It's my area,' Bunch muttered. 'Frampton had no right sending those Land Girls away without informing the area offices. You, of all people, know how imperative it is to have the food production uninterrupted. Just because the convoys are coming in doesn't mean the food situation will get any better.'

'You have been a diplomat's daughter long enough to know how to deal with these things.'

'Sorry, Daddy,' Bunch said. 'I'm a bit out of sorts, what with

Jonny and then these damnable squaddies. You should have heard them earlier. Perfectly awful.'

'I did hear them,' he replied. 'Colonel Kravitz assures me it will not happen again. It will all be different when you move over to the Dower. I know it's demanding for you but this deal with Perringham, and a couple more houses like it, was a huge part of our planning. If we can get America on board with us…'

'Their money isn't to be sniffed at.'

'Rose!'

'Sorry, Daddy.'

'You should be.' He laid a hand on her arm. 'I'm not going to lecture you. God knows, you're not a child. I know you've had a bad time, both you and Dodo. Do try to behave and leave this desperate business with Frampton to the police.'

'*You* said you'd introduce us properly to Kravitz,' Bunch said.

'*You* are changing the subject.'

'*You* aren't answering me. Does he have a problem with women?'

'I think he has a problem with you still being here. He was under the impression we were all leaving last week. Some sort of Whitehall cockup. Nobody seems to know what happened. I really do think you would be better moving out today. He will not make life easy for you.'

'If Dodo can manage Olivia, I can manage this military type.'

'Only just,' Dodo said.

'I know you can, Rose. Now, I must be off. Keep out of trouble. Your mother and I should be on the plane before midnight. We shall send you a telegram when we reach Singapore. I do not want to be asked to turn around and fly back again because you pair have been arrested.'

'Don't be silly, Daddy.' Bunch grinned despite herself. 'We shall be positive angels.'

'Of course we will,' Dodo agreed.

'That will be a first.' He reached out and pulled his girls close for a hug. 'Look after Granny, and yourselves. No more playing with bombs, Rose. Daphne, you are still welcome to join us. The trip would do you good.'

'No thank you, Daddy. Maybe later. It's too soon now.'

'Not letting Olivia Tinsley bully you into staying, are you?' He held Dodo away from him and stared into her face. 'She's always far too concerned with what the neighbours say about her.'

'She can be a little difficult at times but I can manage her, though.'

'That's my girl. Now I really must be going or I shall miss the London train, and then I shall have your mother on the warpath. Goodbye girls.'

'Goodbye Daddy. Take care. Say cheerio to Mummy.'

'I will. Don't come outside, it's far too cold.' He planted a kiss on each of their foreheads in turn, picked up his attaché case and strode out to the waiting car.

❧FIVE❧

Bunch stood at the kitchen window surveying the overnight snowfall with a jaundiced eye, and wondered exactly when in her life fresh snowfall had ceased to fill her with anticipation. 'It's stopped.'

'Do you really need to go out?' Dodo scraped a smear of preserve onto her toast, cut it into neat triangles, and stared at it. 'I wonder how much longer this bloody war is going to last,' she added. 'Sadie Lyle told me we won't have oranges soon because of the U-boats. I can do without the bacon and kidneys, and even kippers, but I so love orange marmalade.'

'Cook says she will be making rosehip chutney instead. Rosehips are just as good for one,' Bunch replied.

'They quite probably are but they're not going to be the same. You didn't answer me, Bunch. Are you going out this morning? There can't be a lot of work anyone can do in this weather.'

'Always something to do and I've already been out once. We can't all lie around all morning, you sluggard.'

'You've only been out to the stables so don't tell fibs.'

'True, but I do need to run up to Perret Shaw as soon as breakfast is over. There are ewes missing and one of the girls thought she heard some up that way yesterday afternoon. I also need to check that the girls have the fencing finished around the main pheasant pens or we'll have no shoot at all since half the heath is ploughed over.'

'Will we be allowed to keep the shoot?' Dodo asked.

'Like to see them bloody well stop us. It's fresh meat, after all. There's not much else we can do with that stretch. It's damn near vertical along most of that side of the coombe.'

'Parsons is supposed to be the steward. He can deal with that, surely?'

'He went over to East Grinstead for the cattle market. We've a half dozen steers up for auction, and I can't expect the old boy to do everything. We have dragged him out of retirement.'

'I don't think he needed much dragging. Anything to keep out of his daughter's way, I gather. Are you taking any of the horses out?'

'No. I need Haynes to accompany me and he doesn't ride.'

'At least you walk at the same pace.' She grinned. 'How is Haynes? Is he recovering?'

Bunch sighed. Dodo was probably the only one who dared rag her sister about her injuries. That did not mean she appreciated it any more. 'He's not the happiest of companions, but healing according to the doctor, though Haynes would tell you otherwise. He's not that eager to return to work, came up with all kinds of excuses not to go with me today. One advantage of being a fellow cripple is that I am the one person on the estate that he can't pull the wounded soldier card on.'

'Well, rather you than me. Knapp said he was really very rude to her just yesterday. He's not the same chap he was, is he? Touch of shellshock, do you think?'

'That's Parson's opinion. Poor chap had a bad time and it's finally getting to him.' Bunch came to sit opposite Dodo to help herself to breakfast. 'I need him to get the feed over to the pens every morning. I wouldn't want the girls wasting time hauling it down there. Can you cope on your own for the morning? Unless you want to come?'

'I can cope. Anything you want me to do here?'

'Not as such. Botting may be arriving to take your statement. I doubt our Chief Inspector will be back. There's not been any traffic along the road this morning, as far as I know.'

'I can't see why they need both of us to say the same thing.' Dodo mopped the last smear of marmalade with a crust. 'I shall see if I can get the car out. In case Knapp needs to shop.'

'We're short of petrol. I've had a couple of runs over to the depot this month and we're out of petrol coupons for the jalopy. Besides, Cook won't need anything today.' Bunch stabbed a slab of bread onto the toasting fork and held it up to the fire, smiling to herself and relaxing as the heat thawed her face and hands. Anyone less likely than their cook to run out of anything would be hard to find. She was already laying in for a siege with bottled this and pickled that, all of which could be backed up with a good supply of rabbit and game, although Bunch didn't consider this to be *hoarding* as such.

Bunch pulled the toasting bread away from the flame and quickly pushed it off the fork onto a plate, speared the browned side again, and held it up to singe. Fireside toast was one of those nursery habits that she could only indulge when her parents were absent.

'Will you be expected on Land Army duty today?'

'What? Oh no, I won't go to HQ this week. Waste of petrol swanning over there in this weather for no good reason. I told them I would be doing less now I have Perringham Estate to deal with.' Bunch swore at the stream of smoke curling up around the bread. 'Dammit. You shouldn't distract me. Burned the wretched stuff again.' She scraped the worst of the charcoal back into the fire and brought the slice to the table.

'You do know that Cook will make you perfectly good toast if you let her,' said Dodo.

'Yes I know. It just doesn't taste the same.' From where Bunch sat she could see most of the garden, wrapped in that curious stillness that snow brought wherever it fell, and she mentally added path clearing, at least out to the woodshed, to her list of jobs to be allocated.

The telephone rang in the next room. She glanced at Dodo, who seemed not to have heard, and strode through to grasp the black handset from the desk. 'Perringham House.'

'Would that be Mrs Courtney?'

'*Miss* Courtney,' she corrected him. 'Who is this?'

'Oh, I'm sorry, *Miss* Courtney. This is Chief Inspector Wright. We have a bit of a run on this morning so I shan't be able to call back as I promised. The Coroner has asked for the files to be completed. Would it be possible for your sister to come in this morning to give us a statement?'

'Well that's unfortunate because I am going to have to say no. Quite impossible.'

There was a silence at the other end of the phone and then a long whoosh of breath. 'Miss Courtney, I know we agreed to delay a little but I am sure you can appreciate we need a little more than your say so.'

'Mr Wright.'

'*Chief Inspector* Wright.'

'Quite so, Mr Wright. Except that I need my petrol coupons whereas you receive yours for police business. My sister will provide you a statement with pleasure, Chief Inspector, if you would be so kind as to send someone here to take it.'

'I'm afraid it's not quite that easy, Miss—'

'Nonsense, man. Unlike the rest of us you can access as much fuel as you need. Send Botting.' She let the handset drop from her fingers back into the cradle. 'Officious oaf,' she muttered. 'He seemed almost human yesterday.'

'Who is it, Bunch darling?'

'Police.' Bunch hurried back into the kitchen rubbing at her arms 'They want your statement. I told him if he wanted to waste his time he would have to come here and do it.'

'Don't you need to keep on his good side?'

'Me? Why on earth would I do that? He agreed to delay. The Coroner needs all statements before he can proceed. If Wright wants our cooperation he needs to earn it.' She pulled a chair up to the table and started to butter her toast with the meagre chunk left in the dish. 'Damn this rationing. How can you have a decent breakfast without butter?'

'Cook said she could trade eggs for a half pound of butter at the shop.'

'Under the counter? Bit risky for Cook, I would've thought.'

'You would be surprised what Cook will do for the sake of the table.'

'Oh, good grief, is it that time already? We've only just got New Year over and done with.' Bunch took the lid of the honey jar and grimaced. 'No honey. Couldn't feed a mouse on this. Thank God we've got toast.'

'The mice do very well, as it happens. I gather the little devils have been tunnelling through the wax tops into Cook's jars of potted meat.'

'How very domestic.' Bunch grinned and earned a punch on the arm.

'Don't be so bloody condescending. Just because you've gone Farmer Giles since you came home from Town. Some of us still like to maintain standards.'

'Not my choice, darling. Blame the bloody war.' She bit into her toast and chewed stolidly on a large mouthful, staring at the wall directly in front of her. 'They will be coming for you next,' she mumbled. 'Daddy said they will be conscripting everyone if Hitler crosses into France.'

'What?' Dodo said slowly. 'I thought being a widow...'

'You're a widow without dependents and not engaged in direct war work. I say, isn't there any more coffee in that pot?'

'What should I do?' Dodo said.

Bunch didn't want to discuss it. She had planned to join the WAF but her injuries had put paid to that idea. It now irked her that Dodo seemed unwilling to step up. She caught a glimpse of Dodo's anxious face from the corner of her eye and batted away her myriad doubts. She swallowed the toast before speaking. 'Not a great deal you can do. Acquire some dependents; it's probably your only option.'

'Bunch!'

'Think yourself lucky you're able to do anything at all.' She looked up at a light rap at the door and set down her cup. 'Can't be the police. Unless they have a *kite* handy.'

'Don't be silly. It's probably Knapp,' Dodo replied, raising her voice to call. 'Come in.'

A blast of air swirled against the fire glow, stealing all the heat in an instant, then the outer door was closed. Frank Haynes paddled into the room. A short wiry individual in his thirties, though work and weather had added ten years to his face. 'Mornin' Mrs Tinsley.' He swept both his oily flat cap and dark balaclava from his head and nodded to Bunch. 'Miss Courtney.' He stood scrunching headgear between his hands and fiddle-footing nervously in woolly-socked feet.

'Ah, Haynes,' said Bunch. 'You're early.'

He nodded slowly. 'Mr Parsons says you was askin' about some missin' ewes.'

'I am. Have you checked the count?'

'Ah, I told Mr Parsons we've got ewes missin', right enough.'

'The girls were quite insistent they heard sheep up in the shaw.'

Haynes frowned, screwing the cap and woollen hat a little harder. 'I went up the rise but I didn't hear nothin'.' He tapped his injured leg and then let his hand fall away under Bunch's glare. 'The main flock was pitched up over t'far side of Stubbs corner. That's two fields over but I reck'n the noise'd carried. The cold will do that.'

'They had to have gone through the winter barley to get there. Weren't the gates shut?' Bunch glanced at Dodo and raised her eyebrows. 'Two shut gates in fact.'

'Poachers, mebbe, left the gates open?' He glanced at his feet and then back to stare Bunch straight in the eye. 'One o' your land maids reck'ned she heard shots the day afore that.'

'I see.' Bunch looked down at her toast and worked hard to calm herself. Moving some of the herd had been all about protecting them from just this kind of predation. 'Is poaching likely to be a problem?'

'Dunno, Miss,' he mumbled.

Bunch glanced at Dodo, who shrugged. Treating Haynes with kid gloves was all very well but his surliness had categorically veered into rampant insubordination. She wondered if he would have spoken to her father in that same way. Somehow she doubted it. 'You think our missing ewes might have gone into a local stew pot?'

He shrugged. 'Mebbe.'

'Were the sheep near where—' She found herself reluctant even to mention the death. *Pull yourself together, Bunch.* 'Was it near the shooting?'

'Tracks go back down the crossways.' He shrugged again. 'No tellin' when snow's druvven all which ways. That was a few hours back. I didn't go all the way down.' He glanced at his maimed leg. 'If them sheep're in the wood they'll be safe enough. Best left. We can get 'em out easier when the tracks're cleared.'

Bunch stood up, brushing crumbs emphatically from her own injured leg. 'I still think we should go and take a look.'

'Today, Miss?' Haynes gestured at the window. 'I can send one of them maids up to walk the fence. You know what sheep're like. They'll be sittin' lee side've a hedge somewhere.'

His efforts to avoid exertion were a red rag to Bunch. Her own injury made it a task. Nevertheless if she could make it up there then so could he. 'The girls have enough to do getting the flock back out of the barley. I think you and I can risk a quiet stroll.' She smiled at him. 'You are our stockman not the gamekeeper. We don't even have one of those any more. More's the pity. It's sheep we are chasing, not pheasants. That will be all, Haynes. I shall be along shortly and we can investigate it then.'

'Should we call for Botting?' Dodo asked. 'Even if the sheep are safe we can't have wholesale poaching getting out of hand.'

'They didn't look too closely when a man was found dead up at Hascombe Wood, I really doubt they will turn out for a couple of sheep.' Bunch heard the bitter edge in her voice and saw Dodo flinch. 'Sorry, old thing. You will have to wait in in case the police do decide to turn up.'

‹ SIX ›

As Bunch emerged into the yard that lay between bothy, barn and outbuildings a snowball smacked against the wooden doors. The six Land Girls straggled to a halt as they spotted her. 'What-ho boss,' Kate called.

'Good morning girls,' Bunch replied. 'There may be an extra job for you after lunch if it doesn't start snowing again. Not a terribly nice one, I'm afraid. I'm going to check out your reports of sheep up in the woods and if they have broken in there we may need to move the main flock closer, which is not going to be simple in these conditions. Have you seen Haynes? He was supposed to be waiting for me here.'

'He was taking a trailer load of hay up to the beef steers. Said he'd be back soon,' said Kate.

'Really.' Bunch stared out toward the distant barns housing the few beef cattle that remained with them. She had been quite emphatic about meeting Haynes and there was no excuse for him to go off on some other job in direct defiance of her orders.

'Any chance I can take the shot-gun up to the woods?' Kate asked her. 'See if we can bag a few bunnies for the pot?' Kate Woolridge, along with Patricia Quinton, were county girls, though from Warwickshire rather than the local Sussex area. They had joined up at the same time and somehow managed to stay together. Both liked to ride and shoot, given the chance.

'What?'

'Rabbits?'

'We are supposed to catch poachers, Katy. Not train up new ones.'

'I'm not skinnin' no rabbits. Can't stand rabbits. 'Orrible smelly things.' Mary Tucker patted her peroxide hair that was swept back in carefully sculpted victory rolls on either side of her head, with a wide scarf tied over the top.

Bunch always wondered what time the girl got up every morning to effect the elaborate hair and make-up, and why, given the job she and the rest did. Elsie was dark-haired with slightly less of the movie star about her but was no less noisy. Very different from Ruth Cole, the mousey Londoner, or the brawny Yorkshire lass, Annie Marsden. They were a mixed tribe, to be sure, but a close-knit crew living together in one of the empty cottages, and working side by side seven days a week. Bunch had observed very few arguments despite all that, and attributed it to Kate's innate head-girl persona.

'Give us the nod,' Kate said. 'If it's on estate land it's not poaching.'

'All right. Once you've done a sweep along the edge of the shaw,' Bunch said.

'We're sorry to hear about your friend, Mr Frampton.' Patricia came close so that her soft voice carried the distance. 'Such a horrible way to go.'

'Thank you.' Bunch could barely believe that news had got around so quickly since the police had not issued a statement, so far as she knew, and the local paper had yet to come out. It was a shock and it made her angry that Jonathan's reputation could go down the drain quite so quickly.

'Mary said that he killed himself,' said Kate. 'Is that true? The poor man. What would drive somebody to do such an awful thing?'

Bunch regarded Mary coldly. Hearing the official police line voiced as common gossip was a stab to the body. 'Mary Tucker, you have no call to say such things and it is not for discussion.'

'I'm sorry. We don't mean to pry,' Patricia said. 'You should probably know there was nothing else talked about all last night in the Seven Stars. Especially the Reverend. He indulged in a great deal of sinning-against-the-soul rhetoric before his fifth pint and staggered back to the rectory. Old hypocrite.'

Bunch's mind swept back to her conversation with Dodo and she clenched her teeth against some choice words. She was not a religious person herself and did not adhere to the damnation of Jonathan Frampton's eternal soul. His being buried *beyond the wall* was becoming a reality and a terrible and permanent reflection on his memory as a coward, a moral backslider, a failure.

She raised her chin to stare down at Patricia with the full force of her disapproval. 'The Reverend Day would do well to remember where his stipend comes from,' she said finally. 'As would all of you. Mr Frampton was a good friend to me and to my sister. I forbid you to discuss estate business in the Seven Stars. You should not have been there so late, in any event.'

'Free country,' Mary replied. 'Can't stop us going for a few pints. Ain't much to do round 'ere that's fun, as it is. Besides, you see all sorts out there. Like last week.'

'You are permitted to live here and not at the Land Army bothy because you have early starts,' Bunch replied. 'Remember, I am responsible for all of you girls. I am a Land Army officer *and* the landowner, and if anything happens to you I shall the one answering the awkward questions. That includes you, Mary Tucker. You would do well to remember it, unless you want to be transferred.'

Mary regarded her brazenly in a way Bunch was totally unaccustomed to. 'My mum was leavin' me on me own since I was ten.'

'I'm not against you having some fun, girls, but there are rules. I'm supposed to be keeping an eye on you all.'

'The girls at t'ostel have a nine p.m. curfew,' Annie mumbled. 'They get fined 'appen they break it.'

'See? As for drinking with a bunch of soldiers—' Bunch shook her head. 'Do be careful around those chaps. They know they won't be here forever and a lot of them will not be overly concerned about what they leave behind.'

'Yeah? Well that makes 'em no different to any other bloke. I can look after m'self, Miss. Ten of us at 'ome and all younger 'en me. Why d'you fink I volunteered for this mob? This is a doddle compared to them.'

'Not everyone has the benefit of your experience, Mary. I don't want to impose a curfew but I may have no choice. Rein back on the late nights. Is that clear?'

'Yes, Miss Courtney.'

The faces before her were variously sullen and chagrined. She almost regretted such sweeping critique. The girls were only repeating tap room chatter. If it were not someone as close to her as Jonathan Frampton she would be just as eager to chew over the scant details. She liked these girls and hated to come down on them hard, or have them see her as a cold and heartless toff, but she could see where the general opinion was headed. Jonny was already being pilloried as a moral coward in their eyes and it hurt her deeply. How was she ever to convince them of what she knew to be true?

'For the record, I spoke with the Chief Inspector myself and the circumstances are not certain by any means. If you hear any rumours or gossip I'd be grateful if you let me know. It needs to be nipped in the bud before it gets any worse.'

'Other than 'e killed 'imself?' Mary demanded. 'Can't see 'ow you can get worse gossip than that.'

'We won't know what happened to him until after the inquest so please reserve judgement until then. I am sure if one of you met with an accident, or worse, and that would not appear to be out of the question if you roam the lanes late at night, you would not want people trampling your good name underfoot. I'd appreciate knowing anything else that's said about him.'

'Will do,' said Kate.

'Thank you. Tell Haynes to come and find me the moment he gets back with that tractor. I shall be in the stables. Oh, and tell Parsons I'd like a word when he gets back from the market.'

She walked back into the teeth of the wind. It was blowing harder, driving fresh snow against the brick and tar-blackened boards of the barn walls. More snow gave her more time but hindered her movements.

To be honest, she was a little disappointed that the girls had not heard more. She had come to rely on them for local news now that below-stairs was all but a distant memory. She realised she may have been a little rough on them but she hoped Kate and Patricia, at least, would have informed her of anything they thought she needed to know. Mary was all mouth and trousers according to the rest of the gang, and not very bright, relying on her peroxide starlet looks and natural cunning to get by. *Not that cunning isn't a useful gift.*

She glanced back at the barns where sounds of snowball fighting had resumed. A fresh flurry of snow stung her face. Bunch thrust her hands deep into the pockets of her duster, hunched her head into her shoulders, and strode to the stable block without looking left or right.

The yard was empty and she walked straight into the stables and to Perry's stall. He thrust his head over the half-door and pushed against her shoulder, snickering quietly from deep in his considerable chest. Bunch scrubbed the horse's forehead with her knuckles, kissing the forelock tuft that hung half way down his face as she muttered soothing words. 'No treats today. You will get fat standing around your box all day. I know, you're bored but we can't go out in this weather every day. You're not as young as you were.' She smoothed his velvety muzzle, scratching the sides where grey hairs were peppering dark patches. He was not the thoroughbred hunter her peers would have chosen, as her father and sister had chosen. Bunch knew people looked down their noses at Perry but she had been riding him for a long while and he was her pride and joy. Roger pushed against her legs, paddling his feet and whining. 'Oh, shut up you jealous old fool. We're going indoors very soon and then you'll get fed.'

The light chestnut hunter stretched her head from the door of the next box and whinnied, echoed by a deeper snorting from a dark dapple-grey stabled further down again. 'I know, Sheba, and you as well, Robbo.' Bunch reached out and patted Sheba's nose. 'It's not nearly feed time. You will all have to wait.'

Bunch busied herself refilling trickle nets and checking water buckets, then stood for a while longer in the centre of the stalls, soaking in the sweet scents of horse and hay. All her life the stables had been her retreat in times of stress, somewhere that she could offload her troubles without fear of reproof. It was also warm in there, even though there were only three horses when there had been six just two years before. Barty Tinsley was not the only one to have reduced his stable. With the onset of war and the requisitioning of Perringham, and despite all her arguments, her father had reduced their string to just three mounts. Enough for the odd ride out with the hunt. The other mares and the stallion had been loaned out to a breeder over in Somerset. She missed them but didn't imagine the arrangement would be permanent.

She wished she had remembered some titbits to offer her three charges. 'I'll sneak you out some apple in the morning,' she muttered.

'He can have some right now.'

Bunch jumped causing Perry to back up, tossing his head peevishly.

'Sorry Ma'am. I didn't mean to startle you.' The blonde officer she had seen the previous day stood in the doorway holding out a weighted paper bag. 'I saw you come in and figured these guys could do with a treat.'

'They could, thank you...?'

'Lieutenant, Ma'am. Seb Johansson.' He walked forward with the bag. 'Apples,' he said. 'Mary said you'd welcome a few for your boys.'

'Thank you, Lieutenant.' She eyed his uniform, seeing that of a British cavalry subaltern that belied his accent. *European,* she thought. *Dutch?* That she doubted. *Norwegian maybe, by the name.* She had seen uniforms of all nationalities at the clubs up in Town. *What could he be doing in British togs?* She took the bag and rummaged inside to pull out a couple of pieces of fruit. 'Two boys and a girl, as it happens,' she said.

'And I can tell which is which.' He walked forward and patted Sheba firmly on the neck. 'Hey there. You're quite the lady aren't you? Just like your mistress, I bet.'

Sheba backed up, tossing her head in agitation and Bunch smiled to herself. 'Technically, Sheba belongs to my sister,' she said. 'Her father-in-law doesn't want to stable her.'

Johansson glanced up at the name plate over the door. 'Sheba. Not just a princess. She's a Queen of the Nile.' He pulled an apple from his pocket and offered it to the horse, which she took eagerly but stepped back again to crunch it in private. Johansson also stepped back to get a good look at Robbie and then Perry – and then at Bunch, who watched him warily. 'Can I feed him?' he said. 'Get to know him?'

'Of course.' She tossed him an apple from the bag, which he caught expertly with one hand. He grinned and winked as he turned to feed Robbie.

'Cricket?' she asked

'Hell no, 'scusing my language. Handball.'

She nodded. 'That's like netball, isn't it?'

He shrugged 'Maybe just. I think more basketball.'

'Of course, I should have known.' She fed Perry his apple in silence. She resented this stranger in her private temple. He was too cocky by far, but she could not look the gift-fruit in the horse's mouth.

Johansson slapped Robbie's neck as the hunter munched. 'He's a fine boy,' he said. He came to stand by Perry and eyed him up and down. 'And this is Peregrine.' He peered at the name plate over the door. 'A pretty name for such a solid beast.' The lieutenant smiled a little sheepishly. 'Good upper strength. Solid conformation.'

'You mean he's not what you'd expected to find in here,' she said. 'Perry is a Fell pony and he's top notch. He'll hunt all day and hardly break out in a sweat. He's totally bomb proof on the roads and he has a mouth like velvet.'

'Woah.' He raised both hands in surrender, that trademark grin widening even further. 'I wasn't meaning any insult. Truly. We have horses like him at home. Haflingers and Fjorders. Good animals. I only meant that—'

Norwegian, then. She nodded. 'You think a posh gel like me shouldn't be riding an old nag? Better people than you have told me that. Including the Hunt Master, who happens to be an Earl, I might add. I see you know horses but the stables are off limits. Nothing personal.'

'I know. I only came over because Mary said—'

'Mary? She says far too much.'

Johansson frowned. 'Mary's a good kid. She said I should tell you something about the night your friend died. Frampton was he called? Do you want to hear it?'

'Oh, sorry, yes. Yes I do.'

'Okay then.' He leaned against the stall post, untwisting tangled strings from Perry's net. 'I was walking back from the pub, with Mary, and I – we – we saw some guys parked up where the road cuts between the two woods.'

'Army?'

'No, I don't think so. Civilian. Two vehicles…'

'Anything else?'

'One was big. A van, an old Bedford – maybe? It was hard to tell. Neither had their lights on.' He frowned. 'I thought nothing unusual at the time. The Blackout, you know. But this one guy hanging around, he ducked away pretty quick when he spotted us, back into the trees on his side of the woods. Mary wanted to go after him, had this idea she knew him, maybe.' He rubbed at his neck and smiled sheepishly. 'She's one hell of a girl.'

'Mary comes from a colourful background. She will get angry before she is frightened.'

'Don't I know it! Anyhow, when I saw her just now she was kind of anxious that you should know.'

'Yes, thank you.' Bunch wondered why Mary had said nothing herself earlier but let it lie. The girl was naturally secretive when it came to dealing with authority.

'Does that mean anything to you?'

'Not a great deal. Possibly nothing more than some chaps meeting up for a bit of poaching. Though a van might be a tad optimistic. Did you see what colour what it was? The van, I mean.'

'Maybe red or brown? Hard to say in the dark. It did have a name on the door but I didn't see it that clearly. I had other things on my mind.' Johansson paused, flushing slightly. 'I think it said *Something and Sons*. Could be Reddingham? Bucking-ham? Something ending with *ham*, for sure.'

'That should narrow it down to a few dozen,' Bunch replied. 'Sorry, I didn't mean to be brusque. It may help. Thank you, Mister Johansson. Thank Mary for me, as well.'

'My pleasure.' He pushed away from the post and swung her a lazy salute before sauntering away.

Bunch watched him go with very mixed feelings. He seemed willing and helpful enough. She gave Perry a final pat. This was an interesting development, especially when she had an idea who owned the van. Many of the local butchers had their own farms and their own slaughter house, which also served other farms in the area. One such was the local village butcher, Beckenham's. Bunch had no notion whether Saul Frampton utilised their facilities. She knew that Parsons, her own steward, had not used them after a scandal some ten years before over horse meat. Except that Frampton was not a man with the same kinds of sensibilities.

No time to worry about it for the moment, with missing sheep to trace, she decided. Bunch strode from the stable in search of the recalcitrant Haynes.

❧SEVEN❧

Bunch allowed Haynes to set the pace along the ancient trackway leading to the spot where the girls had claimed hearing sheep. The progress was slow, partly due to the snow but mostly down to Haynes' disability. She tried not to sigh at their slow progress. She had been something of a strider before her own clash with the gods of war so she had some sympathy and she did try very hard to hide her impatience. She had given in to a rather uncharitable sense that his disabilities were frequently convenient, and she knew it to be unfair.

'I'm sorry, Haynes,' she said as he stumbled yet again on a hidden obstacle. 'I didn't think how difficult this route would be for you. If you want to start back I can find it on my own, I expect. I do know these woods.'

'Mebbe,' he grunted. 'The Guvn'r'd have me strung up if I was to let you out here on your own.'

'Mr Courtney is away,' she replied. 'He'll never know.'

'Mebbe.' He shot her a scowl. 'I bain't lettin' you go wanderin' about on your own.'

Her sympathy for his struggle against the snow evaporated under his dogged adherence to masculine authority. It layered frustration on top of irritability, atop of a restlessness that she was uncertain how to address. She had come up against it in her WLA duties, this unshakable certainty in some minds that, despite her birthright and status, she really could not take charge whilst her father was alive. Even then, she had the certainty that in many eyes she would only be stewarding until a man could be found to marry her and take over. She was the heir because both of her brothers had died in the flu pandemic, and though there was no entail the assumption remained that her father would question every move she made, whether it was a logical decision or not; it was as if the Property Acts had never been passed.

Bunch had made her exasperation with such casual misogyny well known yet today was not the day for making such points, however. All she wanted was to find the damned sheep and get back home into the warm. She huddled into her waxed coat and tugged her scarf up around her chin to cheat the brisk wind blowing up along the coombes from the general direction of the English Channel, and wished she had saddled up Perry despite Haynes' presence.

She eased the shotgun, held close over her elbow, and plunged toward the cover of the trees. Roger lolloped through the drifts, vanishing now and then when he flopped into a deeper snow-bank, only to plough through the other side and carry on. Snow still whispered through the meshed ceiling of bare branches, falling as a finer powder than in open fields, yet still accumulating in the little glades and dells and swirling around the tree trunks to fill the gullies. Further into the woods it had yet to lie with any serious intent but still managed respectable drifts where some fallen titan had left a break in the canopy.

'Back end o' the rise that tops the road,' Haynes said, and came to a halt, resting on his rough-hewn stave and waiting quietly. 'That's where they maids wuz workin'.'

'Up through the hazel coppice?' Bunch asked. 'Can you manage that, Haynes?'

He glowered at her. 'Tisn't easy going for you, neither.' He paused and peered skywards. 'Big fall on its way,' he said. 'Might be better t'leave it fer today.'

'The snow is precisely why we need to go now,' she replied. 'We could go around the other side if it makes it easier, though it will take a lot longer.'

Haynes grunted. 'I've bin up an' down this coombe all my life, Miss. We'll take a while but I c'n manage. We'll go up this bank right 'ere. Tis safe enough.'

Bunch looked back the way they had come and then up to the top of the rise. He was right. Going around would add the best part of an hour, probably far more given his slow progress.

'More haste an' less speed or one of us'll be breakin' a leg. This bank has been a warren fer as long as anyone knows and tis riddled with scrapes an' burrows.' Haynes shot her an accusing reproach and she pulled a face. 'You can't see 'em under the snow.'

'We should certainly take care.' She grabbed the base of a hazel stand to pull herself up onto the bank's rim and paused. 'Did you hear that?' she whispered.

'Miss?' he called too loudly though she was not ten feet away.

'Quiet. There's someone up there,' she hissed. They both listened intently.

'Sheep over the coombe,' Haynes called. 'They do sounds 'uman a' times.'

'That is not sheep.' She was certain the noises she could hear were human and wondered if it was wise to go further. She looked at Roger, busy digging into the bank after some buried rodent. He seemed not to have noticed, but the wind was to their backs and his hearing was not so acute as it had once been. She strained to hear what the voices might be saying but it was just a mutter, rousing into a chorus of raucous laughter, before sinking back to a bass grumbling. 'You hear that?' she hissed at Haynes.

'Ah,' he said, more loudly than she thought wise.

'Wait there,' she said. 'I'll just take a quick peek.'

'Don't take the risk, Miss.' Haynes slapped at his leg with his stick. 'You're faster on yer feet than me, but still... I'll stay an' watch so you c'n go and fetch old Botting.'

'That will take an hour or more,' she replied. 'No, I'll just take a look.'

'But Miss...'

'I can manage. You stay,' she said again, and turned away to hide her smile when Roger sat abruptly on her command. 'I won't be long.' Bunch could understand Haynes' frustration at being told to remain behind, and she empathised. She hauled herself up the last ten feet to peer across the clearing. The uneven slope was laid out beneath a swathe of ancient woodland beyond the coppiced hazels.

Three figures were gathered between the woodland stand and a sprawl of invading rhododendrons that sheltered them from the worst of the wind. The ground around them was red brown with a compote of newly disturbed leaf litter and blood, with splashes of newly red gore adding to the mix. The tallest of the three, a tall man by any standards, was, despite the cold, stripped down to bloodied shirt sleeves, a makeshift sacking apron tied around his waist with twine. He was wielding a fletching knife efficiently, hacking through sinews that held flesh to bone. He bent to pick up a ruddy lump and dropped it into a sack held open by a shorter muscular countryman.

Bunch peered at them; they were vaguely familiar to her but not sufficiently enough to register names. The third man, only partially visible, was rolling the skinned fleeces into portable bundles and throwing them down the slope behind him.

Another two dead beasts lay close by, and beside those was an alarmingly large heap of entrails and heads. This was not deer being poached for local tables, as far as she could see. All of the glazed eyes staring from decapitated heads were sheep, stolen from her own flock, she did not doubt. Quite apart from the money they represented, these were rationable goods being removed from the precious national stock. She felt less nervous and increasingly angry at the complete wrongness of it all. Even then she hesitated. There were three intruders and Bunch was acutely aware that her shotgun only had two barrels.

She felt, almost clinically, her pulse crashing through her veins, and wondered why the notion of shooting these men came to her so readily. After all, they were apparently armed only with knives and at such a distance not much a threat. Perhaps it was the image of Jonathan's corpse, stiff and bloodied in a clearing not a half mile from where she stood, that hung stubbornly in her mind. Or her instincts picked up on something far more dangerous than local lads stealing for the pot. There was also the very real possibility that she was over reacting. Her mind raced through all these thoughts and permutations in a split second. At the end of it she snapped her shotgun closed with a practised flick, flinching at the noise that was not as loud but certainly more piercing than the crack of a broken twig.

Before she could do anything further, Roger had crested the rise and lumbered past her. Bunch hissed at him to *heel*. The dog halted, peering back at her for a moment, and then looked toward the intruders with their tantalising odour of meat and blood. His uncertainty at being confronted by strangers was apparent and he reacted the only way he knew how. His hackles rose in a scrubbing brush ridge all along his spine and he let loose a volley of deep barks.

The thicker-set man dropped the sack, snatched up his coat, and started to run, screaming, 'Bugger, booy, it's that Courtney maid!' The other two stared at Roger standing half-way, and then to Bunch at the edge of the trees.

'Bugger, booy!' The tall butcher repeated, staring at Bunch in total confusion.

The thick-set man backtracked to grab the tall butcher by the arm, and dived back into the thickness of the evergreen shrubs and was lost to view in bare seconds. The remaining poacher stood half obscured by thin hazel stems, frozen, staring across the clearing at the dog and its owner.

'Who are you?' Bunch called. 'This is private land. Hey! You there!' She started forward. Encouraged by her firm tone and, possibly, also by the smell of fresh meat, Roger lurched to his feet and lunged after them.

The final poacher dropped the lengths of twine he had been holding and dived for a coat piled a few paces away. He came up brandishing a pistol, spinning round to point it at Bunch. 'Call off that bloody dog! Or I'll fuckin' shoot 'im!'

'No don't, please. Roger,' Bunch shouted. 'Roger, heel!'

'Miss Courtney?' Haynes called. 'Miss Rose!'

'Stay there,' Bunch shouted. She stared across at the gunman, sound fading to the rush of blood in her ears, vision tunnelling onto that face now turned to the dog. Across the fifteen or so yards separating them she had time, in an oddly stretched moment, to note his cheek bones jutting like blades from beneath a wide-brimmed hat jammed low on his forehead. Once again a stirring of recognition tickled at the back of her brain, though she was more fixed on the pistol that he held between clasped hands; arms stretched forward with the gun barrel jutting at her like an arrow.

Bunch had time to wonder if she could raise her gun, flick away the safety, and fire before he did. It was a passing thought and no more.

He swivelled the pistol between her and the dog, glancing from side to side. There was no panic in those actions, and it did not need a Master at Arms to see that the poacher was ready and quite willing to fire at any threat, perceived or real. They stood at a stalemate and Bunch feared that a shooting was far from unlikely. The only movement, other than the sweeping gun, came from across the clearing with the wind whipping through the branches. She had not heard him cock the weapon but that proved nothing. She felt she should say something calming, as she'd seen in the movies. Something like 'everything is fine' or 'put the gun down', but all she could think to utter was a feeble 'hello?'

He relaxed by a fraction though the gun did not lower so much as a quarter-inch. He stared, his face half-obscured now by the tree cover and hat in equal measure. She was convinced she could see his eyes glittering but knew that to be impossible at such a distance. Yet something about his attitude shrieked of mockery.

The bastard's laughing at me.

Haynes could be heard scrambling up the slope, followed by muffled cussing as he reached the clearing. The gunman loosed a shot toward him.

Bunch threw herself down but Roger, excited by gunfire, lurched forward. A second shot barked out, answered by a canine shriek. She saw Roger collapsed on the ground, peddling his legs madly, thrashing snow to raspberry pink as blood streamed from a wound along his back.

'No!' Bunch stood and launched herself across the dell, falling to her knees beside the stricken animal. 'Roger!' She struggled to hold him against her body to still his thrashing limbs, oblivious to the blood coursing over her arms and chest, and waiting for the adrenalin to stop firing her heart and nerves. 'Hush, hush, good boy, steady now. Steady, old chap. Shh...' Roger calmed gradually at her voice.

The shooter had gone, following the same path as his partners, and Haynes just stood at the side of the clearing looking after them. He then limped across to pick up her discarded shotgun and came to stand over her.

'Gone?' She shook her head, stating the obvious. 'Sorry. Obviously they have. Did you see which way they went?'

'Down to the road,' Haynes replied. He eased himself down to look at the dog. 'Tis fortunate,' he said. 'It'll leave its mark but 'e bain't dead.' He heaved himself up and scraped some snow away from the base of a tree to peel up a large handful of moss.

Together, and in near silence, they packed the wound with moss, covered it with strips of sacking he found lying nearby, and tied it firmly in place with Bunch's scarf.

Haynes seldom said a great deal and Bunch felt too shaken for chatter. She had been close enough to explosions to feel their heat but bombs had never seemed personal. That was war. Being shot at on her own land was as personal as it could get, and it had shaken her to the marrow. The battle-hardened Haynes seemed more stoic, at least on the surface, but she saw how his hands shook as they worked on the Labrador's wounds.

'Poaching?' she said. 'Or just after the sheep?'

'Sheep,' Haynes replied. 'Lot more'n we've lost. I reck'n they'm gathering stock from all over.'

'Stolen in broad daylight. They have bravado,' she said.

'Ah,' he agreed. 'They know there's no men left on the farms. Easy pickins. They'll be Lundun spivs.'

'Will they be back for this, do you think?' She waved at the mess of bloody carcases and discarded viscera.

'Not fer a bit. We'll get up 'ere and fetch the meat. An' I'll get the girls to move the flock closer to the lower yard. Better fer feedin' in snow, if'n you agrees, Miss.'

'I concur. We should get back now and call the police.'

'Shall I take the old lad, Miss?' Haynes said.

'No, you take the gun.' She stood up and Roger struggled to his feet. 'Roger has other ideas. He seems to be coping.'

'He'll be all right Miss. Tis no more than a graze but he needs a vitnary.'

'I know.' She looked around the dell, seeing it clearly for the first time, seeing the temporary sheep pen fettled from old wattles, and the clumps of yellowish wool, tainted with gore, dotting the well-churned woodland earth. She looked back at Haynes and then up through the branches at the heavy yellow-tinted clouds. Granular snow spittered onto her face. It would be hours before a constable could be standing where she was now, by which time, as with the murder scene across the woods, there would be nothing left to see. 'We should get Roger back quickly. You have the Land Girls move the flock. They won't be able to do much else today.'

He brushed his forefinger along the brim of his cap in a salute that was somewhere between military and feudal. 'We neither o' us need to stand around here, Miss. There's a sight more snow to come an' there's work to do. That ol' dog needs lookin' at.' Haynes limped over to check the discarded sheep heads for markings clipped to their ears. 'There's some've ours,' he said. 'Mebbe six. T'others bain't.' He kicked at the heap and exposed a further heads. 'Some Hascombe stock,' he muttered. 'That one there's from Fenny Barns. Bin a lot've thievin' all over, accordin' to my ole dad.'

'Yes.' She glanced in the direction in Hascombe Hill. Perret Shaw had once been a part of that woodland and was only divided from it by the roadway and a small strip of flat land currently being cleared by the Land Army girls for beet crops. 'They are money on legs, and you know as well as I there is every chance whoever did this will be back.' She bent down to pick Roger up in a double-armed hug. He was heavy, as she knew he would be, but there was no way that the crippled Haynes could carry him. *At least*, she told herself, *it's downhill most of the way.*

Haynes regarded her passively, leaning heavily on his stick as he rubbed at his thigh. The message was clear: he was in pain and didn't want to stand around in the cold any more than she did.

She shook her thoughts out of the rut that they seemed intent on falling in. The drone of engines, somewhere way beyond the wood, reminded her oddly of her stint in France. She took a deep breath and watched, staring up for a glimpse of the planes high above the trees, and at the same time poised for action. The sounds came no closer, passing away toward Parham airfield. She eased her stance and calmed herself, angry at her reaction to the noise from the planes. *That was months ago, dammit, woman.* 'Let's get back.'

'Yes, Miss.'

Bunch turned and walked around the edge of the rise without speaking, breathing heavily with the strain of carrying the heavy dog. She was mulling over the previous night's events as they walked. There had been a raid down on the coast, she knew, loud enough and bright enough to be seen for miles inland, and more than a few stray ordnances had fallen close enough to shudder loose fittings. People would not notice the clatter or bangs on the Downs on such a night, but even so it would have been a bold team that stayed out in that and had not felt the need to head for shelter.

The men had butchered a dozen sheep, perhaps many more, and that could not have been done without some lights, even with the faux luminance that snow provided. Lights that the ever-present Home Guard at the spotter station on Pikes Hill must surely have seen, not to mention the ARP. Her farm had been fined three weeks running for an alleged chink of light leaking from a warped door to one of the barns last autumn, a fact that still rankled. In Bunch's opinion there wasn't a barn in the county that was waterproof for lack of repair, never mind lightproof.

By unspoken agreement Haynes moved ahead, forging a trail back through the snow for her to follow, and for that she was grateful. The shock of being fired upon was beginning to sink in; she knew the tremble in her limbs was not entirely down to her burden. Bunch tried to concentrate on putting one foot in front of the other and to blot out the memory of that gun snouting in her direction. She thought more of the man behind it. He was a Londoner based from the few words he had uttered. The other two men she had glimpsed, on the other hand, had seemed to know her, which suggested they were local. She could name half a dozen and more men from the estate's pre-war staff who could efficiently butcher game without a second thought.

Bunch stopped near a stile, kneeling carefully to lay the dog on the snow. Roger whined and licked at her hand. 'All right boy. We'll get you home as quick as we can.' She stroked his head gently. 'A moment Haynes, I need to catch my breath!'

The stockman walked back and leaned on his stick. 'We can't let 'im get chilled, Miss.'

'I know, just a few seconds. That dog weighs a ton.' Bunch rubbed at her aching arms. 'I was rather thinking,' she said, 'if they intended to take or leave all those sheep heads, or if they were in a hurry? I imagine they were disturbed last night, as well. But by whom? Do you think they were slaughtered around the same time as Saul's animals? Or had they returned later for more high-end butchery bonus?' She knew her thoughts were all of a jumble.

'Couldn't say, Miss.' He shrugged. 'Folks will buy no matter how high the prices go. Folks that should know bet—' He paused, his face setting in harder lines. 'People will be feelin' the pinch soon enough and there's those as knows how to ease it fer 'em.'

'Quite probably.' Bunch stared around the hillside though she was not sure what she was looking for. This side of the hill tailed down into small meadow and continued across the lane into Frampton's land. Was it too much of a coincidence that sheep had been stolen and a man shot to death on the same night? It would not be a huge leap of imagination to assume it was the same gang. If this did not convince Chief Inspector Wright that Jonathan had been a victim of another man's hand, she did not know what would.

An almost leaden quiet, of the kind that only snow could produce, made her uneasy. She listened. Snow whispered on cold ground; a solitary crow called somewhere higher up the hill; but no sound of human activity could be heard. The gang had picked their spot: somewhere few people came, especially at this time of year.

❧EIGHT❧

'Miss Courtney? Chief Inspector Wright.'

'Inspector. I had been expecting you to call last night.'

'I am sorry for not getting up to you, myself. I do have a transcript of the incident telephoned in by WRC Dyer. His report is on my desk. We logged this as a firearms incident and of course we shall continue with our routine investigations, but other than the statements from yourself and Mr Haynes we have little to go on so far.'

'Is that all I'm to expect?' Her comment was met with a long pause sprinkled with muffled clicks and buzzings at the other end of the line. She imagined Wright holding the receiver against his jacket to mute her as he spoke to some unknown person at his end. 'May I remind you that I was fired upon?' She raised her voice to overcome the impedance. 'It was only by chance that my poor dog was injured or worse, and not me.'

'I can assure you that we take this very seriously, Miss Courtney. Botting and Dyer are conducting enquiries in the area, and we *do* have your statements. Until we have gathered any additional information there is little we can do. We had several other serious incidents overnight—'

'Armed men on my property is not serious?' Bunch remarked. There was another silence. She would have given a lot to speak to the Chief Inspector face to face and not merely as a voice at the other end of the line.

'I seem to be doing a lot of apologising to you. You don't need me to tell you that the road conditions are bad. In my defence, my superior has deemed two *actual* murders down on the coast a higher priority. It's not an excuse seen from your perspective, I realise. The crime committed against you *is* very serious but fortunately you were not hurt.'

'Leaving aside my chance escape from a near miss with a

bullet, these men were stealing livestock and not rabbits for the pot. Need I remind you of the gravity of that?'

There was another short silence. 'Oh, the report I have only states poaching. That does change things somewhat,' Wright said.

'As if my being fired upon was not enough.'

A longer silence and then, 'I am destined to apologise to you at every turn.' The rush of his sigh across the mouthpiece rustled like the crushing of coarse paper. 'Policing can be a bloody business and obviously doubly so in wartime. We can lose sight of how things affect people, and…' His voice was fading a little with fatigue, yet his sincerity was all too apparent.

Bunch found herself feeling sorry for him. 'I appreciate that,' she said. 'I suppose you think me a bit of a pill, Inspector.' Bunch tried to sound conciliatory. 'I appreciate it could have been worse. Nevertheless, it's not something to be shrugged off, whatever our station in life. Having a gun pointed at my face felt serious enough.'

'Miss Courtney, *any* civilian being fired on is serious.'

Bunch waited for more but Wright had fallen silent, with only the general static of the telephone greeting her ear; and with it the knowledge that the village telephonist would be hanging onto every word.

'Better the weapon you can see than one dropping out of the sky?' he suggested at last.

'Maybe something like that.' She picked up her teacup, grimacing at the skin forming on the surface. It quaked gently in her grasp. She took a sip anyway and watched her hand curiously as it continued its St Vitus' gyrations. She hadn't been aware of her trembling until that point. Shock, she knew, and tea was the prescribed panacea; sweet tea, though this was anything but that. She found herself to be unafraid now, not the least bit nervous on any sensible level, so that the physical evidence of her unsteady hands to the contrary was deeply irritating. Bunch was annoyed by this betrayal of her reaction. She was feeling inordinately glad that Wright was due to give evidence at the Crown Court in another case within the hour and thus he would be unable to visit and see her in such a state. *Not that he's important or anything,* she told herself, *but I'd rather he didn't see me being quite such a ditz.* 'I did give my statement to Botting, as you know,' she said aloud.

'I've read it. Look, these two local men, are you sure you did not recognise them?'

'No, I only had a glimpse.'

'Yet they appeared to know you.'

She lodged the handset between ear and shoulder to free both her hands, lit a cigarette and pulled hard on it, blinking smoke from her eyes and allowing the heady rush to wash through her. 'They seemed to,' she said. 'If they were local they'd be bound to know who I am.'

'You think they might work on the estate?' he asked.

She took another lungful of smoke and tilted her head back to exhale at the ceiling, watching the greyness rush upward in a long stream. 'Not everyone in the village works for Daddy,' she said. 'They would recognise me, though.'

'They would?'

She laughed lightly, realising how arrogant that must sound and was unexpectedly eager for him to see her in a better light. 'Occupational hazard, I'm afraid. I am a Courtney. People around here know us by sight, at the very least.'

She could hear Wright sigh and imagined him rubbing a hand through his hair as she had noticed him do so when deep in thought. 'I'll come up tomorrow,' he said.

Bunch smiled as she took another long drag then stubbed the cigarette out. 'I shall look forward to seeing you.'

'Thank you Miss—'

'Rose,' she said. 'Bunch to my pals. Till tomorrow.' She tipped the handset into the cradle and sat back adjusting the blanket she had slung around her shoulders. The office was not the warmest place in the house; she had not set a fire on the grounds that she wouldn't be in this particular room for much longer. The face-warming call from the good Chief Inspector was about to go to waste as she shivered deep to her core.

She needed to visit Saul Frampton and discuss the slaughter of his sheep on her land. She did not want to go. Twice in as many days was more than she ever wanted of that man's company, yet it was a conversation that could not possibly be conducted over the telephone. She'd take Dodo along; her sister was far better with charm offensives.

~~~

Frampton seemed not to have moved since they had left him the previous day, except perhaps to seek out two more bottles of whisky to join the one he had proffered to them on their earlier visit. His clothes were more rumpled and his face unshaven. *Or not even acquainted with soap and water,* Bunch thought, *unless the water he might be mixing with his scotch counts for anything.*

'What do you two want?' he growled. 'Hanging around the place like a pair of bloody ghouls. He's dead, dammit. Gone. Now you two can do the same.'

It was a challenge that Bunch did not quite comprehend even though he was a man in grief and, in her experience, grief so often caused hiccups between brain and mouth. 'Sorry to intrude,' she said, 'but we found out something we thought you should know.'

'Nothing I don't know already, I'll be damned,' he snarled. 'Bugger off, the pair of you.' He leered at Bunch and dropped his oily cleaning cloth long enough to pick up the glass sitting next to the tin of gun oil. 'He was never interested in you. Did you know that?'

Dodo pulled her sister delicately to one side and stepped closer to the table. 'Losing someone close, it's painful. I know that all too well. We don't mean to pester you, Mr Frampton, but there are a few things we thought you should know, or rather ask you, about missing stock.'

'I don't give a damn about bloody stock.' He tossed back the inch of scotch that the glass had contained without any noticeable effect on his throat. 'I don't need pity off some milksop widow. Why should I care about a handful of bloody sheep when the vultures are moving in? I have nothing to say to you or anybody. Just clear out, will you.'

Bunch noted how steady his hand was as he set down the glass and reverted to his methodical cleaning. He had plainly been drinking all day, possibly all night, yet was apparently stone cold sober, on the surface it appeared. Bunch laid a hand on Dodo's arm as a warning. She did not blame Saul for losing himself in the bottom of a bottle but he was crossing lines, even for a man deep in the cups. That he could not be reasoned with nor cajoled into better humour was best ignored for now. They should target the practicalities of life. He had a farm to run, just as she did, and few staff to do it with. 'Who's dealing with your stock?' Bunch glanced at Dodo in the silence that followed. Dodo only shrugged. 'Mr Frampton? Do you need anyone to help out?'

'I pay people to work.' He raised his head to meet her gaze revealing bloodshot eyes that now struggled to focus. His hand might be steady but he was clearly inebriated, Bunch assumed, and unlikely to make any real sense.

'Do you have indoor staff?' Dodo asked. 'Is your housekeeper coming in today?'

'She came,' he said. 'Told her to clear off. Can't be dealing with interfering women.' He glared at her meaningfully, half rising and slumping back when his legs refused to support him. 'I don't want you here and I'm bloody sure *you* don't want to *be* here.' He frowned into the short silence before adding, 'Why are you here, anyway?'

'We need to talk about your stock. And we also thought you might need help with the funeral.' Dodo touched his shoulder. 'I know how it is. I've lost Georgie and it's awful. Like a huge chunk of me has been ripped away. We have to carry on, though.'

'Do we?' He snorted and wrestled the bottle from Dodo when she tried to move it away. 'There is no *we*. That grasping, hypocritical, do-gooder stupid little bastard threw it all away. Everything I've worked for. He *threw* me to the sodding wolves.' Frampton splashed scotch at the glass. 'You know nothing and you don't want to know. Go back to your bloody palace and stop asking me bloody stupid questions about things you'll never bloody understand.'

Bunch slapped the table with her palm making the oil can jump, bringing Frampton's fuddled attention to her and away from the shaking Dodo. 'Now look here, Frampton, you can't talk to my sister like that. I won't have it.'

'George's special little pal?' he tipped his head back to roar out a fume-laden bellowing laugh.

Bunch tugged the bottle away from him, stowing it at the far end of the dresser. 'Snap out of it, Saul. Jonny is dead, and that is awful, but there are things that you need to do Checking your flocks is a must because there are men rustling on a big scale.'

Frampton stared at the table top for a long moment before raising his head yet again to meet her eye, far more soberly than she would have thought feasible. 'Why would you think that concerns me?'

'Because we found sheep heads with Hascombe ear clips, and because one of my WLA girls and her young man were out in the lane and saw vehicles parked below the wood,' she replied. 'I think they had something to do with what happened to Jonny. Tell me this: which abattoir do you use?'

Frampton's shoulders began to shake and then he opened his mouth and bellowed humourless mirth into the chilled kitchen air. 'Bloody abattoirs? She's telling me to call funeral parlour and you're all for the knackers' yard. Not that it wouldn't do for him.' He waved a hand at them. 'It's none of your damned business who slaughters my beasts. Don't be poking about in a man's business when you don't know what his business is.'

'It is very much my business.' Bunch kept her tone level and her hands firmly in her pockets before the urge to slap him overtook her. She had never warmed to Saul Frampton, few did, but today he was really crossing all the lines of decent and civilised behaviour. She could ignore the insult to herself but, even his being deep in the arms of Bacchus, could not excuse the insults he poured on his own flesh and blood. 'Jonny did not kill himself,' she said, 'and I will prove it. You of all people should have reason to help me.'

He lurched to his feet and retrieved the bottle. 'You know something, *Miss* Courtney? You want to know something?' He put the bottle to his lips and took a long swallow, pausing as even his anaesthetised throat was stung by the sheer volume. 'You know why you are always going to be the county's most eligible spinster? You know why?' He swayed dangerously and slumped into his chair once more. 'Cos you wasted your time mooning after my boy.' Frampton took another long drink from the bottle and stared up at the ceiling. 'You might be blind and stupid, Rose Courtney, but I knew all about his unnatural acts.' He turned to Dodo and stabbed a finger at her. 'Him and your flyboy and the rest. All at it. Bloody public schools. I told him, I said to him, there's never gonna be anyone to pass it onto. No damned point—' The bottle slipped from his grasp and shattered as it hit the floor, the last of its contents spilling across the stone flags. Frampton beamed at the two women and slowly slid to the floor to join it.

Neither woman could bear to look at each other in that sudden hiatus. They just gazed at the gently snoring heap that was Saul Frampton. It was Bunch who finally broke the tableau. 'He's drunk,' she muttered. 'He was not talking sense.'

'Drunks will always tell the truth,' Dodo whispered. 'Daddy always told us a man will show his true hand from the bottom of a bottle.' She held her hand over her mouth as if to stem whatever else she wanted to say. Her eyes were liquid with fresh tears. 'How could he say such awful things? Vile terrible things.'

'He was only lashing out.' Frampton's rantings were less of a bombshell to Bunch. She knew several men in their circle who generally preferred the company of other men, but it was never discussed. She had known, in that same unspoken fashion, that Jonathan was one of that group – and she had dabbled in lesbian passions of her own at school. George Tinsley, however, was a complete surprise to her. 'Damnably cruel of him, nevertheless.' She prodded Frampton with the toe of her boot. 'We should just leave him. He can wallow in his own filth and sleep it off.'

'Which makes us no better,' Dodo replied. 'He may be a pig but we can't just leave him.'

'I suppose you are right. And Dodo, don't breathe a word to anyone about this, especially to Chief Inspector Wright.'

'He should know. It might be relevant.'

'It's also bloody illegal and at this stage nothing more than a spiteful old man's rumour. Jonathan's case is on sticky ground as it is. Say nothing unless it's absolutely necessary. Agreed?'

'Agreed.'

Bunch stared down at Frampton and then to the door into the rest of the house. 'We should get this lump into his bed.'

'I know but I'm not taking his clothes off.'

'We only need to get him onto his cot and let him sleep it off there.'

It took some while to drag the inert body onto his bed. Dodo pulled off his boots and flipped blankets over him. Bunch watched her with no comment beyond, 'Thank God he's not using the upstairs any more. We'll go and find Pole. Meanwhile, I know Jonny had an aunt near Arundel. She should be aware of the sort of state Saul's in. I'll have a quick rummage around his office and see if I can find a number.' She moved from the bedroom to the rear of the house, to the room that Frampton used as an office. She was mildly surprised at the order that reigned in there. Most estate offices she had seen were a mess of files and papers left by the outdoors men who begrudged time pushing pens rather than dealing with the real work.

She peered at the box folders neatly lining the shelves on one wall, each labelled by year and function. The ledgers would doubtless be in the squat safe brooding in the far corner, but receipts were a different matter. Bunch took down the file labelled STOCK SALES/1939.

Inside were wads of receipts neatly pinned or stapled together in bundles. She picked one at random and scuffed through the small sheaf. Mostly vet bills and invoices from market auctions. She picked up the next bundle and leafed through it. In the middle was a handwritten invoice ripped from a cheap receipt book. Stamped across the top in faded purplish ink was *Pollard & Sons, Superior Butchers*. It was a receipt for slaughtering charges on fifteen spring lambs. The exact amount was blurred, deliberately so, she suspected, but the actual cost did not interest her. Beckenham's had been her suspicion over the rustling and this seemed to throw that theory out with the bathwater. Saul was not dealing with the potential owner of the mysterious van, at least not in writing. She realised one receipt proved nothing but it did decrease the odds against it. If you had receipts for all the sheep slaughtered then, she was certain, selling them on the black market in any quantity was hardly likely.

Voices from outside made her pause. Dodo had found Len Pole. 'Dammit.' She rammed the papers back into the box, shoved it back on the shelf, and started rummaging in desk drawers for an address book. She turned to greet Dodo and the farm foreman, with a battered black leather book in her hand.

'Ah, you found him, Dodo. Good show. Good afternoon, Pole. I was looking for an address for Jonny's Aunt Constance.'

'Afternoon, Miss. There'll be no need for you to worry. I saw as how Mr Frampton was getting in a bit of a state so I called Mr Frampton's family yesterday. I need to know how to run things.'

'Of course you do. Quite right. Capital.' She waved the book in vague circles, smiling and feeling she must look like a gurning idiot, whereas Pole was not an idiot of any sort. 'Someone will be helping Mr Frampton out?'

'I daresay someone will be *throwin'* him out. After all, the estate belonged to Mr Jonathan.'

'It did?' said Dodo. 'He never breathed a word. Was it all Jonny's?'

'Yes, Miss. It's came through his mother's bloodline. Mr Saul's was a good family, mind, but they never 'ad a ha'penny after the Great War.'

'Meaning Hascombe now belongs to…?'

'His cousin Rupert.' Pole moved into the space between Bunch and the desk and gently took the book from her. 'I shall get someone t'keep any eye on the Guvnor for tonight. Don't you worry about 'im. Likely he'll just sleep it off.'

Bunch nodded. The passing of her friend seemed to have opened no end of worm cans. Under those circumstances the arguments since Jonathan had graduated made Saul's actions almost explicable. She wondered why Saul had stayed at all; and why Jonathan had not taken more of a hand. Perhaps, like Dodo's pal Lizzie Benson, he would not receive his inheritance until he reached a set age beyond the normal twenty-one. 'Wills can be such bloody awful bores,' she muttered aloud.

'They can, Miss,' Pole agreed. 'I shall be in charge for now, until Master Rupert has it all sorted out. That'll be a few days yet.'

'Then you should know we found the remains of your stock in our woodland. I came to tell Mr Frampton but he wasn't listening.'

He nodded. 'I shall get the flock moved closer in where we can keep an eye. I appreciated you comin' out to tell us in this weather.'

'Did you know he fired his housekeeper?'

'I did, Miss. Don't worry yourself. All taken care of.'

She found that Pole had manoeuvred them back to the kitchen as quietly as would any sheepdog or a polished butler. She had to admire that skill. The gun still lay across the table and she pointed to it. 'I think maybe you should lock that up somewhere. Don't want another death.'

'I will, Miss.'

'Okay, we shall be off then. Let me know if you need

anything.'

'Yes, Miss.'

The sisters found themselves out on the step in the teeth of a rising, snow-laden wind, with the door firmly shutting behind them. Bunch blinked a few times and looked at Dodo. 'Well, what do you make of that? It's been a while since I was shown the door quite so emphatically.'

'Or politely.'

'Indeed.' She fished in her pockets for gloves and hat and buttoned up her coat against the cold, looking around her all the while.

❧NINE❧

Frampton's declaration had plainly affected Dodo so profoundly that she had fallen into stunned quiet since dinner, and Bunch could not blame her younger sibling for that. No amount of insisting how much George loved her was going to lessen Dodo's feeling that her marriage was, in fact, a sham and, moreover, that he had indulged in an affair which was not only illicit but illegal.

Bunch glanced at her sister relaxing before the fire. The magazine across Dodo's lap had been open at the same fashion spread for at least half an hour. There was a time when the girl would have been chattering on about this fashion or that, but tonight she had been as close to silent as she ever came.

Bunch had mastered the same ice-cool, unflappable, facade that their mother had perfected in a lifetime of embassies and Foreign Office stations. She had found the carry-on chaps bravado oddly comforting and Frampton's outburst had not shocked her in quite the same way as it did Dodo. She had fewer illusions and enough contact with the public-school brigade to know the ways of the world. Her affair with Jonny had not culminated in a trip to the altar, as she might have wished. Rumours about his sexuality had been repeated often enough for her to be realistic on that score. Revelations about George, on the other hand, were a complete surprise and thus, in her experience, likely to be unfounded. Poor Dodo, deep in the rawness of fresh bereavement, was not able to be so sanguine.

Snow was piling rapidly against the terrace wall and Bunch estimated six inches or more had accumulated over the course of the day, with gobbets of white continuing to brush past the diamond leaded panes. She pushed through the heavy Blackout drapes, which cut the window seat off from the room, just as the clock struck the quarter hour.

Shouting and raucous jazz from elsewhere in the house made

her pause, wondering if she should go out and challenge these interlopers. She had nothing against jazz per se but it wasn't *her* jazz, nor anything to do with any part of *her* household, and in this particular evening its imposition, especially at such volume, was irksome. It was only going to get worse, she was certain of that. 'Want a quick snifter?' She crossed to the side table and sloshed brandy into the balloon goblets waiting on the tray and handed one to Dodo.

'Thanks.' Dodo threw down the magazine and took the glass eagerly. 'Noisy boarders,' she observed.

'Bloody hooligans.' Bunch smiled wryly and bent to stroke Roger's head. He thumped his tail a few times on the heath rug where he lay, his midriff swathed in bandages. The white of the bandages made him look like some blonde and diminutive Galloway calf.

The music changed, blasting out the relentlessly cheery *Dance Cabaret* theme, which was quickly drowned by a sudden roar of raucous laughter from Perringham's new residents. Dodo flinched at the sounds, seemingly perturbed by them and Bunch wondered at how quickly she herself had become accustomed to strangers in the family citadel. 'Bit different to Banyards,' she said as she collapsed into an armchair.

'Different but not necessarily worse,' Dodo replied.

'It's not unpleasant once you get past the odd assortment of accents. Father insisted there were Canadian Pilot Officers moving in but I can assure you there are many more nationalities walking these corridors than Canucks.'

'They at least are not interested in the local gossip. It's been horrible since George died; and worse still since Emma went back to Oxford. Once we'd had the funeral she couldn't get away fast enough.' She swilled the brandy around the goblet and stared at the oily residue left clinging near the rim. 'You know, there are conversations going on in corners that I am not meant to hear. There have been things I *absolutely* know I was not meant to see.' She stifled a sob, her bottom lip trembling for a moment, and then she took down the remaining brandy in a large gulp.

To give her eyes a reason for watering, Bunch thought. 'Barty and Olivia are plotting?' she asked. 'I can believe it of her but it's not really Barty's style, surely.'

'Olivia mostly. It's perfectly beastly. Do you think they've heard those awful rumours about Georgie? And Jonny of course.'

Bunch studied the fire, at its amber flames. Dodo was asking oblique questions beyond the obvious room-dwelling elephant that was her deceased husband's alleged betrayal. She had no idea how to answer those questions, let alone those Dodo had yet to articulate. 'I can understand you are feeling confused,' she said. 'Saul was only being a pill. As for Barty and Olivia, they probably don't know what to say. They lost a son, after all.'

'Oh, I don't know. Perhaps. I always had a sense I don't really belong there. Since Georgie was killed it's been more than a little fraught. There were occasions when Olivia was downright hostile. I think she's surviving on pills, powders and sherry.'

'Oh, really?' Bunch came alert. 'What sort of pills?'

'I have absolutely no idea. Doctor Lewis visits infrequently so I don't know where they come from. She's so foul tempered one moment and flitting around like some aging flapper the next. I've heard her heaps of times creeping around downstairs in the middle of the night. She couldn't sleep, I suppose, which I understand completely because I was awake as well.'

'Olivia pepping up?' Bunch began to laugh. 'Olivia by-the-book Tinsley? You are joking?'

'I probably *am* wrong. It was just an impression. Seen it often enough in the fast crowd.'

'It would seem unlikely. Did Emma say anything?'

'Emma was terribly strange the whole time she was home. You were better chums at school, being the same age, but I thought we'd be closer now that we are sisters. It's all very peculiar.'

'It must be awkward for Olivia and Barty. If you think about it, it's rather like old man Frampton's situation in some ways.'

Dodo drew her brows in, puzzled by the comment. 'Saul? Why on earth would you say that?'

'You heard Pole. Saul Frampton is out of a home due to some entail.' Bunch sipped the last of her brandy, drawing the vapours over her tongue like a cat scenting prey, her lips pursed in a thoughtful moue. She knew it was time to be bald-faced about all of the recent events. Yet, now the opportunity came, Bunch was still loath to say things that might upset her sister's frail calm.

'Whilst George was alive and life was running as it should, it didn't matter that much. He was the heir and all that. Nobody really expected anything to change. If anything happens to Barty the entire estate is all yours, and Olivia and Emma will be cap in hand to you for a roof over their little heads. In the eyes of the law that will only change if you remarry before Barty kicks the bucket.' She shrugged at Dodo's stricken expression. 'Yes, yes, I know, it's bloody. But Olivia Tinsley's heart will never stray far from the family lucre.'

'I'd never have dreamt of that.'

'Then you should, my dear. Love is all very well but this is about money. If I had been knocked off my perch driving for the military last year you would be inheriting this place as well.'

'Bunch!'

'It's cold hard facts, darling. If I don't find a man and produce and heir, then—' She lit a cigarette, coughed a little, and picked a strand of tobacco delicately from the tip of her tongue. 'I must buy a new holder. It's getting harder and harder to get decent gaspers these days. I do enjoy one after dinner but I'm not sure I like these American brands that are now arriving.' She looked at Dodo and half smiled. She loved that her younger sister was such an innocent. Married and widowed but still so lacking in guile.

Dodo had not been forced through the ghastly hoops of boarding school as had Bunch, and not even been properly *finished* before the threat of war had brought her home and the Season had almost come to a halt since the draft board had sequestered all of the eligible men. Bunch's own coming-out had been scuppered by the Great War, though she had only been eight at its close. With a previous generation of men gone there were many more heiresses to be married off than men to marry them, even ten years after Armistice.

Dodo's coming-out season had all the balls and beaus she could have wished for yet she had been married and widowed in less than six months. Bunch hoped she could have been spared that much, yet could not help but be a little jealous of Dodo, despite her sister's grief; and Bunch a kindred spirit now that Jonny's death had given her loss all of her own.

'Sorry, I didn't mean to sound quite so hard nosed. I was thinking aloud, musing on the whole Jonathan thing. Knowing he owned the estate makes it even less likely he'd do himself in.'

'Except for this *new* little thing with George. Olivia can cope with him dying, but heaven forefend the county got a whiff of scandal.'

There was vinegar in that last crack and Bunch revised her opinion. Perhaps Dodo was not quite the little Shirley Temple everyone fondly imagined. Grief had struck a measure of reality into her cosy world. 'That was a bit rough,' she said.

'A *bit* rough? My God! He cheated on me with his best friend, for Christ sake!'

'Sorry Dodo, that was incredibly insensitive of me.'

'Insensitive she says? I've been breaking my heart and all the time he had a— What do we call him exactly? A floozy? A gigolo?!'

'Shh...' Bunch motioned for calm with her palms down. 'We still don't know it's true.'

'You can't blame me for feeling angry, Bunch. It's just so bizarre. I mean to say, Jonathan Frampton. Of all people.'

'Not something *I* want to dwell on any more than you.' Bunch took another long draw on her cigarette, staring into the grate at the flames licking around the large chunks of apple wood she had put there a few minutes before. She needed all the clarity she could summon. 'There was something odd in that kitchen. I should have noticed. I know I am being dense about it and it is driving me insane. I'm equally sure that Pole knows more than he's letting on.'

'George told me Jonny was angry over the way his father handled things,' said Dodo. 'Neither Saul or Pole hinted at more.'

'Family loyalty, I suppose. If Jonny knew he was the legal owner why let Saul run things into the ground?'

'I can only imagine Saul had tenure until Jonny reached a stipulated age,' Dodo suggested.

'And now this cousin will be hot-footing it from Arundel to claim the spoils.' Bunch looked down, considering the matter for a moment. 'It will be rather lovely to see Hascombe in proper working order,' she said. 'A crying shame it all had to end like this because of...'

A tap at the door paused their conversation. 'Come in,' Bunch called.

The door opened on a young soldier in army greens and battle bowler, a rifle slung by its strap over his shoulder. 'Sorry for disturbing you, Miss, but I couldn't find your staff. We've apprehended a girl in the grounds.'

'On whose authority?'

'Standing orders, Ma'am,' he replied. 'This girl said she had to speak with you. Said it was urgent.'

He waved a hand into the corridor behind him and a second soldier appeared clutching Kate Wooldridge by the arm.

'You know her, Ma'am?'

Bunch had a notion he'd have preferred she didn't. 'Kate, what are you doing here at this time? Whatever is the matter?'

Kate shrugged off the soldier's hand and hurried to the fireside to crouch with hands toward the flames. She had plainly come out in a hurry with neither hat nor gloves. There was unmistakable evidence of tears around her eyes. 'It's Mary,' she said. 'We can't raise the police. I think the telephone lines are down again. We tried to get Mr Parsons out but his daughter says he's down at the Seven Stars so I ran up here. We didn't know what else to do. Because it's Mary...'

'Calm down, Kate. Deep breath. Now, what about Mary?'

'She was late in. Not that being late is a problem. I mean, I'm not tattling. You know she is often out but we made her promise after what you said today. You know, about getting sleep and such. Be home by ten, we said. She promised she would. She promised. Crossed her heart and hoped—' Kate broke off in a strangled sob.

'Here.' Dodo poured a brandy and thrust it into the girl's hand then turned to glare at the soldiers. 'You may go. If we need help we'll call.'

'Yes, Ma'am.'

They waited by unspoken consensus until the two men had stepped into the passageway, though no further, Bunch noted.

'Mary's dead.' Kate's statement was bleak, matching the expression in her eyes. Try as she might she could not keep her upper lip as stiff as she was so obviously attempting.

'What?' Bunch was fairly certain her own face was no less tortured. 'Where?'

'We found her on the step. She was covered in snow so I hate to think how long she had been there. Maybe if we had thought to go out to look for her earlier she might still be alive.' Kate drained the glass and stared into its depths. 'We might have saved her.'

'You can't possibly know that.' Bunch patted her arm and smiled reassuringly. 'What happened to her? Did she have an accident or...?'

'She was shot.'

'Oh—' Bunch paused whilst the baldness of the statement sank in. 'Where is she now? Is she still out in the snow?'

'No. We got her inside. We couldn't leave her out there. We were not sure she was dead at first.'

'Of course you couldn't leave her,' Dodo said. 'Could she, Bunch? Nothing else any of you could do.'

Kate nodded vigorously. 'We thought your phone would be working and we could call the police from here so I volunteered to run up – and then your boys stopped me.'

'Not *my* boys. It looks as if they can be a little over zealous.' Bunch got up and hurried to the office room and picked up the telephone, holding the handset to her ear and rattling the cradle. It remained ominously quiet. She went back to the sitting room. 'No phones. The lines must be down. I'm surprised we still have power.' She gestured to the men still hovering just beyond the open doorway. 'One of you will have to go down to the village and raise PC Botting.'

They looked at each other and indulged in some foot shuffling. 'Very sorry, Ma'am. We're under orders not to leave prisoners unguarded.'

'Prisoner? Oh, for God's sake, man. Kate works here. Go and fetch the police.'

'I can go fetch the duty officer.'

'Hell's teeth, yes all right, if that's what it takes. Hurry up about it. This side of Easter, please. Go.' Bunch watched with righteous satisfaction as he scuttled away. The other soldier remained at the doorway. 'Yes?' She demanded.

'Orders, Ma'am. No unauthorised persons on base without escort.'

'I am telling you that you are dismissed. If your CO has a problem with that tell him to come and see me himself.' She glowered, a look that usually withered men of all stations.

'Can't think why you want to stay in this house for even a day with all those soldiers' Dodo observed. 'It must be bloody unbearable.'

'I'll cope. Not important now. We should get down to the farm; the rest of the girls will be frantic.'

Dodo glanced at the door. 'Shouldn't we wait for the chap to return with his officer?'

'I suppose someone should but I rather go with Kate and wait there for the police. Kravitz and his puppies can catch up.'

'I'll come, too,' said Dodo.

'No, you have to remain here.'

'I'll go mad with worry sitting here on my own.'

'You said so yourself. Someone has to stay and speak with Kravitz when he eventually turns up.'

'Bunch. Rose! It's not fair.'

The anger and frustration was irrefutable in that one word: Dodo never called her Rose, any more than she called her sister Daphne. It was a pact of a lifetime's standing. She leaned forward and planted a kiss on her sister's forehead. 'Stay here, Dodo. Hold the fort. Please?'

'I...' Dodo deflated. 'All right.'

'You're a good egg.' Bunch gave her a quick hug. 'I want you to keep trying the phone for Doctor Lewis or the Police House. I won't be too long. I hope.'

❧TEN❧

The vast bulk of the Sussex Barn eventually gave Bunch a land-mark to navigate her way to the furthest end of the terrace. A muddy path ran along the front of the row of tile-hung cottages, with shorter brick-paved pathways branching off to each of the six porches. Bunch shone her torch to the doorway of number six. The snow covering on the path itself was a mass of boot prints around where the body – *Mary*, Bunch reminded herself – had been found.

She walked a few paces toward the front step to inspect the depression left by the body in the snow. There was an irregular patch of dark staining that she assumed would be blood, but beyond that the area was too much disturbed to provide any sort of narrative.

Snow settled in sizable clumps filling the footprints before her eyes and she knew that whatever might have been seen would soon vanish. Whoever came to investigate would doubtless wail about the scene being spoiled but Bunch couldn't really see how it could have been saved. 'Probably shouldn't tread it down any more than it is already,' she said to Kate. 'We'll go around to the back.'

She let Kate lead the way to the back door, or side door in this case, which opened into the scullery. As the bootjack was buried deep in the drifts the two women scrambled indoors before attempting to kick off their gum boots and hurry through to the kitchen, which was warm despite the late hour. A recently revived fire was spitting in the range. The room smelled of baked bread made earlier in the day. Annie sat at the scrubbed wood table, which took up much of the floor space, chewing her way through a door-step slab of toast.

Ruth and Patricia were clamouring for answers the moment their boss had stepped across the threshold. 'Are the police coming?' 'Where can we go?' 'I can't stay 'ere.' 'It ain't safe.' 'Who would do such an 'orrible thing?'

'Shh…' Bunch held up both hands for silence. 'We've sent for help but I have no idea when it will reach us. Where is Mary?'

'Front room, Miss Courtney,' said Elsie.

Bunch frowned. 'She wasn't alive when you brought her in?'

'We thought she was,' Kate said. 'Or rather we hoped she might have been but the moment we had her laid out it was pretty obvious she'd already gone.'

'You probably shouldn't have moved her,' Bunch said.

'We couldn't leave her out in the cold, Miss. An' Pat thought maybe we should get 'er in an' make sure she was, you know…' Elsie trailed off. Her face was pale with the burnt-cork mascara, liberally applied for a night at the pub, now smeared across her cheeks.

'Understandable,' said Bunch. 'I would have done the same thing, I should think. Anyone here First Aid trained?' There was a general shaking of heads. 'Right then.' She headed straight into the front room. Mary's neatly laid out body was anonymous beneath an Army-issue blanket.

Of all the girls that would be out at night it would be Mary, but this is not right. This should not happen at all, Bunch thought. *This is simply not right.* She knelt and gently peeled back the covering far enough to see Mary's face and could not help noticing the girl's make up was smudged. She had never seen Mary anything but immaculate. It was who she was: a cockney sparrow, as colourful and dapper as any kingfisher. The smeared lipstick and tear-stained powder seemed incongruous and yet only emphasised the girl's pretty features.

Bunch resisted the impulse to pull out her handkerchief and wipe the grime from Mary's cheek. She pulled the blanket back a little further, instead, to reveal the red stains covering the girl's abdomen already drying and turning brown at the edges. She noted the neat hole in the front of the mid-blue swing coat.

Fashion-conscious as ever, Bunch thought. *That's a good coat, but bullet holes are optional.* She dismissed her own flippancy, annoyed that she could be so callous even in her own thoughts. It seemed cruel to think the worst of the girl at such a time.

She lifted the coat aside and noted a corresponding neat

puncture through the front of her woollen dress. This was not the peppering effect of a shotgun. *This was made by a rifle.* She considered turning the body over but was very much aware of the girls crowding at the door, watching her every move, and she did not want to do anything to spook them any more than they already were. She replaced the blanket and stood up, dusting her hands thoughtfully. 'Why didn't she come back with the rest of you?'

'She was wiv Seb,' Elsie replied. 'Smooching. She never brought 'im back here this late, an' 'e couldn't exactly take 'er back to his place.'

'Is that Johansson?'

'That's 'im.'

'No sign of him since, I take it?'

'Not since we left the pub.'

Bunch studied the crowd of faces looking for answers, and felt angry at herself for having none to give them. 'I can't believe you all went out on a night like this,' she said. 'What possessed you?'

'Not all of us went,' said Patricia. 'Only the musketeers. I told them they had to be mad but they went down in a truck with some boys from the base – I mean the house – so I thought they'd be all right. I mean if they got stuck in the snow they had strong backs to dig them out.'

'Me an' Ruthie got a lift back about nine cos the weather had turned,' said Elsie. 'Mary didn't come cos she was wiv Seb. He'd borrowed a staff car.'

'I thought you said you all went down together.'

'Yeah. She went down wiv us cos Seb was on duty. He met us down there.'

Bunch looked from one worried face to another and sighed. 'I hope that sentry did what he was told and went down to the Police House.'

'He did but not on your say so, Miss Courtney.'

Bunch swivelled around to face the officer as he muscled his way through the knot of girls. Colonel Kravitz reminded her of Uncle Wentworth though the resemblance was purely skin deep. Kravitz had none of Wentworth's bumbling charm, though she could see from the way her girls reacted that he had charisma of a kind. She felt her own instincts rise to do battle.

Kravitz removed his hat and brushed snow from his coat. 'The duty officer told me what was going on so I thought I should come down and see if I can help in any way. I'm sorry about your girl. Never easy to lose a man – or a woman.' He bowed with the ghost of a self-deprecating smile. 'What happened here?'

'I should have thought that perfectly obvious. One of my Land Girls has been shot. Murdered, in point of fact. We shall wait for the police before we draw any further conclusions.' Bunch glared at him, annoyed at his assumption of authority. He may have stolen Perringham House from her but he had no jurisdiction here.

'That's too bad.' He stared down at the blanket-covered form, working his lips in apparent concern and puzzlement. 'I dispatched a detail to fetch your local *bobby*. Not that he's going to be much help. Shouldn't your Scotland Yard get called in for a shooting?'

'Not necessarily,' she replied. 'I imagine that the police from Brighton would be called first.'

'I bow to your knowledge. You've no idea how this happened? Was it an accident?'

'Hardly. Looking at the blood on her clothes I would say she was shot from very close quarters.' Bunch didn't know if that was true or not.

'In this cottage?' He looked at the women ranged around the doorway and frowned. 'Right here?'

'God, no,' Kate replied. 'We never even heard gunshots so wherever it happened must have been some way off.'

'She was shot and she just walked here? She's just a kid.'

'We don't have any details, Colonel.' Bunch held a hand toward the girls daring them to say more. 'It is neither our place nor yours to indulge in further speculation.' She placed an emphasis on the *yours*. 'It would be best to leave all of that for the police. The girls here say she was last seen with one of your men. What happened between leaving the pub and Mary turning up here, we have no idea.'

He looked around him. 'Where *is* Lieutenant Johansson?'

Bunch smiled inwardly, and without humour. So that was it. The only reason Kravitz would be roaming around in these conditions, she realised, was to protect his own. She couldn't blame him for that, she supposed; it was his job, after all. That did not prevent her irritation that his pretence of caring had anything whatsoever to do with good will. 'I might ask you the same thing,' she replied. 'Johansson was the last person this poor child was seen with. The police will want to ask him a great deal more.'

'We shall have to see. You're certain she was murdered?'

'Yes,' Bunch replied. 'I may not be a soldier but I assure you, I can recognise a bullet wound when I see it.'

He squatted on his heels and lifted the edge of the blanket to peer beneath it. 'I'm sorry, I did not mean to doubt you. Poor child. I only spoke to her once and she seemed like a sweet girl.'

'You have only been here for week, as has Johansson.' Bunch tweaked the blanket from his fingers and straightened it over the girl's inert form. 'Mary was a good person and yes, a child. Barely eighteen.'

'Terrible. Is there anything I can do to help?' Kravitz said.

Bunch did not want to appear churlish and yet she found the Colonel's reactions peculiar in their situation. 'No thank you, Colonel. We will just wait for the police to arrive.'

'It's a bad night to walk alone. Should I leave you my driver?'

'No need. I do know the way.'

'You are sure? I have to return and organise a search patrol for Johansson. He was supposed to have reported in two hours ago so he is officially AWOL. Given he was with this girl we have to assume he was caught up in the same ambush.'

'An ambush?' Bunch said. 'This could be a lovers' tiff gone very wrong, for Mary, at least.' She heard the collective intake of breath from the Land Girls chorus, for she had voiced the unthinkable, that Johansson had murdered Mary and fled. She was certain it would be exactly what the police would be assuming in the absence of either Johansson's body and the staff car he and Mary had left the pub in.

Kravitz raised his chin to squint down his hooked nose at her. 'Johansson is a good officer,' he snapped. 'A valuable officer. In fact, there are many more reasons why he himself might be a target for an enemy agent rather than—' He glanced at Mary's body and clamped his lips against phrasing the obvious comparison. 'Until we know otherwise I shall assume something has happened to him.' He straightened up abruptly. 'That aside, Miss Courtney, this is not the night for young women to be stumbling around on foot. More so now if there is a killer loose. I would feel a lot happier knowing you reach home safely.'

'I appreciate your concern but I do not need help on my own estate.' Bunch felt no guilt in her acidity. Kravitz was on damage limitation, she thought; it also occurred to her that he would be as eager to prove his young adjutant's innocence as she was to exonerate Jonny.

'With due respect,' he growled, 'I would appreciate it if you climbed down off of that high horse. You might be as strong as that damned ugly pony of yours but the weather out there is something fierce. I shall leave you my driver.'

'Then you would have to walk back and as the stranger in these parts you are at far greater risk of getting lost. I shall be quite all right. Thank you.'

He laughed a deep, cigar-roughened rumble. 'Where I come from this is just a sugar sprinkle. You might be a cob horse but I am an old ploughman's nag.' He tipped his hand to his brow. 'But if you're sure? Good night, Miss Courtney. Ladies.'

✍ELEVEN❧

Bunch watched as Mary's was lifted onto a stretcher and tried not to focus on the obvious shape outlined by the blanket. 'Shouldn't the Coroner be here to verify cause of death?' she asked.

'Under normal circumstances, yes.' Chief Inspector Wright spread his hands and closed his own eyes for a moment. 'The GP was able to pronounce death otherwise we would have to leave her here. The Coroner's office is still snowed under, no pun intended. To compound the problem another five trained officers joined up this week and not a single replacement, though we've been promised some ATS drivers. You're fortunate *I* was able to get here. The force isn't just stretched, it's beginning to fall apart.' He paused to bow his head as the two ambulance girls lifted the stretcher and ferried it out of the door. He gestured after them as the door closed. 'Their service is suffering just as badly. Not right to expect young women to do these things.'

'I know. I've done my share of driving,' she replied.

'Of course. You were invalided out.' Wright touched her shoulder lightly. 'Forgive me, I didn't mean to sound patronising. People often don't understand the problems.'

His knowing her background made Bunch uneasy. Did she have a police file, she wondered. *Had he been asking around? Either way,* she thought, *might prove he is starting to take me seriously.* 'It isn't important,' she murmured. 'Have you finished here? I mean you don't need to take finger prints or … oh, I don't know. Whatever it is you chaps do.'

'Not for this case,' he replied. 'Even if we had the men, which we don't, this is obviously not the crime scene. She was shot elsewhere. Shame the path got so trampled on.'

'Can the girls go to bed now?' Bunch said. 'They have to get up again in a few hours.'

Wright looked through the kitchen door toward the young

women huddled around the table. 'If the constable has taken down all they know – God knows it's little enough – then yes. Even if he hasn't he knows where to find them.' He raised his voice a little. 'You should get some sleep, ladies. Nothing else to be done now.'

'Goodnight girls,' Bunch said. 'I know it's been awful but yes, do try and get some sleep. You need to be up in just a few hours. I shall be down later today, if you remember anything else.'

The women filed past to the staircase mumbling goodnights as they went. All of them avoided looking at the spot where Mary had lain. Bunch waited until the latch rattled closed behind the Land Girls and their footsteps had clumped all the way up to the landing before she hustled Wright into the kitchen. 'I was going to ask you to call today; I have some things to tell you. According to that Johansson, the two of them saw people parked on the road below the woods the night Jonny was killed.'

'You think that may be relevant?'

'Isn't it a rather large coincidence when all of this happens the very next day?' She watched him carefully, certain that he would join the dots as she already had. Investigations were his business, after all. 'You have to admit it all seems to fit.'

Wright grunted as he fastened his coat. 'I can't make any headway on guesswork. I need to speak with the Colonel before I can interview this young subaltern of his,' he said. 'Until I hear it from him it is conjecture. Hearsay does not stand up in court. Shall I walk you back to the house?' He pulled on his hat and paused. 'What's he like, your Colonel?'

'Arrogant,' she replied. 'Full of his own self-importance.'

'He's a colonel, the station commander. Doesn't that go with the rank?'

'Does it? I know a few colonels and a couple of them might be a tad pompous but none of them are quite like Kravitz.'

'You don't like him?'

She paused to consider. It would be too easy to blame the Colonel for all that had happened at Perringham House, the loss of privacy, of feeling under siege in her own home. It would be easy to judge his actions in looking out for his men as selfish, but she was sure her father would have done the same thing. 'Not exactly that,' she said. 'I think he is rather more ambitious than most – and political. A dangerous trait in a military man, isn't it? However, I haven't had enough contact with him to form a proper opinion. Do you know anything about him?'

'Only that he's attached to some sort of special operations department. I'm not nearly high enough up the ladder to be told anything important.' He waved her toward the door. 'Your family connections may have better means of finding out more than me. Now, shall we go?'

Early morning had calmed the storm with snow reduced to just a few tiny flurries on a lazier wind. Bunch and Wright walked along the lane to the main house in silence, with scarves wrapped across their faces against sub-zero air. The ambulance had left deep tracks in the lane that made easy going, at least as far as the gates veering off to the stable end of Perringham.

She avoided his gaze, pausing at the step to scrape off her boots against the iron boot jack just inside the vestibule. She tried to decide if his silence was some kind of insolence or some a strange interrogation technique. Perhaps it was a little of both. She was looking forward to playing word games with him, which surprised her; it was something she missed in what had become the very female world in which she had found herself over the past six months. 'It's this way, Chief Inspector. The dining room will be warmest at this time of day.'

'Warm?' Wright struggled to remove his own wellingtons with the fumbling awkwardness of a city dweller. 'Is this mausoleum ever warm?'

'Of course.' She opened the dining room door and hurried across to the recently lit fire, holding her feet in turns toward its building warmth. 'In summer it's quite delightful.'

'I wonder what your military guests think about it.'

'I care more about what my people think. Our butler left three weeks after we first knew these people would move in, and after twenty years in our service, which probably tells you a lot. Kravitz wants to install central heating.'

'On their slate? Why not let them.'

'They want to tear up all of the carved panelling and most of the original floors to do it.'

'Ah.'

'If Gibbs were still here, of course, they wouldn't stand a

chance. Daddy did try to stop him from leaving but he had already signed up.'

'Twenty years a butler? Wasn't he rather old to sign up?'

Bunch laughed. 'Officially, yes he was. He served as General Foswick's batman in the Great War and before that, I believe. Fossy was called back to run a department by the War Office and when he snapped his fingers Gibbs was suddenly back to being his batman. As Fossy is Mummy's cousin Gibbs could still claim family loyalty as well as to the regiment.' She rubbed her hands together and held them in front of the flames, her gaze at the fire a little unfocused. 'Probably best in the long run. We only have a few rooms to ourselves and Knapp can deal with those. Now my parents are off to Singapore and we're decamping to the Dower House I don't have time to entertain. Not that the call-up is leaving anyone left to entertain. Gibbs would have nothing to do but field complaints from Kravitz and his chums. It's a different world now, Inspector.'

'You do know it's *Chief* Inspector?'

'Of course it is.' She smiled, eyeing him sideways on. 'Such a mouthful, don't you think?'

The door opened wafting cold air in on the conversation. 'Oh, Miss Rose. I didn't know you were up.'

'I haven't made it to bed yet, Knapp. There was a major kerfuffle at the farm last night.'

'So I understand, Miss.'

'Dodo has gone for a lie down, I understand.' Bunch glanced at Wright and pulled a face. 'She never used to be such a delicate thing but she's been finding a lot of things rather upsetting since George died. To be expected, I suppose. Knapp, could you get a tray taken up to her please? Chief Inspector Wright will be taking breakfast here with me.'

Knapp glared at the Chief Inspector but nodded. 'Yes, Miss. It will be a few minutes. Cook is only just stoking the range.'

'That's fine. If you could bring some tea that would be splendid.'

'Of course, Miss. Will that be all?'

'Yes, thank you Knapp.' She waited for the door to close before laughing quietly. 'You realise she's gathered completely the wrong impression?'

'About what?'

'About you. She will be checking the bed for warm spots.'

'She thinks that I—'

'Oh, don't look so horrified. It's not at all flattering.'

'Yes. I mean no. I...'

She tapped his arm firmly. 'You should learn to take a joke, Inspector.'

'I can take a joke, Miss Courtney. I just can't take a risk.'

'Oh, your middle-class morals are showing *Chief Inspector*. Never a good thing to have. A flair for indiscretion is far more fun.'

'Morals?' He quirked his lips in a half grin. 'Truth to tell, it isn't something I see a lot of in this job. Suspicion is far more usual. Beside, it's not seemly for me to fraternise with people involved in a case.'

'Against regulations?'

'Only if you were suspected of a crime.'

'By that reckoning one could be forgiven in assuming I'm in the frame. Am I?'

'So far that has not been the case.' He glanced at the door as it was pushed open and Roger waddled through to greet his mistress. 'How's the dog?'

'He's just fine.' She bent down to give Roger a gentle pat to his shoulder and waved him off toward the fireside. 'Lie down Rog.' The dog flopped onto his side before the hearth. 'See? Not worried in the slightest. It takes a brain to worry and poor old Roger has always been a bit short in that department.'

'What about you?' Wright asked. 'Have *you* recovered? Being shot at is no joke.'

Bunch snorted loudly, slapping her knee and making the table shudder. She wasn't up to talking about her own experience except in the most basic, making-a-statement sort of way, and laughing it off was always her best defence. 'I will survive. Shaken but unbowed.'

'Of course.' His tone was light, almost flippant. 'Now, you said back at the farm that Mary and her lieutenant saw a van.'

'I thought you weren't interested in vehicles.'

'It's not much of a lead and besides, it's not just walls that have ears. Those Land Girls have ten between them.'

'Which might matter if they knew that much about vans,' Bunch replied. 'I believe it was only Mary and her young man who saw it.'

'Nevertheless.'

'As I understand it, the van had a name on the side. *Something-ham and Son.* Neither Mary nor the lieutenant saw the name clearly enough to read it fully. They said the fellow standing next to it vanished into the woods on the Hascombe side the moment he saw them.'

'This was the night Frampton killed himself?' Wright shrugged under her glare. 'That's the Coroner's official opinion until I – we – have proven otherwise.'

'There have been some other developments that may change that.' She crossed to the sideboard and lifting the lid of the rosewood box took a cigarette, lighting it with sharp movements and puffing on it several times before stubbing it out with equal venom. She felt Wright must be watching and judging her. 'We found the remains of butchered sheep in our side of the woods,' she said at last. 'Remember, we've had animals go missing of late, so our stockman was checking although he doesn't usually walk that far. Invalided out of the Navy last year.'

'Sheep have been rustled from your land?'

'Indeed they have. Deer poaching has been a problem for a while. Daddy said venison is appearing more and more on the club menus so we know where it's going. Sheep are something else entirely. When we checked the ear marks on the carcasses left behind we found clips for Frampton's flock as well.'

'That is something we can look into. Were these remains found close to the road where these vehicles were parked?'

'They were on the upper slopes directly above. There would be less chance of being spotted by walkers. Close enough as crows fly. If it wasn't for the snow and the girls seeing tracks I doubt it would have occurred to me or Haynes to go and search there.'

'Haynes?'

'The stockman.' She put her hand on the rosewood box and withdrew another cigarette, spinning on her heels to face him. 'Do sit down,' she said. 'Sorry, no manners this morning.'

Wright sat, skewing the chair away from the table a little and pulling another out for her presumably, Bunch assumed, to be able to look her in the face. 'These remains were in your woods. Yet the unidentified man took off into the other side of the road, which is a different estate,' he said.

Bunch stared down at the sideboard idly straightening the cigarette box and ash tray. 'Apparently so,' she murmured. 'I can't think why that would be. You need to ask Mar—' She stopped, clicking her tongue in exasperation. Mary wasn't there to ask. 'Johansson is the one to tell you, if you can find him. He told me that there were two vehicles which means *at least* two men. I saw three men in that clearing butchering my sheep, although there could have been any number of chaps to butcher and carry all those carcasses down to the transport. Surely that in itself is proof enough: who would try to kill himself in a place that was crawling with people? Do you think someone may have thought Mary and her chap saw more than they actually did?'

'It cannot be ruled out. It's a theory, though at this precise moment theory is all we have.'

'Not if you accept that Jonny was murdered. It is not much of a step to assume the same people killed Mary. It would be a huge coincidence, otherwise.'

'The law does not work on assumptions,' he replied.

'The War Department would appear to.' Wright gave her a warning frown and she chuckled. 'They were very eager to shut it down when they thought it was something to do with their hush-hush games. You now agree that there is a suspicion it has nothing to do with his job, after all, and everything to do with criminals?'

He nodded, hesitantly at first and then a firm tucking of his chin into his chest and up again to look Bunch in the eye. 'Yes, I think you have a reasonable theory.'

'Thank you. Thank you. Thank you. That is an absolute relief to know.'

'Too soon for that,' he replied. 'I can promise nothing as yet. All I can do is relay my – our – suspicions to the Coroner's office and ask him to keep it in mind.'

'That would be wonderful. I will be in your debt.'

'Hmm.' Wright shook his head. 'Don't expect too much. We can't do anything about Mr Frampton's death until the Coroner has had the opportunity to review the case. Mary Tucker, on the other hand, was quite obviously murdered.'

The maid came in with the tea tray and set it on the sideboard. 'Thank you, Sheila. I shall pour,' Bunch told her.

'Yes, Miss Rose. Cook says breakfast will be a good ten minutes.' The girl bobbed a brief curtsy, saucer eyes fixed on Wright, before retreating rapidly.

'The staff has a bad case of the jitters,' Bunch observed as she sat down opposite Wright and poured tea into cups, hand hovering over the sugar for a moment. So few people took sugar in tea now it had almost become rude to offer. 'The indoor *and* outdoor servants, and it takes a lot to have them all singing from the same hymn book. War is one thing. They all know of someone who has lost someone and I suppose it isn't going to get better all that soon. But war takes place somewhere else but murders right here on the estate; that is different and they're all terribly afraid.'

'Normal people find murder unthinkable.'

'Yet murder is your living.' Bunch chuckled. 'I am rather glad it is you or I might have had a complete clod on the case.'

'Thank you,' he replied. 'I think.' He leaned forward to take the proffered cup and saucer. 'Did the girls get on with each other? No rivalries that you know of?'

'Nothing that came to my attention. They would be able to answer that question themselves more easily.'

'We have their statements or will have soon. I only wondered if you had heard of any major disagreements that they might not want to mention to me.'

Bunch expelled a loud breath and shook her head. 'They have their squabbles, of course. When you have six young women living cheek by jowl it would be more unusual if they didn't. If you mean had any of them rowed with Mary violently enough to want to kill her, then I should jolly well say not. She could be a bit of a hellcat, I heard, and an incorrigible flirt. But there were no stolen boyfriends or anything of that sort. I am fairly certain I would know of anything of that magnitude. Girls take that sort of thing terribly seriously. Mary was obsessed with the pictures and fashion; you know how girls can be. I don't think it was anything out of the usual, however.'

'What about this man of hers. Norwegian I understand? What do you know about him?'

Bunch shrugged. 'I know he's missing.'

'I know that much, but have you met him?'

'Once. No, twice.'

'And?'

She puffed and shook her head. 'Pleasant enough. A little full of himself but then so many of them are.'

'You don't like him.'

'Like?' She stared at the top of her tea. She couldn't think what to say. She had not formed an expert opinion on a so little acquaintance but he had seemed genuinely fond of Mary and concerned for her. Was that enough? She was dead and he was missing. A suspicious person might see a connection. 'I barely knew him,' she said at last. 'He seemed to know his horses. Beyond that I really could not say. The girls should know much more.'

A tap on the door was a blessed interruption. 'Excuse me, Miss Rose.' Sheila sidled in and stood just inside the door. 'Sorry Miss, but a message from Colonel Kravitz. He wants to see you.'

'He does? Very well, show him into the morning room,' Bunch replied.

Sheila looked stricken. 'He's not here, Miss Rose. He sent a message for you to go and see him.'

'Did he, indeed? Take a message to the Colonel that if he has something to say he can come here and say it.'

'Miss?'

'You are not deaf, girl. Now, is breakfast ready yet? Tell Cook to hurry, will you? I have a feeling today is going to be a bit of a rush.'

'Yes, Miss.'

Bunch waited until the door had shut before she let rip. She slammed her hand on the table top. 'Damn the man. Who does he think he is, sending for me in my own house?'

'I doubt he sees it that way,' Wright replied. 'In his eyes this is his domain.'

'I honestly do not care what he sees. Actually I do. It's all quite ghastly. If it wasn't for the horses…' She slammed her hand down once again. 'He thinks I am one of his damnable flyboys at his beck and call. I can't move without everyone in the place knowing it. I wonder if the Geneva Conventions cover civilian hosts because I'm damned sure POWs have more privacy than I do!' She glared at Wright, breathing stiffly, daring him to contradict, and then looked away aware that her eyes were filling up despite all she could do.

She stood abruptly and went to the window. The sky was getting lighter to the east. Pallid blue streaked with wisps of rosy hued clouds. She stared blindly at the dawn and steeled herself against emotion. One thing that her upbringing had taught her was iron control, and she exerted that with all the will she possessed. It had been a bad night. A bad week. A bad year. Possibly even a bad decade; but she was a Courtney. 'Red sky in the morning,' she said, grateful that her voice behaved itself and did not crack. 'Doesn't bode well.'

'Shepherd's warning?' Wright said.

'Yes. Or what was the other one Nanny always used? Rain before seven, fine before eleven.' She looked back at him. 'Sorry. I won't have helped you at all by poking the tiger with a stick. You might want to go and see the Colonel another day. I can't see him being very helpful now.'

'Oh, I've dealt with a colonel or two.' Wright grinned and held up his cup. 'You promised me breakfast. Any more tea?'

Breakfast was almost over before Colonel Kravitz strode unannounced into the room. Bunch glanced up at him coolly, a glance that became glacial at his lack of apology. 'Colonel. Good morning. How good of you to come and see me. Tea? Or we have coffee.'

He grimaced. 'Tea? No. I ate two hours ago.'

'How nice for you.' Bunch stretched for another slice of toast, slathering liberally with jam, ignoring Wright's surprise at her profligacy. 'You've met Inspector Wright?'

'*Chief* Inspector Wright.' Wright rose and proffered his hand.

'Good morning,' Kravitz said.

The men shook briefly, a sharp tug from both sides that was an obvious testing of strength. *Each weighing up the other*, Bunch thought, *with the expertise of long years*.

She concentrated on her toast to hide her amusement. 'You must excuse my grubbiness, Colonel,' she said. 'We had a long night sorting things out at the farm after you left. Only just got back. Of course you know that already. Your little soldiers will have told you when I came home.' She smiled sweetly and took a large bite from the toast and chewed slowly, dabbing excess jam delicately from her lips.

'I came to ask if you had any news on what happened to the young Land girl,' Kravitz said. 'Mary.'

She bided her time, allowing the mantle clock to mark its passage whilst she took a swallow of tea, schooling herself not to wince at its chill. *Mary.* She was surprised that Kravitz would remember her name, and doubly that he would use it. 'She was taken to the mortuary. The Chief Inspector will be able to tell you more in time.'

'Okay, good, thank you. Chief Inspector.' Kravitz nodded a brief acknowledgement.

Wright sat back, taking a sip from his own cup. 'I'm glad to meet you, Colonel Kravitz. I need to speak with you about one Lieutenant Johansson. I understand he was the last person seen with the deceased.'

'Says who?'

'Several sources,' Wright replied. 'We will need to eliminate your officer from our enquiries.'

'That won't be possible, I'm afraid, Chief Inspector. You cannot question him or any of my men without direct orders from Whitehall.'

'I would beg to differ. In the case of murder I have authority to question all people of concern.'

'In peacetime that would be true, but these boys will be laying their lives on the line and they do not need distractions. I am sorry about the girl but the needs of the many...'

Bunch watched the two men facing off once more like a pair of stray dogs over a lamp post, each with growing impatience. Neither appeared keen on the subject being skirted around but they were dammed if they would give ground to the other. On another occasion she would have found it amusing but this was a long way past humour. 'The Chief Inspector only needs to speak with him,' she snapped. 'It is not going to be a problem, surely.'

'If it's a problem,' Kravitz replied, 'it isn't mine. I had direct orders from the Chief of Staff this morning. All legal matters regarding my personnel to go through official channels. He pointed at the rug between his feet. 'This place, this house, is now covered by official secrets.'

'This is my home.'

'Ma'am.' Kravitz sighed impatiently. 'Miss Courtney, your father, your Government in fact, signed it over to my unit for the duration. We agreed you could stay for a few days because we arrived a little earlier than planned but the security situation has changed. I can't allow you further privileges and we don't want a repeat of last night with one of your girls being detained. She was lucky. Next time the guard may be a little more trigger happy.' He nodded a half salute and turned to leave and then paused, looking back over his shoulder. 'We shall be increasing perimeter patrols as of this morning. All civilians going in or out will need a pass signed by me or my staffers every time they pass our sentries.'

'You can't do that,' Bunch breathed, 'I have an estate to run. The Ministry of Agriculture will require access to my office and you cannot stop them.'

'I think you'll find I can. Within the house and immediate grounds, at the very least. Good morning, Miss Courtney. Chief Inspector.'

There was a stunned silence when the door clicked shut behind him.

'I said he was arrogant but that was well beyond the pale,' Bunch said finally.

'He's not bluffing,' Wright replied. 'He's just protecting his own.'

'From people like you? Me?'

'He's playing for time. The question is why.'

'He had his orders, it would seem.'

'Their young pilot is missing and it points to his guilt or deep suspicion of his involvement. Their easiest option is to close up ranks and hide behind general orders.'

Bunch nodded. 'What can you do about it?'

'I have little jurisdiction over military establishments unless I can bring a good case. We don't even know where Mary's murder took place.'

'So you can't even question this Johansson?' she asked. 'Meanwhile, whilst all you boys are playing your playground bragging contests, I am going to find it impossible to get in or out of my own home. It was one of my girls who was apprehended last night when she came to tell me about Mary. That was before Kravitz knew of her murder.'

'I doubt there is very little your Colonel does not know,' Wright mused. 'It would have been a good idea to have you in here to keep an eye on him, but your family must have property close by where you can set up home.'

'I'm going to be living at the Dower House.' She pulled a face. 'With Granny.'

'On the estate?'

'The Dower is about half a mile on the other side of the farm. My reluctance has more to do with the present incumbent.'

'Your grandmother? What's wrong with her?'

'Oh, she's a sweetie. Getting madly eccentric in her dotage. I find her, well, I'm sure you'll discover for yourself. She was supposed to be living in the house when Dodo and I were young to keep an eye on us while our parents were away, but she was firmly of the opinion that was why we had a nanny.'

'As were my parents. I was always happy with that. My nanny was a good woman. A Highlander. She had a cottage on the edge of the town.'

'You had a nanny?' Bunch could not keep the astonishment out of her voice. 'Really?'

Wright flushed slightly. 'At the least you do know your grandmother.'

'Too well.' She could see he wanted to change the subject and she wondered what story lay behind a man with family means now serving as a lowly Chief Inspector. His expression warned her off the subject, *For the moment,* she thought. Bunch sighed. 'I suppose we all have to make sacrifices. There is a war on. Now, if you'll excuse me, I need to pack.'

❧TWELVE❧

Bunch was happy to leave the removal of what remained of the Courtney household to the capable Knapp, but she regarded the relocation of her three horses to the Dower's stable block as far more personal. The Dower stables had not been used for animals in several years and the clearing of lumber, the scrubbing of stalls and transference of tack, straw, hay and feed took a long while.

She led Perry from his old home taking a slow walk along the runnels where tyres had ground the snow to ice. Kate and Patricia led the other two horses, all under the watchful eye of tense and silent military guards. None of the watchers offered to help and in truth she was not sure she would have accepted any had it been offered. It felt like a betrayal, being evicted from her home by alien occupiers, and she felt some sympathy for the refugees both across the Channel and in England itself.

It was long past dusk and beginning to snow once again by the time she had everything arranged to her satisfaction. She gave Sheba's rug a final tug and scratched the mare's ears. The hunter nodded her head, snickering loudly in reply. The animal was clearly unhappy with her surroundings or, as Kate suggested, it reflected the mood of her owner. Robbo pulled wisps from his hay net and nodded his head in empathy; little ever stirred the gelding beyond what time supper arrived.

Bunch walked along the line of horses, fed Perry a final carrot from her pocket and slapped his neck firmly. There was nothing more she could do for them at the moment. It was down to the animals themselves to become accustomed to the new stalls. The advantage of relocating them as dusk was falling was that they would have warm mash to combat the chill and then the night in which to assimilate the smells and sounds of their new lodgings, and moving all three together ensured that they would have each other to answer any nervous calls in the cover of darkness. Now it was time for Bunch to settle her own accommodation needs.

'That's it for the night, girls. Thank you for staying on. I do appreciate it when you had so little sleep last night.'

Kate and Patricia waited as Bunch pushed the doors shut and then walked across the yard in step with her. By tacit agreement they had not referred to Mary's death all the while they had been working although the mood had been sombre, with little of the idle banter that usually echoed around the yards. Perhaps, Bunch reflected, it was a mark of how much Mary had been the dynamo powering the gang since they had all arrived the previous autumn. The lack of sleep had been obvious in the girls' faces, along with the grief they all felt for Mary.

She guessed they were both eager to know what news there might be but were afraid to ask. They hung back and that surprised her a little. As Mary's close friend, Bunch had assumed Elsie would be the one to demand answers at every turn, but she and Ruth had vanished at the first opportunity. The taciturn Annie had melted away soon after them leaving just Kate and Patricia behind.

'Have you heard anything?' Kate murmured at last, as they reached the yard's gateway and their parting of ways.

'Not a thing,' Bunch said. 'I don't suppose we will for a bit.'

'And if it *was* him,' said Patricia, 'what then?'

'Do you believe it was?' Bunch asked.

Patricia shook her head. 'No, he seemed as smitten as she was.'

'Then we shall have to wait. When the police find him we'll get some answers.'

'But if they don't?' Patricia persisted.

They wanted answers yet at this time she had nothing to offer to ease their pain. She certainly did not want to mention the growing suspicion in her mind that the deaths of Mary and Jonny were linked, and that the killer was unlikely to be Lieutenant Johansson – meaning there was a murderer in the vicinity who may not hesitate to strike again.

'If you're right and he was as smitten...' Bunch shrugged. 'I'm not sure I want to take any guesses at this point.' She clapped Kate on the shoulder. 'Go home, have supper, get a good night's sleep, and don't waste your time on guessing games. I promise if I hear anything I'll let you know. Good night girls.'

'Good night, Miss Courtney.'

Bunch watched them trudge away through the snow-spittled dark; she rubbed a few accumulated salt drops from her eyes. She was as exhausted as they were and as much at a loss. They had lost a friend and she had lost a home. She looked toward Perringham House. Little could be seen in the darkness yet she felt its presence, so near and so far. She gave herself a mental shake. Maundering on what she could not change was not going to help, and a pile of bricks was nothing to the loss of flesh and blood. She was being self-indulgent. Selfish, even.

The snow was freezing hard now and slippery under foot, with stinging wind-driven flakes adding to accumulations already laying and obscuring Perringham's distant outlines in a pale haze.

The Dower House was a square, red brick building typical of its Regency origins. In better times its long windows would have lit her way but Blackout curtains blocked every chink. Only reflected snow and her trusty torch gave her a hint of where to tread. Home was where the heart was but Bunch wasn't yet convinced the Dower was it. She felt her chest tighten and her eyes seep water once again and told herself it was only the cold wind in her lungs and on her face.

'Pull yourself together,' she growled. 'It's the Dower, not the trenches. There millions of refugees and conscripts out there tonight and they have no idea where they will be laying their heads.' Her pep talk did not help her feel any less self-pitying but it did stem the immediate outbreak of unwanted emotion. She rather hoped that dinner would already be underway so that etiquette would permit her eating alone in her own room. She avoided the front door with that aim in mind and hurried down the rear steps into the scullery, to slink along the service corridor as she'd done so many times in her younger years. Head down, she walked briskly past the kitchen and had almost made it to the rear staircase before Knapp spotted her.

'You are expected in the drawing room, Miss Rose. Mrs Courtney wants a word.'

'I have no doubt she does,' Bunch replied. 'I am absolutely fagged and I cannot appear in the drawing room looking like this. Granny would have an absolute fit.' She gestured at her stable-stained jodhpurs and ran a hand through her hair to dislodge clouds of grime. 'Nobody has so much as walked into those stalls for ten years and I swear I'm wearing half the cobwebs. Don't tell her you've seen me. I'll have a tray, if you can manage that?'

'The ship has sailed on an alone supper, I'm afraid, Miss. Nothing gets past the old lady. She saw you crossing the yard and told me you are expected to dine. She has held supper for half an hour.'

'Of course she has. Damn it, I really don't want one of those tedious dinners today.'

'Your grandmother was concerned, Miss.' Knapp smiled an apology. 'I think she has found the upheaval a little distressing herself. You know she likes to keep with tradition, and you do have time to dress.'

Rose took a deep breath. Between Beatrice Courtney and Knapp, she was being managed, just as she feared she would be. 'Oh well, nothing to be done about it.'

'As you say, Miss.'

Bunch started up the stairs with Knapp close on her heels. 'Everything else running smoothly? No staff wars breaking out with Granny's household?'

'No, Miss. Fortunately we only had a couple of full-timers left and the Dower House has been short-staffed for a while. We have a slight excess now but Mrs Breen, the Dower's cook-housekeeper, retired last month. Mrs Crane has been coming in from the village but she has been anticipating our Mrs Westgate to be taking over the kitchen. From what I have heard she sees this as an opportunity to follow Mrs Breen into retirement. She has a sister in Shropshire, I believe.' Knapp waved a hand in a general sweep of the house. 'I gather your grandmother let a couple of outdoor staff go quite recently. Two young men whom Mrs Courtney strongly suspected of ... *nefarious activity* was her exact term.'

Bunch had been letting the household tedium pass her by but that snippet rang a bell. 'They were stealing?' she said.

'I gather they had been living beyond their means.'

'Interesting. Do you know, did they make any fuss at all?'

Knapp frowned. 'Not as much as one might have expected, Miss. Other than that it has been a smooth transition.'

Bunch had a good idea to whom Knapp referred. For a moment she tried connecting them to the men she had seen running from the woods but there didn't seem to be any obvious likeness. 'Convenient all around,' she said

'Yes, Miss, and if it's equally convenient I shall continue as lady's maid for yourself to avoid crossing too many duties with Mrs Crane, until she goes.'

'If you think that works best.' Bunch smiled mechanically and looked around her, aware of something missing. 'Where's Roger?'

'In the kitchen. He has a nice warm corner and he'll be no trouble there. Mrs Courtney was concerned about the upstairs rugs.'

'Was she? We shall see about that. I imagine he will be happy where the food is, for now. Dodo is still here, I take it? I could have done with her help in the yard.'

'She told your grandmother she intended to stay, Miss.' Knapp waved a hand at the stairs. 'But your grandmother has made very pointed comments. She seems to feel Mrs Tinsley should, as she put it, *show some spunk*.'

'Sounds like Granny.'

'Yes, Miss. Now, I've laid out the green Pollard gown for you and your bath is running.' She smiled an apology. 'Your grandmother wasn't the only one to see you talking to the girls across the yard. I took the liberty given the day you've had.'

'Knapp, you are an angel. I'm in the Blue Room I take it?'

'Yes.'

'Wonderful. I can keep an eye on the stables from there. Sheba's in a bit of a tizz over the move.' Bunch took the rest of stairs two at a time and headed straight for the large guest room at the rear of the house. It was a familiar space to her, having stayed there on occasion as a child when her parents were overseas. It was, as the name suggested, decorated in hues of blue. The walls papered in soft turquoise, Morrison prints of acanthus and flowers that were echoed in the duck-egg and white damask bedding. The rugs were a rich royal blue, patterned in an eastern style, and the curtains were of the darkest, almost navy blue, velvet. Some said blue was a cool colour but the overall effect was of calmness and welcome, and the newly lit fire crackling in the grate gave an illusion of warmth even though it had yet to raise the thermometer.

Her green dinner evening gown lay across the bed. Bunch pulled a face. It was Knapp's little joke to name the frock by its designer, a joke at Bunch's expense when there were more jodhpurs to her name than evening gowns. She owned a few gowns from necessity, having little interest in fashion, but the acknowledgement of her wardrobe deficiencies brought to mind Frampton's dig about her eligible spinsterhood. She realised that invitations were getting fewer and most of those were with an eye to her considerable inheritance. She found it hard to decide whether that bothered her or not.

Bunch crossed to the window and risked the Blackout to peek down at the stable yard. All was quiet. Without the distant booming of coastal raids, darkness was lulling even the flighty Sheba into quiet. She pulled the Blackout blinds firmly back into place. There was always the risk that there might be an ARP officer out on patrol and she didn't want to get black marks on her first night in residence.

From the door on the other side of the room the sound of water and wisps of steam escaped into her boudoir, reminding her how much she needed to be clean. She hurried toward it discarding clothing as she went, turned off the taps and shed the last of her clothes to step into the bath. After the chill of the yard it was a luxury to sink into warm and fragrant water. There was a brand-new bar of Yardley's Lavender sitting in the shell-shaped porcelain soap dish. It was not her usual brand but she was grateful for it, all the same, and also for the bottle of shampoo on the ledge. She wished she could have taken the time to soak away the aches along with the dirt but she dared not be too late for dinner on her first evening. She washed quickly and emerged to find Knapp waiting for her.

'Will you be wanting something for your hair, Miss Rose?' she asked.

Bunch rubbed vigorously with a towel and glanced in the mirror at the eminently practical bob currently standing in a spiked rabble across her scalp. 'No, it'll dry quick enough.'

'As you wish.'

Bunch glanced at Knapp, trying to decide how judgemental the older woman was being with that coded admonishment.

Knapp had been working for the family from the moment she had left school before the Great War, moving up to housekeeper by being the epitome of perfect staff. It was unlike her to speak her mind without cause, and however obliquely. 'But?' Bunch murmured.

'There is an extra place at table.'

'Oh? For whom?'

'Major Tinsley, Miss.'

'You think Barty Tinsley warrants added pizzazz? Hardly.' She stepped into her dress and waited as Knapp buttoned and hooked and adjusted. It was a while since she had been *dressed*. School had made her more independent than many of her peers, and war and the loss of staff had seen ladies' maids further depleted. Her mother had one, of course, and Dodo preferred to have assistance. She herself was not sure she required a maid. Dressing felt such a nonsense when she spent her days wielding shovels and brooms, and then to come home and go through the motions of being a woman of leisure. A year finishing in Switzerland and more recently her training in FANY had given her a level of self-sufficiency that suited her. She submitted because she was tired and because she sensed that the process was as much for Knapp's peace of mind as her own comfort.

'What does Tinsley want here, anyway?' She sat at the dressing table and allowed Knapp to finish drying her hair and moulding it into shape with brisk strokes of the silver-backed brush.

'He came to collect Mrs Tinsley.'

'Did he indeed?' Bunch turned, narrowly avoiding a mouthful of bristles, to stare at Knapp. 'Dodo never said she was returning to Banyards today.'

'I think she was as surprised by his arrival as anyone.'

'I don't doubt it. When *did* he arrive?'

'About an hour ago, Miss Rose. He didn't seem keen to stay but Mrs Courtney can be very persuasive.'

'Good old Granny.' Bunch almost felt sorry for him. There were few who could gainsay her grandmother's ruthlessly sweet little old lady act. She dabbed some powder on her face and leaned forward to peer in the mirror as she applied a smear of lipstick, pursing her lips and angling her head from side to side to examine the effect. She was exhausted and would have been happier with a glass of milk and a sandwich – and a lot of sleep – but that was no longer an option. With Barty Tinsley gracing the table it made dinner an even less attractive prospect. 'Is she going?' she said.

'Is who going where, Miss?'

'Is my sister going back to Banyards?'

'I rather got the impression she was evading the issue, Miss. I was going to send for you but Mrs Courtney was quite adamant that you finish your day's work.'

'I bet she was.'

'Yes, Miss.'

Bunch stood up and twirled with hands held palms out in a cat-walk parody. 'Will I do, do you think, Knapp?'

'Your hair is still a little damp. Are you sure you wouldn't like to try the gold and green turban? Or I could pin up a snood?'

'Steady, Knapp. You'll have me looking like some young deb and I'm a little bit past all of that.' She scooped up a pair of earrings and snapped them onto her lobes. 'There, should do.' She paused at the sound of the front-door bell and found herself flushing, wondering if her earlier thought about the ARP was about to backfire. 'Visitors?' she said. 'At this hour?'

Both women listened intently to the maid ushering in a visitor. Bunch recognised a voice. 'If I am not mistaken, that is Chief Inspector Wright,' she said. 'What can he want? Cook will be cross having to lay yet another place at table.' She grinned at Knapp and winked. 'I might go down before the final gong, after all.' She snatched up the wrap that was laid out for her on the end of the bed and swung it around her shoulders as she walked onto the gallery.

She watched Wright shed his coat and hat before following the girl across the mosaic floor to the drawing room. Something urgent must have brought him here in person rather than his using the telephone, as any sane person would on such a night. She was tempted to call out to him. However, she did not want to be viewed as gauche so she waited for a count of twenty, sufficient time for Wright to be announced, before descending the stairs and heading for the Roman arena that a country-house dinner sometimes became.

The drawing room was an oasis of warmth compared with the

relative chill of her bedroom. Its focus was the twin armchairs and an ancient chesterfield flanking the hearth. Dodo was deep in conversation with Wright whilst Tinsley sat silently at her other side, clutching a glass of sherry and doing a good impersonation of a recalcitrant chorister. Bunch noted how Dodo and Barty sat as far from each other as the sofa permitted and wondered again why Tinsley had decided his daughter-in-law's presence at Banyard Manor was so urgently needed tonight.

'Good evening everyone.'

All heads turned to Bunch. 'Rose, my dear.' Beatrice Courtney stood gracefully and held out her right hand, her left clutching a silver topped cane. She was slim and tall, with pale hair that was pure white around her face but still retaining some of its former darkness to the back. She had a good bone structure that kept her face handsome for a woman rapidly approaching her eightieth year. 'Just in time. Second gong will be sounding any moment. Come here and let me see you properly.'

'Yes, Granny.' Bunch dutifully approached the fireside and allowed the elderly woman to kiss her on the cheek. 'I am so sorry to be late. Such a lot to get done.'

'Allowances can be made in times of war. Wet hair, on the other hand, will get you a chill.' Beatrice turned to Wright with an arch smile. 'Old habits, Chief Inspector. I was a nurse in the last war, you know. Then, Perringham became a convalescence home from the middle of nineteen-sixteen.'

'As did I, Mrs Courtney, though not as a nurse obviously. King's Own. Just for the last year.'

'Surely not. You can't be old enough.'

He laughed and bowed to her. 'Too kind. I only saw six months in France, it's true. That was enough.' He looked down at the rug for a moment. 'And you, Major?'

'Grenadiers,' Barty retorted. 'Not something—' The gong in the hallway clattered and Tinsley rose quickly. 'Ah, dinner.' He offered his arm to Bunch. 'Shall we?'

Bunch glanced over her shoulder at Wright with wry apology. She understood Barty's dismissal of Wright even as she was annoyed by it. His snub of her grandmother, on the other hand, was harder to interpret. The unease bristling between Beatrice and Barty Tinsley was obvious and she wondered yet again why the man seemed hell-bent on whisking his daughter-in-law back to Banyard Manor with such little notice.

His proprietary attitude was irritating although not, she knew, out of character, and Bunch was not above tossing a touch of oil into the flame. 'Granny has asked Dodo to stay here for a few days, Barty,' she said. 'She misses proper society something awful. Isn't that so, Granny? I'm a poor substitute, you see. Never out of the stables long enough to waste time with socialising.'

The old lady fixed Bunch with a gimlet stare, her lips twitching amusement, before she inclined her head. 'Rose my dear, I have always been in the set, and many of Daphne's friends are still single. She will never have trouble finding a seat.'

Bunch pulled a face. She was all too aware that dinner invitations as a single woman among married friends were getting few and far between. 'What are you implying, Granny?'

'That you are not a young thing, my dear girl. Though it's never too late for a woman of means, if such is required.'

'I'm too busy for all that now.' Bunch smiled sweetly and gave silent thanks for the final dinner gong before her Grandmother could saddle one of her favourite hobbyhorses.

Dinner was a brittle affair of stilted conversation and with simmering questions that could not be asked. It was Bunch who inevitably switched the focus to Tinsley. 'Barty, you'd be good enough to send some of Dodo's things over?'

'That would be topping,' Dodo added. 'It would be nice to spend a few days with Granny.'

'I am afraid we really do need you at Banyards,' Tinsley replied. 'We have some legal papers concerning the family that need all of our signatures. I realise you are still in shock but we must deal with George's will.'

'You couldn't bring the papers here?' said Bunch.

Barty flushed around the collar. 'Olivia's nerves are shot to pieces these past few weeks. With Emma going back at Oxford so soon, Banyards needs someone to organise the house. As I have already said, there are legal matters to attend to.'

Dodo nodded reluctantly. 'Of course.'

Her apparent capitulation was a surprise to Bunch. The younger woman's manner had been subdued since George's passing but this bordered on servile. 'There can't be anything that urgent, surely?'

'It isn't just that Olivia needs Daphne's help. She was beside herself when she heard about the farm girl getting killed. Olivia is convinced Daphne will be safer with her.' He blushed a deeper shade of red at admitting his wife's shortcomings and turned to Dodo with a genuine helplessness. 'The doctor does what he can to keep her calm and I know it has been as challenging for all of us, but it has been harder still for her or I wouldn't have come to fetch you in this weather.'

'I am sure Olivia can cope for a few more days.' Bunch was aware Olivia would never allow another woman to *run* her household; but her objecting for the fear of Dodo and her inheritance slipping the leash, now that Bunch could well believe. 'The doctor thought the change would do Dodo some good and I am inclined to agree with him.'

'Doctor Lewis never mentioned it to me.'

'Oh, not that old dinosaur. I meant Doctor Ephrin, our family consultant up in Town. He's a cousin of Mummy's.'

'I know him,' Barty replied. 'Played in the same eleven at Oxford. I'll give him a call tomorrow. Chap can't object to a girl being with her family.'

It was an odd reaction and Bunch could tell his heart was not entirely behind the comment, despite his bluster. She had always thought Barty insufferably pompous and could not imagine what it would be like to be forced to share a roof with him and, though he might appear ignorant on occasion, he was not an idiot. The only explanation she could think of was that he was acting on orders from Olivia. She glanced at her sister who pulled a face, attempting amusement and only highlighting a deep unhappiness in her eyes. Bunch felt she quite understood why Dodo was desperate to escape Banyard Manor. 'Perhaps we should retire to more comfortable surroundings. Granny?' she said, hoping the older woman would take the cue.

'Excellent idea. We can all stand a glass of port, I am sure.' Beatrice folded her napkin, rose abruptly, and looked at the maid. 'We needn't stand on ceremony tonight. We shall also take coffee in the drawing room.' She led the way to the next room, seated herself close to the fire, and waited for the visitors to be seated. 'Chief Inspector,' she said, 'you have been charming but terribly quiet all evening and I've completely avoided the obvious question until now. What brought you all this way on such a dreadful evening? Have you some answers for us?'

'Nothing new, sorry to say. We've hit a bit of a wall, so to speak.' He glanced around the room and smiled grimly.

'Can't stop for a bit of snow,' Tinsley said. 'It's a murder, by God.'

'I think the Colonel is worried at how it all looks with his chaps caught up in all of this before the base has even become operational.' Wright spread his hands. 'I can see his point now that this Johansson has vanished. However, fostering goodwill toward our allies is crucial.'

'It does make the pilot look guilty, by any mark,' Tinsley said. 'Chap slopes off when his girl has been shot. It looks pretty damned bad.'

'Which is exactly why Kravitz is playing by the book,' said Wright. 'Waiting either for Johansson to turn up or for further orders, whichever comes first. I would do the same in his place.'

Tinsley snorted. 'You'd just hang around waiting? That's not how we do things here.'

Wright glanced at Bunch and she was almost certain that he winked at her.

'We've a few rules of our own that we can wave about. I've made application through the Ministry to speak with special services, and the Chief Constable is pulling a few strings to get the Coroner's report hurried through.' He nodded at Bunch. 'Seems you have some influence there. Officially, we don't know how the girl met her end.' He sighed. 'You seem to be one of the last persons outside of the base who spoke to Mr Johansson. I was rather hoping you might have remembered some more details.'

Bunch paused for a moment to consider the possibilities. 'So you think that what he told me about those vehicles actually *is* tied up with Mary's death?'

'An alternative theory is that Miss Tucker was killed by her young man who promptly went on the run. From what I've been able to ascertain he was not a violent man. There is no link between Johansson and Frampton that we have discovered, yet there seems to be some suggestion that the two events are somehow connected. I have no idea why the lieutenant has gone AWOL but I am not convinced he murdered Mary Tucker.'

'I'd agree with that,' Bunch said. 'He seemed a nice enough chap. Knew his horses.'

'He *has* gone missing,' Tinsley growled. 'You can't deny that. I've been a magistrate for almost ten years, I will have you know. In my experience that is the act of a guilty man. Odd, this chap turning up just before Frampton does what he did.'

'He remains innocent until proven otherwise,' Wright replied. 'That has been the main tenet of my twenty-year policing career, as it should be yours.'

'Can't ignore the obvious, Chief Inspector. It's one huge coincidence that the man's little fancy piece is killed whilst he conveniently vanishes. Seen it many times with soldiers away from barracks. He's a bad one. I'd bet a month's pay on it.'

'Steady on.' Bunch tapped her finger nails on the chair arm. 'Mary Tucker was genuinely fond of this man and according to everyone we've spoken with that affection was returned. Why would you even think that?'

'I went up to the house first because you never told us you were moving out,' Tinsley replied, 'and spoke with Kravitz. He is a good chap. He's joined the golf club. Kravitz assured me that Johansson's family would not welcome some illiterate urchin straight out of the East End into their fold, even once this war is over.'

'His background and his money are hardly relevant.' Wright leaned forward in his chair and fixed Tinsley with a disarmingly bland smile. 'The lieutenant will remain a suspect until such time as he is available for questioning, but *only* a suspect. We have no evidence he was involved beyond the circumstantial. Until such time as we have proof, one way or another, I am inclined to think there are other forces at work beyond a lover's tiff.'

'Such as?'

'Such as whoever slaughtered at least three dozen sheep in those woodlands over the course of the past few weeks.' He paused whilst the maid brought in coffee and had retreat once more. 'The Ministry has a lot of problems with rustling over recent months. These rackets are being run out of London for the most part, which is also where the meat is going.'

'Perhaps the lieutenant was a part of that.' Tinsley gave the coffee Dodo handed him considerable attention and took a sip, grimacing slightly. 'You know there are some very good suppliers of coffee still in operation?'

'I don't think—' Bunch was interrupted by the telephone. Evening calls were invariably the harbinger of bad news.

The maid sidled into the room and bobbed a curtsy. 'Beggin' pardon, but there's a call for the Chief Inspector.'

'Thank you. If you'll excuse me.' Wright hurried after the maid and a curious quiet fell over the room as they all attempted unsuccessfully to eavesdrop.

'You were saying about coffee,' Bunch mentioned at last. 'I'm told we shall need coupons for everything soon. Naturally, pillars of the establishment such as ourselves would surely not circumnavigate the process.'

Tinsley's chins wobbled as he searched for words. 'I merely have a very efficient system on my estate for obtaining supplies in bulk. A man in my position would be mad to go anywhere near the black market.'

'Nobody is accusing you of anything, Barty,' said Beatrice. 'Though I am increasingly worried about the reports of hoarding; aren't you?'

'Is it likely?' Dodo asked. 'I mean, all households make jam and butter don't they?'

Beatrice examined her youngest granddaughter curiously. 'I suspect it is all a matter of proportions. The WVS has been sending out literature to its members. A little jam is one thing, a few sacks of sugar is quite another. People were imprisoned for that kind of thing in the Great War and I have no doubt there will be such occurrences again. I hear some MPs are calling for it to be a capital offence.'

'Hoarding?' Tinsley frowned at her. 'Yes, of course. Hadn't considered that. It depends on how long this war goes on for, of course. You and I should not be unduly perturbed by it.'

'Not perturbed? Quite the contrary. From what I hear, I should have thought you and Olivia would have more cause to be concerned than myself.' Beatrice sat back, sipping at her coffee and meeting Tinsley's arctic glare with one of her own.

An ancient enmity had always existed between these two but,

even so, Bunch was surprised that her gracious grandmother would deliver such a sting. She had no time to pursue her thoughts before Wright had returned.

'That was my station sergeant. He rang through some preliminary results from the Coroner.' Wright sat down to finish his coffee; then, running a hand through his hair, said, 'The weapon used to kill Mary Tucker had a .22 calibre, which would appear to rule out the lieutenant. He would have possessed a standard issue, larger calibre sidearm.'

'There is still the matter of his going missing,' Tinsley replied. 'Bloody suspicious, if you ask me.'

'I doubt he would go to the lengths of buying a local weapon. Our best theory returns to the matter of stolen livestock.'

'That is a different leap of faith,' said Tinsley. 'Why would someone gun down an innocent young woman because she saw some vehicles parked by the roadway? It makes no sense.'

'Is this the same East End illiterate you were talking about earlier, Barty?' Bunch asked. 'She can't be both. Dodo, what do you think?'

Dodo shook her head. 'I didn't know her. It seems unfair to talk about the poor creature when she is not even in her grave. I mean, I don't think any of us really knew her.' She held a hand to her forehead. 'You know, I suddenly have the most frightful headache. If it's all the same to you I think I shall go to bed.'

Tinsley rapidly hauled himself to his feet. 'We can be home in a quarter of an hour, my dear. We should go before the weather gets any worse.'

'I don't think I could face going outside. I have a room here all made up for me, so I shall stay.'

'Daphne, I came all this way in this weather to fetch you, and if we leave now we may avoid being snowed in and we'll be home before ten. Don't be difficult.'

Bunch watched Tinsley's face darken. He was plainly angry and she wondered why it mattered so much where her sister stayed. 'Dodo's with her family,' she said. 'Or have you forgotten that? She really doesn't look well, Barty. I am sure going out in this weather will not do her any good.'

'Don't fuss, Rose. This is Sussex not Siberia. We shall be fine.' He slipped his arm under Dodo's elbow and guided her toward the door; Dodo could not avoid accompanying him without causing offence.

Dodo walked with him to the front door, waiting nervously as the maid fetched outdoor clothing for them both. 'I'll come and see you soon, Bunch. If you need me just give me a ring.' She paused. 'In fact, I could still stay here for another day.'

'We need to go now, Daphne,' Barty grumbled.

'You do not have to leave,' Bunch hissed.

Dodo gave Bunch a hug and a kiss on her cheek. 'I will call you tomorrow.'

Bunch and Wright watched Tinsley and Dodo get into the car and pull away. 'Odd reaction,' Wright murmured, 'and it's a shocking night to be driving around unnecessarily.'

'I thought so, despite Barty's assertions. Heaven knows how he ever got his over-stuffed arse on the Magistrate's Bench, even if he is only a part-timer.'

'I was thinking more of your sister,' he replied. 'She did not seem keen to go with him.'

'You noticed that?'

'I think he wanted to get her away from here far too much. Is he the controlling type?'

'He never used to be and I'm not convinced he is now. I rather think he had orders from on high. Olivia Tinsley is quite the queen of that castle,' Bunch replied.

☙THIRTEEN☙

Chief Inspector Wright poured himself more tea and stirred in a few grains of sugar. 'I am very grateful to your grandmother for offering me accommodation last night. Will she join us for breakfast? I would like to thank her.'

Bunch looked at the mantle clock. 'At seven o'clock in the morning? She's still in bed, I imagine. Granny is getting on a bit for early mornings. I'm only up because I have to see to the horses. Plus this fresh snowfall is going to cause all kinds of problems for the stock. The telephone lines are down again, incidentally. Knapp said the engineers are out repairing them as we speak so we should have the lines back by lunchtime.'

'I intend to be back in Brighton by then.'

'Hopefully the snow ploughs will have cleared the main roads,' she replied, 'provided we don't get another heavy fall before then.' She looked at the window, with its Blackout curtains that would stay drawn until full sunrise. 'That was something of a blow we had last night wasn't it? It kept me awake half the night!'

'I hope your sister and the Major got home in one piece.'

'I am absolutely certain we would have heard by now if they hadn't.'

'Tinsley is an ex-soldier.'

Bunch snorted, scraping at her toast with added vigour. 'Daddy says he never got past the stores in Aldershot.'

'Not quite true. I checked his records: he was invalided out in January 1917 with shell shock.' Wright shrugged. 'I gather he spent quite a while in a sanatorium.'

'Really? Poor chap.' She stared into blank space for a moment. 'I feel a bit of a toad now.' She resumed her attempts to smear butter fit for one slice across the two on her plate.

'Happened to a lot of men. Most recovered eventually, more or less.' Wright gulped the last of his tea and mopped his lips. 'I have to dash. I have military types to deal with.'

'Good luck with Kravitz. Keep me informed?'

'I will if I can.'

She had hoped to pick Wright's brains over the case but was sure he was not going to say more without a tussle. It was not that she expected to be party to every detail; she had been around her father's table long enough to know some things were not for general chatter, but she had been used to being accommodated on most subjects. Being thwarted so effectively was a novel and uncomfortable experience.

~ ~ ~

Bunch finished her breakfast and hurried down to the stables where all three horses greeted her loudly. 'Just me, I'm afraid, chaps. Sadly, I can only take one out.' She gave Sheba and Robbo a pat before walking to the end box where Perry was tacked up and waiting. She was pleased to see that Parsons had added a larger quarter sheet despite the pony's naturally shaggy coat.

The air was crisply cold even though a pale sun took the edge off the sharp wind. Bunch pulled her duster tight around her neck, stepped up onto the mounting block and gathered the reins in one hand before climbing into the saddle.

The tracks made by Wright's snow-chained tyres made an easy walk until she reached the first gateway which stood open onto a field of unbroken snow. It was beyond temptation, that childish need to make her mark on a pristine landscape. She nudged Perry into the gap and started across the space.

There was nothing to see and hear but the sh-sh-sh of wind sliding between the bare trees dotted along the hedgerows; drifting frozen granules scraping wavy undulations into the white desert; the crunch and squeak of Perry's soup-plate hooves; and his breath coming in steamy snorts of exertion. Forging a path through the fresh undisturbed snow was heavy going, even for him, and Bunch realised she would not be travelling as far, nor as fast, as she had intended; but even this steady plod was exhilarating.

She rode to the top of the coombe and looked down the valley at a white landscape crisscrossed with a spider web of neatly snow-mounded hedges. Away to her left the two woods on either side of the road made an unbroken expanse of ancient forest canopy. Somewhere in the distance there came the steady drone of an engine but she heard no other sounds of human occupation, and she realised how war and weather had denuded the landscape of people. An entire platoon could wander through this side of the vale and the chances were nobody would see them.

She rose up in the stirrups and stared at the dip just to the south of the woods and saw a thin column of smoke twisting upwards. It was as though the sleeping giant beneath every hill, as folklore would have it, lay just beyond sight enjoying a leisurely cigar. She could not see the cottages that nestled in the hollow, but cottages and occupants there were.

Bunch turned toward the farm, cutting across to the next field and coming around the rear of the yards. There was none of the usual banter ringing around the barns as she slid from the saddle and led her mount across the cobbled yard and into the stables. The only person she could find there was Kate stacking hay in the feed store.

'Has Chief Inspector Wright come to talk with you at all since that night?'

'No, but then we didn't really see anything.' Kate looked away, drawing breath sharply, but not before Bunch had seen the wobble in the girl's expression.

'Everything all right?' she asked. 'Anything any of you need?'

Kate cast her a grateful look and then stared down at her boots. 'It's so weird in the cottage,' she murmured. 'Poor Elsie is heart-broken. She might benefit from a spot of compassionate leave. Can you spare her just to see her family for a week or two?'

'We can arrange that.' Bunch paused, unsure of her facts, wanting to make sure she didn't promise what she could not achieve. 'I doubt the Coroner will release Mary's remains until after the inquest and that may take a little while yet. But I do agree, Elsie would benefit from some time off before then. It's not as if we are all that busy this time of year. Tell her she can take two weeks.'

'Oh, that would be marvellous. Thank you. We all miss her but Elsie and Mary were like sisters.'

'Understandable, of course.' Bunch smiled at her and avoided making anything of the Land Girl's unshed tears. She leaned into

Perry's side to lift a hind hoof to pick out impacted snow with the attachment on her pocket knife. 'This is why I usually avoid snow riding. Plays the devil with their feet especially when it becomes ice, like this.' Bunch said. 'It was such a bind when our farrier was drafted, and then hunting season disintegrating into nothing, so we never managed to get winter shoes fitted. We don't always have this amount of snow. Riding Perry was a bad decision, as it turns out.' She let the hoof drop and patted the horse's rump before moving round to check the other hind foot. 'I was in the same boat about Mary and that Norwegian chap,' Bunch continued. 'Hearsay and rumour. Couldn't tell Wright very much. It made me feel a bit useless. I ought to know what you girls are up to, shouldn't I? Duty of care and all that.' She glanced at Kate and smiled. 'How are the rest of you coping?'

'Pretty grim. All feeling it. Not like Elsie of course, but we live cheek by jowl and it's hard not to.'

'It must be difficult.'

Kate let out a long breath. 'It's been a bad week for you, as well. You knew Mr Frampton, and before that there was Mrs Tinsley's loss. With luck that's our run of three bad things.'

'We can hope. Did Mary mention anything about the vehicles she spotted in the cut?'

'The ones she and Seb saw? Yes, so far as it went which wasn't much. Mary was always winding the rest up with nonsense about Seb's uncle being a private detective in California. Which is nonsense when he isn't even American.'

'A lot of people living in America aren't. Why would that matter?'

Kate laughed in spite of herself. 'She made him out to be the next best thing to Basil Rathbone. Said he jotted things down in notebooks. He was always taking notes, she would tell us. Kept them on him like a policeman would.'

'Really? Did you ever see these books?'

'Of course not.' Kate managed a lopsided grin. 'It was just Mary having the rest of them on. You know how she liked to spin a yarn.'

'She did?' said Bunch. 'Well, don't worry about it. I am more concerned with what we have now. Keep your eyes open for anything *off* that's going on, will you?'

'Do you think the poachers will be back?'

It was not something Bunch had given much thought to even though it was such an obvious question. She had been working on the assumption that the black marketeers would operate until apprehended, but now… 'I doubt it,' she said finally. 'We are probably bolting the stable door after the event. Doubtless they will move on if they have any sense at all. However, it won't hurt to keep eyes and ears open.'

'Haynes told us last night that you saw some local men,' said Kate.

'Then Haynes told you far too much. That was supposed to be police business and in any case it's not precisely true. I have no idea who they were but they apparently knew me. Have you heard any more?'

'I haven't but Haynes seemed angry about it.'

'How could you possibly tell? He's angry most of the time. Tell him I'd like to see him, will you? Now if you girls can just concentrate on the basic animal care today. Can't see much else getting done beyond feeding, milking and mucking out.' Bunch went to the door and looked out into the yard. It was uncannily quiet, just a few low calls from the byre that gave any hint of animals and farming. 'Where is everyone?' she asked.

'Elsie and Pat are milking and Ruth and Annie took the tractor out to fill the hay hoppers for the sheep.'

'Isn't that Haynes's job?'

Kate shrugged. 'Nobody's seen him this morning. Parsons went to the top barns to check the beef steers.'

'Well, if you find him tell him I want a word. Anything else I need to know?'

Kate shrugged. 'We can't use the top drive. We're having to go in and out by the lower track because the military put up a barrier just inside the iron gates and they were busy repairing the old gate house.'

'Really?'

'It looks like they're making it into a proper guard hut. There's another barrier on their side of the lane from here to the house and what looks suspiciously like the small summerhouse plonked down beside it, but I could be wrong. I couldn't get close enough to see properly. The security seems a bit steep just for a billet. We went to a dance thrown by the Canucks down at Storrington House and it was nothing like this.'

Bunch had similar thoughts herself. The mix of nationalities and lack of heavy equipment did not tally with Perringham merely housing regular Army, officers or not. 'War,' she muttered. 'I am told we're all having to make sacrifices.'

'Doesn't seem fair, though.'

'At least Perringham is still standing and we will get it back,' Bunch replied. 'Eventually.'

'Meanwhile we have to go a mile out of our way to get to the village.'

'I hadn't thought of that. It's a dashed awful road.'

'Anne saw the police inspector go by earlier and she said he didn't look very happy about it,' Kate said.

Bunch pulled the door to and came to stand at Perry's head. She trusted Kate as much as she would most people who worked for her but how much was too much? *Walls*, she thought, *may well have ears*. 'Yes, he was heading to the main house when I left to ride out.' She concentrated on rubbing her knuckles on the horse's forehead, taking comfort in the animal's vibrating rumbles of pleasure. 'I expect he went to talk with Colonel Kravitz.'

'Given the amount of time he was there he couldn't have even got out of his car.'

'Interesting. Well, I'm returning to the Dower now. I've a hundred things to sort out. Unpacking and such. If you girls need anything do ask. I shall let the WLA know that Elsie will be off for two week's leave.'

'Thank you. She will be ever so glad to get away for a bit. The rest of us can cope, I'm sure, and things will get better. The man on the wireless said the weather is turning. Once that gets back to normal surely everything will be different.' Kate spread her hands.

❧FOURTEEN❧

As she completed another set of forms, and despite all she had to do, Bunch's mind wandered back time and again to Dodo. She had not heard from her sister since Barty had bullied Dodo into returning to Banyard Manor, and that troubled her. Even in her harshest grief Dodo would seldom let a day pass without a calling or making a visit.

Bunch dumped a bundle of papers into the out tray, pausing to look at a handful of sales receipts for stock. Some came from the stock market but others directly from the local butcher's slaughter man, and it set her thinking about the van Mary and Johansson had seen. The more she thought about it the more she was convinced. *That's the key, or one of them.*

She yawned and stretched. Her morning had begun with a visit from Parsons to say that Haynes had yet again not reported for another day's work. Bunch was not surprised in the slightest; Haynes' parents had informed Kate of his bitterness since his return from war. PC Botting had decided his absence was explicable by the state of his mind, and since Haynes had only been missing for thirty-six hours there was no missing persons case to be filed. Since Haynes had taken his valued possessions with him it would seem to rule out immediate risks of self-harm.

Bunch did not like to contemplate a third option. *Two bodies are quite enough,* she thought. She stretched, feeling her joints popping from inactivity. A ride was on the cards and she knew just where to go: the one place where someone might possibly have seen something but would have shied away from sharing it with the police.

~~~

Perringham Cottages sat in sweet seclusion in the fold of the hill. Bunch could smell wood smoke tainted with a hint of singeing fur, and she smiled. Fred and Roly Jenner were getting rid of the evidence. Evidence of what, she did not care. Rabbits were their usual quarry, plus pigeons and a few hares, or the very occasional deer. She knew they were not averse to taking a pheasant or two, if they thought the coast was clear. They were countrymen who did not consider the taking of nature's largesse as theft; but they were not rustlers – livestock was not something they would even consider.

The brothers lived in adjoining cottages that had belonged to the Jenner family for decades. Roly and Edna, his wife of many years, lived in one of the cottages whilst in the other was Fred, a confirmed bachelor. These two Jenners had been plying their various trades for more than half a century, and Bunch had huge respect for their venerable woodsmen's skills.

The family had been woodsmen for generations, carving a living from the woodlands, odd jobbing hedging and ditching in season; making willow and hazel hurdles and cut poles; and constructing rustic furniture. If it could be made of wood or from woodland produce, Fred and Roly Jenner could turn a hand to it. Being too old for conscription, the brothers spent their time as they pleased, which mostly meant being out in the woods every day – as well as a lot of the nights. Bunch was certain they would not willingly offer up information to the police unless forced to under oath; both of them had been apprehended on numerous charges of poaching over the years.

The fire she smelled was burning in an old metal oil barrel wedged up on bricks at the rear of the cottages. Tending it was an elderly man dressed in tweed jacket, moleskin trousers and battered work boots and puttees. Roly Jenner was possessed of that whipcord physique of the long-time outdoorsman: lean and lined with slightly bowed legs – bowed as was his back. *Not exactly dressed for the weather,* Bunch thought, *given his age. But he's a tough old bird.* She adjusted Perry's quarter sheet to ensure he would not get chilled and walked down the side of the house.

'Good morning, Mr Jenner,' she called. 'How are you today?'

He barely moved, only turned his head to look at her and offer a slow nod; he carried on prodding at the fire with a stout length of ash. 'Miss Courtney,' he murmured.

'I thought I should ride past and see how you were coping. I brought this to keep the cold out.' She took a half-bottle of scotch from her coat pocket and handed it across the divide and grinned to see the old man's eyes light up. *Nothing like a little bribery,* she thought. 'Do you need anything out here? I can send someone over with essentials.'

'No, Miss, the missus keeps a good larder.'

'Not even fetching groceries from the village? It's cold and neither of you are getting any younger.'

'Bless you Miss, but no.' He eyed the bottle and slipped it into his own pocket. 'Tis a cold day to be sure but we shall abide,' he said.

'I would not be out and about myself but old Perry needs fresh air most days or he gets box-crazed.'

'That beast 'as got a good head,' Jenner observed. 'I'm've the same mind. Can't abide stayin' shut up.'

'You are out all weathers, I suppose.'

'Not so much, now. I gets eaten up with them rheumatics. I bain't as young as I was.'

'Cold can be awful,' she agreed. 'Nice blaze you have there.'

'Ah,' he said. 'Seein' as we're stuck in, old Fred's bin stripping ash for makin' a chair or two.' He nodded toward the workshop at the far end of the garden where the sound of a lathe pinpointed the whereabouts of the second Jenner.

'The weather's turning,' she said. 'Hopefully we shall see the back of this lot soon.'

He nodded and said, 'That'll be a help. Can't do much when everything's under a foot o' white stuff.'

'I can imagine.' She walked upwind of the smoke and held her gloved hands toward the fire, edging close enough to see inside. The remains of a rabbit pelt was just visible under freshly added wood chippings. 'I suppose it's been quiet for you this past week with so little traffic up and down.'

'Them snow ploughs don't do these biddy lanes much. Just the big roads.'

It was a veiled criticism which she ignored. Her own estate was one of the plough keepers for the area and yes, they paid most attention to the major thoroughfares. Perringham Cottages lay on a tiny single track lane that was not a priority to any save the few that lived along its route.

'There's been some excitement, though,' she said. 'Very sad of course.'

'Master Frampton and then that land gal.' He sniffed loudly. 'Seen 'er down the Seven Stars. Flighty yellow-haired piece.' He poked at the embers thoughtfully. 'They'm all flighty bits, roamin' about at night drinkin' an' cussin' like you please.'

'Times change,' said Bunch, 'and these girls are very different creatures from the old days.'

'Ah.' He pulled a pipe from his coat pocket and lit it with the burning end of his ash poker, narrowing his eyes against the smoke and heat. 'Got one of 'em killed dead though,' he mumbled around the pipe stem.

'Hardly her fault. It could happen to anyone. Take Jonny Frampton for one.'

'I 'eared he shot hisself.' His tone was careful, not so much the sharing of gossip, rather bordering on a question.

'No,' she snapped, and then more gently. 'No he didn't, Mr Jenner. I'm certain of that. He had no reason. As a matter of fact it's one reason I dropped by. To ask you a few things. I am going to show the authorities it was not suicide or an accident.' Her tone became conspiratorial as she leaned closer to him. She was taking the chance that mentioning the means to thwart red tape would get Roly Jenner on her side. 'They'll just take the easy road. Jonathan Frampton did not take his own life. I would lay good odds on it.'

The old man nodded sagely. 'That's a sadness and a joy, Miss,' he said. 'Bain't right for a young man to take his own life. Tis against all reason and God. But he'll get a decent send-off in con-see-cratered ground if it were by some other hand.'

'I am so glad you agree.' She rubbed her gloved hands together and held them to the fire once more. 'Jonathan Frampton was a nice man. A good man.'

'More than could be said for his old dad. Saul Frampton's always been a *snuffy* sort of a gent. If it wersent for his havin' Len Pole for his steward he'd 'ave no workers left at all.'

'I still feel sorry for him losing his son that way. Murder is an ugly thing.'

'Tis an' all.' Jenner puffed at his pipe, sending his own smoke column up to join the burning rabbit remains. Bunch was wondering how to get around to asking about Jonny and that fateful night in the woods when he added, 'Fred saw old Saul an' that lad of his. Right old ding-dong they were 'avin'.'

'Really? When – where – was that?' It seemed too much like luck to have the answers land in her lap unasked, but she could see the smile playing around his eyes and knew he was telling her for a specific reason. 'You never told the police,' she said.

'Botting never asked an' I didn't tell him. I'd never tell that pathery lad nothin',' he grumbled. 'Nor Fred wouldn't, neither. He busy runnin' about bodgering innocent men with daft questions.'

She nodded sagely and fought to keep the smile off her face. When it came to innocence these two old rogues were not even in the running. She could believe the local rumours that Roly and Fred Jenner were out poaching long before they could talk. 'So you saw them having some sort of argument?' she asked.

'Not me. It were Fred.'

'May I speak with Fred? It would be a big help.'

'Ah,' he said. 'Fred! Miss Courtney wants a word.'

A long silence was broken by the shed door banging open against the frontage. Fred was as like Roly as it was possible to be without being a twin. He stood in the doorway eying Bunch up and down before nodding abruptly. 'Miss Courtney,' he rumbled.

'Good morning, Mr Jenner. Roly here was telling me you saw the Framptons the night Jonathan died.'

'I did, ah.' Fred made his way to the fire and held his hands out to its warmth, closing one eye against the fumes as he puffed on the blackened pipe clamped between his teeth.

The stench of shag tobacco laced with some hedgerow substitute was noxious, even managing to overlay the acridity of charred remains from the bonfire. Bunch shifted slightly to get upwind. 'Do you know what they were shouting about?'

'Couldn't say. I wersent hangin' about to listen. Soon as I 'eard them I crossed the road, quick as you like, an' came home. It was snowin' hard. Bad night for being out an' about.'

'I'll bet.' She looked at the woods. 'Were there no words you caught at all? It could be really important.'

'I'm not one fer gossip, Miss Rose. Not even to a highbred maid like yourself. An' why should I 'elp their sort? Not after them fines. That Hascombe Woods've got more rabbits than you c'n shake a stick at. Old Frampton don't miss a few. Don't know what it 'as to do with the likes o' Tinsley.'

'Poaching fines?'

'I takes a couple of rabbits over to the Crown a few nights back and that Tinsley bloke was in there. An' him being a magistrate.' Fred scowled at her.

'No love lost then?'

'Could say that.' Roly laid the ash stick on a sawing-horse close to hand. 'Bit rum when you thinks of it. I know his cook bain't afrit of getting a bit extra.' He leaned forward to tap her arm. 'I 'eard how there's one of them spivs was sellin' all sorts.'

'Really?'

He frowned. 'There's all kinds of things they're sayin' about them. Jealous mostly. They'm got the money and food. Ah, an' petrol.'

'Oh, I've heard people complain,' Bunch replied. 'I've heard the rumours but I would say most of it is just that. Rumours.' She tugged at her scarf, looking into the flames and smoke for a few moments. 'Did you see anyone else that night?' she asked at last. 'Other than the Framptons having a row in the middle of the woods, did you see anything else that was out of place?'

'I saw old Tinsleys car go up past us just afore that,' Fred replied. 'It were up by the crossin' an' all. Weren't 'im though. Whoever 'twas, they were a sight smaller than the Major.'

That is new, she thought, *only a few people at Banyards have access to the garage.* 'Really?' she said. 'Gosh. Did you see anyone else?' The brothers looked at each other and back to her. She knew they were hiding something. 'It's important,' she said. 'Anyone else at all? Anything?'

'Couple've them Land Girls went past early. Off down the Stars,' Fred replied. He looked at Roly who nodded. 'And there were some lads poachin'. Useless young tikes crashin' about like ruttin stags.'

'Who?'

'I thought one of 'em were yer Frank Haynes, only he were hoppin' about a lot more then he usually do.'

'And the others?'

'Couldn't say fer sure. One might've bin his cousin Harry. And the other one, he were a bit more careful. I says to Roly, next mornin', I never thought I'd see that Percy Guest bloke round 'ere agin.'

'Guest?'

'Ah. That chap as the Major sent packin' a while back.'

'Oh, I think I might have met him once.'

'Well, it were dark so mebbe not 'im. If it wersen't 'im it were very like.'

'Very interesting; and these chaps were poaching? Do you think they could hear the Framptons?'

'Must've heard, seein' how they were goin' at it 'ammer and tongs, until Len Pole broke 'em up.'

'Are you sure you didn't hear what they were rowing over? Not even a word or two?'

Fred smiled artfully. 'Same thing's always, I reck'n. They argued over the farm and the Mrs F as was. And other stuff as bain't fer a maid's ears.'

Bunch nodded. 'Family rows were a common occurrence with them?'

'So Len Pole reck'ns.'

'Pole was there for how long?'

'Not long. Says as he took old Saul home cos the daft bugger were drunk as a lord.' Jenner gazed toward the woods, clicking his tongue. 'It were fair crammed up them woods that night.' He said after a long pause. 'I came 'ome early cos the *robbuts* weren't goin' to be about much with all them crashin' round.'

'Were all of them on foot?'

'No. There were them with that *gurt* big van an' all.'

'Just one van?'

Fred glowered at her, puffing steadily at his pipe. 'I bain't that bookish, Miss Rose, but I can count to the sum've my fingers. If I says there were one van then there were one. One van – an' one motor car.'

'Of course. Mary thought she saw two vehicles on her way to the pub.' Bunch was not looking at the old man directly, pulling her gloves up tighter on her wrists as unconcerned as she was able to appear. 'Or maybe she was wrong. It was dark. But she said the van had a name on it. I suppose you didn't happen to notice whose it was? I mean was it local?'

'It were writ there in big white letters clear as you like, even in the dark. I says to Roly when I gets back, we can't get a gallon to work our lathe fer love nor money, and there's folks wastin' it traipsin' down from all over.'

'Not local then?' A trill of anticipation had her fighting to maintain her facade of cool disinterest. 'Perhaps they'd run out of fuel,' she said. 'It's not that far up to town but far enough if you don't have the coupons to spare.'

Roly laughed a wheezing whisper of a laugh. 'If they 'ad coupons in mind it wasn't their own. They was sat there with the engine runnin', a-wastin' juice. Reckon they was just sittin' in t'cab to keep their sorry selves from a bit o'chill.'

'I suppose you can't blame them. It was a cold day. You say this was early on in the evening, Fred?'

'Ah,' he assured her. 'I was in before that Henry Hall were on the wireless. I likes 'im. Never misses it.'

'So you were back in by what, eight o'clock?'

'I s'pose I was.'

She nodded, smiling. 'Mrs Knapp and Cook like Henry Hall as well. I get hurried through my dinner so they can listen to him. Or I did.'

'I 'eard you got moved into the Dower,' Roly said. 'Cryin' shame. Them guverment types movin' your family out the big house. Bain't right.'

She shrugged. 'Daddy arranged it all. I suspect he never actually had a choice. When the War Office decides something it doesn't matter who your family is.' She shrugged. 'There's a war on, we're reminded. Having us all in the Dower House will save on bills. Speaking of which, I trust the Army are still buying their wood from you? It would seem wrong not to.'

'Dunno,' Fred mumbled. 'You may've seen more of 'em than us. Their quartermaster chap, he's a rum'n. Bit of a rogue, I'd say. I'll bet he charges his boss more'n he pays me.'

'Quite possibly.' Bunch frowned. 'So neither of you saw anything more than that?'

'No, Miss, jus' that van an' the car. An' the Major's car, as well. Made a 'ell of a row getting along the lane. They didn't have no chains on. Heavy goin' fer 'em along here.'

'It would be. Who in their right mind would try?' She knew it to be a rhetorical question when the lane was little used, it being barely a cart's width and full of potholes. Its only function now was to serve Perringham Cottages, or rarely as a route to avoid driving through the village and past the Police House. That in itself spoke volumes to her. 'Well, I'd best be off. Perry will be getting chilled if he stands about in this wind. Thank you for the chat. If you do remember anything more about the writing on the van will you run up to the Dower and let me know?'

Roly winked slowly. 'You'd best be off for your dinner. I'll bet it'll be a nice pie or some such.'

'Doubtless,' Bunch said, allowing herself to smile in silent understanding, and shook his hand.

~ ~ ~

The ride back was a longer one. Parallel tracks belonging to the Jenner's old horse and wagon had cut lines in the snow and she followed these along the track to the junction and onto the other, wider road where the much-discussed vehicles had parked. The road was freshly scraped with lay-by and verges under heaps of snow peeled to the edges by the ploughs. Try as she might she could not see any evidence that anything had parked there a few nights previously. The thieves had apparently not been back since the London lad had taken a pot shot at her.

She looked left and right at the banks enveloped in their protective woody canopy. There was no sign of human activity, which was as she had come to expect, but somehow wished differently. She felt that the answers to the myriad questions – who and why? – should be written in the snowy banks. Errant fancy, obviously, but a reflection of the frustration she felt in not knowing. In the plus column, she had persuaded the police, or Wright at least, that Jonathan's case was not one of simple suicide, if suicide could ever be seen as simple. Yet the mess that it had become attached to was worse and closer to home in very uncomfortable ways. She also felt sorry for Dodo and guilty that she had not sought out her sister's company, however difficult Olivia was being. She should have provided the sisterly shoulder to cry on.

'That I can remedy.' She nudged Perry into action and headed home at a slightly brisker pace than before, eager to be back in the warmth of the Dower House before dusk.

✣FIFTEEN✣

Beatrice Courtney was sitting at the largest of the morning room's occasional tables sorting hanks of chunky white and blue wool.

'Good morning, Granny.' Bunch leaned down to kiss the proffered cheek.

'You were out very early. Good to know that you don't lounge around the house all day. I am sure you will also be pleased to know that the telephone lines have been repaired and the dratted thing has barely ceased to ring since you went out. I've taken the liberty of calling the telephone company for a second apparatus. We can have it installed in a quieter part of the house where you will have some privacy. Knapp can answer it for you when you are out.'

Bunch hid a smile. *Trust Granny to organise me.* One of the reasons Bunch had not wanted to move to the Dower was that her grandmother, quite rightly, regarded it as her bastion and insisted on full control of everything that went on within its walls. She empathised to some degree. This old lady had, after all, been the beating heart of the Perringham estate until her husband's death had whisked power from her grasp. Now age and war had truncated her endless adventuring to the far-flung corners of the world. Bunch and Beatrice were kindred spirits, which was why they found it hard to exist under the same roof, but at least the old lady understood her eldest granddaughter's nonconformist ways.

Bunch was all too aware of how her own mother regarded her refusal to marry as a failure in furthering the family line. *Not my fault that flu wiped away the line of succession,* she thought. *Perhaps if things with Jonathan had gone the way Mother had assumed they would, then she and I might even like each other.*

'I believe Knapp has the full list of the calls you were not here to take. Rose, dear, are you listening?'

Beatrice's energetic tones dragged Bunch back to the present. 'Sorry Granny. I trust you slept well?'

'I did, despite that infernal telephone,' Beatrice replied. 'All of those calls were for you. Come and sit by the fire, my dear. You look frozen. I'll ring for some tea.'

'Super.' Bunch crossed to stand with her back to the fire, warming her frozen legs. 'So who called for me?'

'There was a Mr Tane, according to Knapp. No idea what he wanted.'

'He's a land owner over Horsham way. Bit outside my area. Anyone else?' She worked at keeping the wasp from her tone. *The old girl's scented some poor quarry. A few phone calls wouldn't rouse her up like this.*

'That Chief Inspector called. Apparently he was rather excited about something. He said he'd call back.'

There we have it, all about our Mr Wright. Don't take the bait. 'No one else?' she said.

'That idiot Barty,' Beatrice replied. 'He called to say he and Daphne got home, rather belatedly, I thought. I was very cross about him dragging her away. Of course we all know who wanted her back. Olivia has never been able to run a house. She hated it when Emma chose a vocation in Oxford. She lost her whipping dog. Barty is too dim to notice she is manipulating him.'

'You have worked out Dodo's life as well as mine?'

Beatrice regarded her quizzically. 'You're not the only one in the family doing their bit. Daphne has been such a help to me. In her own way.'

'I had no idea,' Bunch replied. 'Dodo spoke about WI stuff back in the autumn, but not so much lately.'

'I've also taken on the local WVS and I could do so much more with her to help out. It's quite obvious from all your telephone calls that you will not be at home. Daphne would have been perfect.'

'Of course.' Bunch grinned at her and pondered the reasons behind these plans. Though occasionally victim to a mild heart condition and progressive arthritis, Beatrice was in reasonable shape for her age, well able to stir the local women into action with little more than a phone call or two. Bunch wondered what she knew, or guessed, about Dodo's situation. She was grateful for purely selfish reasons: from her perspective, Dodo would be an extraordinarily convenient buffer to ameliorate the worst effects of living with the Courtneys' Grande Dame.

'So this wool is all WVS stuff?' Bunch asked.

'Socks,' Beatrice replied. 'We have a veritable army of local women all poised for the Knit for the Navy and Air Force campaign.'

Bunch bit back her comments on the tedium of such a project for someone of Beatrice's mind set, but if this gave her some sense of purpose then so be it. 'Splendid, top hole.' She rubbed at her thighs that were just beginning to thaw, ignoring the cold ache in her fingers. 'Well, if it's all right by you I am ready for that tea now.'

'Of course, dear. Ring the bell will you?' She beckoned Bunch closer. 'Something else you should know about Oliva Tinsley,' she said. 'She is not what she seems. No breeding.'

'Don't be such a snob, Granny. She's not from an old family; but still—'

'If she was just new money, my dear, or even trade—' The older woman craned her neck toward the door as if expecting some spy at the keyhole, and added, 'She comes from far more dubious roots.'

'I've heard vague rumours but never the whole story.'

Beatrice laid a hand on her granddaughter's forearm and nodded sagely. 'That fashion plate tells everyone she's from this family and that, but the truth is, she was a music hall girl.'

'Olivia?'

'It was quite the scandal back then. Barty's mother told me the family wanted Barty to pay the girl off. Silly boy wouldn't. Married her in secret. I suppose he felt he had no choice though I'm sure his father would have bought her off, had he known. Anyway, the couple were sent to Malaya to keep them both out of the way until George arrived. The Tinsleys had rubber plantations back then.'

Bunch frowned. There were stories but none so blatantly stated as this. 'Then how is it nobody has ever talked about it?' she asked. 'I mean its juicy goss. You'd think someone would've trotted it out over dinner somewhere. It's hardly like you to worry what the neighbours think.'

'It matters to me because it will worry Daphne. The family was concerned with hushing things up back then and, as I mentioned, sent them abroad for a year. When Barty brought Olivia back to Banyards they already had George. Of course, once the Great War began people had rather more on their minds. Barty worked very hard to keep it under wraps. How times and people can change.' She tapped her lips thoughtfully. 'As it turned out, George was a sweet boy so it could have been a lot worse, but it seems almost as if history is repeating itself.'

'Not the same thing at all! Dodo isn't some vaudeville actress,' said Bunch. 'We all thought it was a little odd, George and Daphne sloping off to a registry office. Without wishing to be crude what would Olivia possibly have to be cross over.'

Beatrice smiled bleakly. 'Jealousy. Olivia fancied herself a bit of a bright young thing after the Great War. Spent a lot of time up in Town but she ended up being dried out in a sanatorium. When Emma came along it slowed her down a little. Barty kept her on a tighter rein when he inherited Banyards. He takes his duty far more seriously these days.'

Bunch thought back to comments Dodo had made and sighed. 'Dodo had a notion something was up,' she said. 'Is that why she didn't want to go back, do you think?'

'Of course.' The door opened and Knapp bustled in with a tray. 'It is very good to have one of my girls here. It has been a while since we had family to stay.'

'Shall I serve, Ma'am?' Knapp said,

'No, that will be all for now. Thank you, Knapp.'

'Yes, Ma'am.' The housekeeper turned to Bunch and added, 'There is one of the farm girls down in the kitchen. She wants to speak with you. Said it was very urgent, Miss.'

'Now?' Bunch looked longingly at the steam curling from the teapot. Tell her I'll be right down.'

'Yes, Miss.'

'Sorry Granny, it's always a bit like this. Tomorrow I'll set up an office in the servants' hall, if that's more convenient?'

'Yes, dear. Perfectly convenient. Whilst I realise you have a job to do, I would be far happier if you will not carry it out in my morning room.'

'I'll pop down and get this sorted and be back in a jiffy. Keep the pot warm for me,' Bunch said and strode away to the kitchen, impatient to deal with whatever panic was brewing.

'Hello boss.' Kate was drinking tea at the kitchen table and made to get to her feet as Bunch entered.

'No, stay where you are.' Bunch indicated the cups. 'I'd love one of those, Knapp. I seem fated to miss the brew today.' She sat down opposite Kate. 'Now then, what is so urgent?'

'Haynes,' Kate replied.

'Still missing?'

'His mother told Mr Parsons that he's not coming back.'

Whatever Bunch had expected this was not it. 'She is absolutely sure about that?'

'Very. Apparently he cleared out her tin. According to Parsons she was very cross about it.'

'Cleared her tin? Is that such a crime?' Bunch leaned down to pet Roger as he lumbered across the kitchen from his temporary bed to greet her.

'It's a Sharp's Toffee tin,' Kate replied. 'She keeps the house-keeping money in it. She's more upset about that than her son doing a runner.'

'Well, that's all a bit unexpected.' A cup of tea was pushed toward her and she took a sip in a daze of deep thought. She did not want to jump to conclusions but Haynes running out at this precise moment looked very suspicious. She stroked the dog's head and wondered if Haynes *had* known what was waiting for her and Roger in that snowy coppice. He had seemed shocked enough, surprised, agitated. No, she was sure he had not led her into a trap but his complicity in the wider crime, if true, was a different matter. 'She has no idea where he went?'

'I think if she did she'd be there beating him over the head with her bakestone.'

'I can well imagine.' Bunch took a sip from the cup and a long look around the room. It was far smaller than the multiplicity of rooms that made up Perringham below stairs: less ancient and yet less modern than the main house, standing squarely in Victoriana with its open range and copper pans. It reminded Bunch of Hascombe Farm, though considerably cleaner. Similar, in fact, to most country house kitchens she had ever glimpsed, though she was not in the habit of venturing into such territory in the houses of her friends. The room felt comforting in its warmth and practicality. 'We should probably call the Constabulary,' she said. 'God, I am so sick of the police. Do you think this week will ever end, Kate?'

'It has been a bad one, Boss.'

She was being humoured, Bunch realised, and knew she was talking to the wrong person. In another place Kate would be close to her social standing but here she was staff, or at very least a subordinate. 'Call Botting,' she said. 'Tell him what you've told me.'

'Not going to ring your Chief Inspector?' Kate asked.

There was a twinkle in that question which made Bunch wonder what gossip was being passed around behind her back. 'I doubt Chief Inspector Wright has anything to do with missing persons,' she replied. 'At the moment all we know is that Haynes has left home. There is no reason for us to think anything has happened to him. Just call Botting and let the police judge whether his disappearance needs to be looked into. As Haynes is missing I shall leave you in charge of the stock management. You and Pat have been here the longest so you are the most knowledgeable in stock feeding. Now off you go. I am going to catch up with that ocean of paperwork the Min Ag keeps sending me.'

Bunch headed back to the morning room. Knapp would oversee the unpacking but the day's bombardment of forms required that she find the time and space without interruptions. Now that she had the estate to run she wondered how long she could keep up the Land Army work.

❧SIXTEEN❧

The estate's stables had been her refuge through her school years; their smells and sounds a salve for anything that had ever bothered her, and Bunch was bothered. She had slept badly and felt muzzy-headed as a result and would have gone out hacking to clear it, but it was not an ideal morning for riding out. The cold she did not mind but never saw the point of getting drenched in the name of pleasure. Added to which, Wright had not returned her telephone calls. She felt sure the new information she learned from the Jenners was important but she was not used to being kept waiting. The station sergeant had assured her Wright was on duty and he had been insistent, on her second call, that he *had left a message on the Chief Inspector's desk*. She refrained from making a third.

She went over the various points in her head as she brushed Perry's coat with twin brushes. Left brush – right brush. *Of course the information about Tinsley's history was not fresh.* Left – right. *Wright himself told me much the same thing.* Left – right. *The Jenner's little revelation about the van and the Frampton family fracas is a step along the way.* She had no idea how they fitted together but it was obvious to her it was something Wright needed to know. Bunch leaned against Perry's muscular hind quarter, staring into the middle distance, trying to picture the van that she might have possibly seen somewhere, at some time. She realised she should have spoken directly to the Jenners sooner.

Perhaps I should have left more details for Wright when I telephoned? She imagined that with so many special constables and part-timers in the police service, procedures might be circumvented and things delayed. She began to convince herself that the promised note had never been written by the sergeant, or that Wright had never read it.

Cold air blasted past her as the door opened and closed.

'Hello? Miss Courtney?' The deep burr of her estate manager Parsons drifted toward her.

Bunch paused her soothing rhythmic grooming and waited in silence. There was always a chance he might just go away.

'Miss Courtney!'

Sheba snorted loudly at the shout and kicked at the side of her box. Bunch knew she would have to speak very soon before the mare injured herself but she waited a few moments longer until she heard the doors gently latched shut. She released the breath she had not realised she was holding.

'Rain or no rain…' She snatched up the half rug and saddle with both arms and re-entered Perry's stall. 'We are going out for a hack, old chap. I am damned sure I need some peace and quiet.' She saddled up and once she was certain there was nobody lying in wait for her led Perry into the yard. The rain was little more than drizzle, really, and her long riding mac was more or less waterproof. If she kept off the hard-packed ice the ride should be easy enough.

With that in mind she slipped out of the stables, mounted up and steered the pony away from the metalled road, taking the cart track between the stables and kitchen gardens to the head of the coombe. Once away from the yard she slowed the brisk trot to a steady walk, keeping to the lee of the high hedges as much as possible and refusing to allow Perry his head, knowing the animal was less eager to be out than she and quite likely to turn tail and head home if he had a hint of opportunity.

She turned off the track and followed the line of a hedge that cut toward the far side of the five acre field, intending to come back through the woods where the trees would offer some shelter. It was not a route she took often, being a rather boring trudge along the headland with no real views, but it was one that allowed her to think without distraction.

Her grandmother's eye-opening revelations about Olivia had her wondering about Dodo's predicament. She had always known Olivia Tinsley to be a stickler for traditions and manners but had never suspected it an act to cover her perceived shortcomings. Looking back she realised how little she knew about the woman. Bunch was lost in thought over what she did and did not recall of Dodo's in-laws. When she came to the end of the hedge she rode straight through the gap where it linked up with another of the many cart-tracks, this one ending at the wood's edge.

The rounded khaki body of a military Austin 10 protruded from the melting mounds. From its position Bunch guessed it had been driven, or pushed, into a deep ditch, one that doubled as a small brook for most of the year but which frequently ran dry during prolonged summers. Today the ditch was beginning to fill with melt water deep enough to reach from beneath its deadening white coverlet.

Bunch slid from the saddle and looped the reins around a gatepost, not wanting to risk Perry slipping into the hidden bank, and waded cautiously through the drifts, testing every step until she reached the accessible side of the vehicle. She grabbed at the handle and twisted. After a brief resistance it gave way and she leaned back to haul it open. The smell that emanated from within did not bode well. She took a few breaths before bending to look inside.

The interior was dingy, but the outline of a slumped figure in the driving seat was unmistakable. The corpse was clothed in the bulky sheepskin of a flying jacket, which was to be expected from a pilot in midwinter. She wrenched the door open a little further and knelt on the passenger seat. The smell of old meat was more pronounced in the confined space. Due to the low temperatures it had not yet reached the rancid sweetness of decay, and for that she was truly glad.

She leaned close to peer at Lieutenant Seb Johansson. The young officer stared straight back with eerily opaque eyes wide open in a slack-jawed face. It seemed to Bunch that he was glaring in silent shock at her invasion of his privacy. Piercing the left side of his skull, between eye and ear, was a neat hole. The cracked window against which he leaned was a mess of dark oxidised blood. It looked as though he had been shot through the head with all the accuracy a gillie would employ in dispatching a stag. Cause of death was not going to be difficult to establish. The obvious mystery was by whom, when and why.

She swallowed hard, leaning back to compose herself, before wriggling out into the snow. Surely the similarities between Johansson's and Frampton's deaths could not be coincidental. 'Murdered,' she said aloud. *Executed might be closer to the truth.* She put both gloved hands to her mouth, peering over her fingers at the vehicle. *What in hell were Seb and Mary doing up here?*

She knew courting couples came here in the summer months. 'But not during the coldest nights of the year,' Bunch murmured. 'There are a dozen places that would be private enough if they wanted to indulge in a little rumpy-pumpy.' She looked around. *This doesn't lead anywhere except the woods and maybe the sheep pens.* 'Sheep!' She raised her eyebrows and tilted her head to the left. *Coincidence?* 'Oh, dear Lord, of course. How could I be so utterly stupid?' The vehicle's partially submerged bulk and its grotesque contents became all the more sinister, which she had not thought possible.

I've been to the pictures and in a Jimmy Cagney film victims are driven into rivers or else burned out in some isolated spot whilst the culprit gains a head start on a long and journey over the Atlantic to Brazil. They aren't usually driven into a ditch and left there. His dying so violently and maybe at the same time as Mary, whom everyone had been assuming was his victim, was difficult to take in. *All roads,* she thought, *lead to an ovine Rome, with sheep at every turn.*

The surrounding fields were quiet on this side of the estate. A stiff breeze now swept pale sheets of sleet and drizzle along the valley obscuring much of the coombe's encompassing slopes. 'It's secluded, just like all the spots where this business has been going on. So what on *earth* brought him here?' She thought back to her one and only conversation with the quiet officer. *Were you and Mary playing detectives? Trying to solve it for yourselves? You silly creatures.* She felt herself colour. What was it Kate claimed Mary had told her? *He was always taking notes. Kept them on him like a police notebook.*

Bunch leant back into the vehicle and stared again at the body. After a moment's hesitation she reached forward to pat his pockets, pulling the sheepskin jacket open to feel the breast and sides of his uniform jacket. The pockets were empty. She took a deep breath and steeled herself to feel his trouser pockets. Not a sign of any notebook. She looked at the foot wells and the map shelves. There were no personal effects, which is what she would normally expect from her time driving motor-pool staff cars.

Nothing whatsoever to link the car to the corpse or a passenger. And nothing at all on him. She frowned at the oddness of that last fact. What sort of chap took a girl to the pub with empty pockets? Not a wallet, nor ID papers. Not even a handkerchief. Whoever had shot him, and presumably also Mary, had picked the scene clean. She thought back to the night Mary had staggered back to the cottage and realised the girl had not been carrying a handbag when she was discovered laying in the snow. The notion of a fashionable girl on a night out without so much as a clutch-bag for her lipstick and comb was unthinkable. Bunch climbed out once again. She hesitated to leave the body unattended but it could be hour – days even – before anyone came within hailing distance of her, and she saw no useful purpose in waiting and catching pneumonia.

Time to call the police and find out if those notebooks ever existed.

~ ~ ~

Mary had shared quarters with Elsie and the briefest glance at their room told Bunch, despite Mary's pretentions toward fashion, neither girl was overburdened with possessions. The notebook Annie had talked of was not to be found. Neither did Mary appear to have shared Johansson's obsession with sleuthing. Her side of the dressing table and her bedside cabinet held a scatter of cosmetics and magazines but nothing to be easily connected with an investigation – except for a hand-drawn map. The writing was small and spidery, nothing like Mary's rounded and rather naïve hand. *Something given to her by the lieutenant?* Bunch folded it up and slipped it into her pocket.

Back at the Dower she opened out the map on a table in the drawing room: a rough map of the estate and village with all of the 'incidents' marked in coloured inks. In the margin were the words *Beckenham and Sons* which was followed by a heavy question mark. The query against the name brought a satisfied smile. She smoothed the paper and examined it closely. Two crosses in the village were heavily scribed. One marked the church and the other a rather vague circle drawn over High Street encompassing most of the shops and a large proportion of the older houses. She turned the paper over to check for any other notes.

She was still pondering on what she had found when a half hour later the maid showed Chief Inspector Wright into the room. Bunch glanced up expectantly and was puzzled when Wright shook his head.

'We were too late,' he said. 'Kravitz's men had collected their car. No sign of the body, either.'

'How did he know about it?'

Wright spread his hands wide. 'I had no choice but to notify him the moment you called.'

'He can just waltz in and steal evidence?'

'MOD says nothing had happened,' Wright replied, 'and as none of my men saw your corpse or the vehicle there is little I can do at the moment. The military even went to the trouble of obliterating the tracks.'

'Where does that leave us?'

'We only have a missing person's report and your word that there was ever a corpse.'

'I should have stayed there,' said Bunch, 'but I was on my own. What else could I do?'

'Nothing at all,' he replied. 'If the military were intent on taking Johansson back to the house I am not sure even I would have had a great deal of sway.'

'It seems so wrong. Can Kravitz really get away with it?'

'He has for now. I've pushed it up the chain for the brass to argue over. It's all I can do under the circumstances.'

Wright ran a hand across his hair, looking down at the rug. It looked to Bunch as if fatigue swamped every inch of him; she wondered if he had slept at all since she had last seen him. She crossed to the bell pull and rang for tea. He was examining the map, leaning his hands on the table on each side of it, as she turned back toward him.

'Did Mary and her lieutenant discover anything useful?'

'Doesn't look like it,' he replied. 'I suppose there could be something in the village to account for these circles but...' he stood up straight to ease the kinks from his back '...on its own it's not a great deal of help. Meanwhile you can shed some light on the lieutenant's death, perhaps.'

'Of course. Do sit down. Ah, tea as well, excellent timing.' Bunch nodded to the maid. 'Thank you, that will be all.'

Bunch poured tea and related all she knew. 'If it is any consolation, you would not have got a great deal. The entire scene was picked clean,' she said at last. 'Whoever shot Johansson wanted to make certain not just that his investigations ended but whatever he knew was not going to be passed on.'

'Proving that amateur sleuthing can be a very dangerous business,' he replied.

'Is that a criticism or a warning? If I recall, you would not investigate Jonathan's death. You gave my enquiry your blessing.'

'Which I am now withdrawing. We need to be very careful, Miss Courtney. You especially need to be careful. Three bodies in a week and you have made no secret of your enquiries.'

'I shall be very careful, believe me.' She poured more tea and waved at the small plate of cakes. 'Sorry we have so little to offer. Sugar rationing has bitten hard and fast out here in the country.'

'It would be rather foolish to offer a policeman more,' he replied and then grinned at her shock. 'I appreciate people out in the more rural spots might in fact fare better. Though tea will be harder to grow around here than churning out a few illicit pats of butter. Now, these Jenners. They seem to know a great deal more than a casual bystander should. I can't imagine why they haven't been interviewed more thoroughly.'

'They don't trust the police so they would be very sure not to be at home if Botting called. He's arrested them before for poaching and his father was arresting them and their father before that. The Jenners may not always be entirely without sin, but I can assure you they would not be a part of anything like this.'

'I think I have the general picture. Would it be any use me going to visit them?'

'Probably not. I think they were being truthful enough with me. We've always got on well enough and the family has some pull with them. I used to see them a lot while out riding when I was young – younger. Interesting that the Framptons were both out in the wood that night and having one of their family battles.'

'They argued a lot?'

'I gather their being together and not having words would have been more notable.'

'You think it possible Frampton killed his own son?'

Bunch sipped slowly at her tea, contemplating the decor as she considered the question. 'No. On the whole I think the rows were quite superficial. Jonny's death meant the estate going to a cousin and Saul would be out on his ear, so I'd say quite the opposite. Saul Frampton may not have liked his son but he had every reason to keep him alive. Jenner seemed adamant that when Len Pole took Saul home Jonny was still very much alive.'

'People don't always do what seems logical on the outside,' Wright murmured. 'Passions run high. Threats go that bit further than intended. It happens between people who actually like each other. If you throw resentment and active dislike into the fray—' He pulled a wry smile 'Bang! In this case quite literally.' He flushed a little around the neck. 'Sorry, that was insensitive. I only meant that people generally don't do the things we expect when under duress.'

'I suppose they don't.'

'In your friend's case it seemed logical that he had taken his own life with that weapon. That gun was not the sort of item to be taken out into a wood at the dead of night for no sensible reason. It was a show weapon for society shoots and looking good in the gun rack. For making a statement.'

She glared and wondered if he was being deliberately provocative. She picked up a biscuit from the plate the maid had brought in with the tea and looked at it curiously. Not because there was anything amiss with it but because it was slowly dawning on her what had been niggling at the back of her mind these past few days. 'Jonny wasn't like that,' she said, 'but he did love his Westley.'

'That he took a bespoke weapon out into the woods is one of the facts that convinced our Chief of a suicide. It is a very handsome weapon for very special occasions. Your own reasoning backs that theory up. When a man like Jonathan Frampton wants to take his own life he does it with some kind of style.'

'A wonderful theory, I have no doubt. Except for two things: he did not take his own life and the gun we found him with may have been the Westley Richards but what about the cartridge casing I found up there, from a .22 gun?' She drew the case from her pocket and set it end up on the map.

Wright peered at her curiously.

'I tried to tell them that same day but Barty was adamant. The weapon Jonny had in the clearing, the one that was lying at his feet when we found him, was a shotgun. Which does not take .22 bullets, as you perfectly well know.' She pointed at the cartridge.

'That tells me he didn't shoot himself.'

'The weapon Botting and Tinsley brought down was the Westley and it had been fired.' Wright's voice took on an official tone that told Bunch how much he did not entirely believe her. 'Botting made a special note of the weapon he recovered from the scene. Tinsley, himself a magistrate, wrapped it and carried it down to the farm.'

'I don't doubt that. Yet someone fired another weapon up there after the snow started. I can assure you that whatever was beside Jonathan Frampton in that clearing, and regardless of the fact that there was shot also peppering that tree, it was not the Westley that killed him.'

'There seems no logic to that act,' he agreed. 'Until we get that Coroner's report we have to make the assumption that he lost his life to the Westley. Why should someone go to the trouble of setting up fake suicide scene if he died hours before you ever came across him?'

'Every new fact brings up a whole raft of new mysteries,' said Bunch. 'Is your job always like this? It must be terribly, terribly frustrating.'

'It can be,' he replied. 'I'm used to it. You and your family must be getting very distressed by it all. You especially. Three bodies in a week, remember?'

'It does seem to be a bit of a habit,' she said. 'But be fair I only found one of them on my own.' She pulled a face. 'The fates appear to think that throwing bodies at me is a good idea. I rather wish they wouldn't.'

'Hopefully there will not be any more. Though the fortunes of war cannot be predicted.'

Bunch nodded. 'More tea?'

'Please.'

'You heard about Haynes, I suppose?'

'Missing I hear, according to Annie.' He checked the note-book resting by his hand.

'Missing quite intentionally, according to his parents.'

'Do you think we should draw conclusions? Is Haynes the kind to kill?'

It was a tough question and one Bunch felt she could not confidently answer. Haynes had changed since he had returned home from the war, but she could hardly blame him for that. He would never walk easily again and it was quite obvious his mind was bruised from the horrors he had witnessed. Looking back, he had been reluctant to accompany her to the wood in search of missing stock, which she had put down to the pain walking that far would cause. He had been genuinely shocked at the shooting of the dog. 'No,' she said, 'although I think he knows some of the whys and wherefores. He may even know who is behind it all. I suspect he had a good idea who the two chaps were that ran away from the slaughter site. Killing a few sheep is something he might see as an acceptable action. I don't think he would murder in cold blood.'

'The kind of experience Haynes went through can change a man, right up to and including the ability to kill. We have put out a search for him though if he has gone to London we have very little chance of finding him. It's chaos up there. So many missing and displaced persons and they are harder pressed for serving officers than we are.' He flipped the notebook shut and slipped it into his pocket. 'I think we've covered all we can and I need to get back to the station.'

❧SEVENTEEN❧

'Come and get me.' Dodo's whisper hissed her urgency through the telephone. 'I can't stay here another night. Please.'

'Are you sure?' Bunch said. 'After all, you agreed to go there with Barty.'

'I would rather not, believe me.'

Bunch stared out of the window listening to a silence punctuated by the sound of stifled breathing crackling from the telephone handset.

'It's so ghastly,' Dodo went on.

'Well of course, darling girl. Nobody expects to be widowed three months after the wedding.'

'Bunch! But not that way. It's about being *here*, about Banyards. George and I talked about it before he— Perhaps I should say George talked and I listened, though at the time I didn't want to think about the possibilities. That's the thing about war, you see. It's why we got married. You never know what's coming. We were right as it turned out.' Dodo sniffled loudly.

'I know.' Bunch's heart reached out to her. She wanted to soothe her sister as she would a twitchy pony. She could understand Dodo's reluctance to stay at Banyard Manor, could only imagine how challenging it was to be daughter-in-law to a woman like Olivia Tinsley. 'Give me half an hour and I'll be with you.'

'Sooner rather than later. Olivia will be back soon.'

'I shall be as quick as I can. We're more than a match for Olivia when we combine forces.'

'You are a match.' Dodo allowed herself a nervous giggle. 'She scares the death out of me.'

'Is that so?' Bunch wondered again what it was that she had not been told. Something had been gnawing at her sister ever since George's funeral. Bunch had put it down to grief but she was less sure now. She didn't doubt Olivia Tinsley could make life difficult for any woman who dared to marry her only son, and she was certain grief would not make that the least bit easier, especially when Dodo could be so very nervous by nature. She could almost hear her sister trembling at the very thought of remaining with her in-laws. 'You pack a bag,' she said, 'just a few personal things.' She started to laugh. 'I could go and fetch Granny. She would sort them out.'

Dodo sniggered despite herself. 'As a guard dog, you mean?'

'Exactly. Not even your ma-in-law would be able to resist. Don't fret, my sweetness. Hang the petrol coupons, I'll drive over there very shortly.'

~ ~ ~

Banyard Manor was a comfortable Jacobean manor house built of red Wealden brick. Its long façade was punctuated regularly with diamond-paned windows; it had sharply angled gables, and a plethora of tall chimneys reaching above the Sussex stone roof.

Bunch had barely halted the shooting brake at the front of the manor before the studded-oak doors opened and Mason, the Tinsleys' elderly butler, lurched across the slushy space.

'Good afternoon, Miss Courtney,' he droned, bowing as he yanked open the car door.

'Thank you, Mason.' Bunch stepped delicately onto the freshly cleared flagstones in front of the steps and shivered at the wind blowing up from the coast. 'Who's at home today?'

'The Major is presiding on the Bench. Both the Mrs Tinsleys are at home, however.'

Bunch wondered if that made this a wasted journey. Dodo had seemed quite insistent that she should leave before Olivia returned from the village. 'I am here to speak to my sister.' She drew her own collar up against the south-westerly breeze. 'Good grief, this place is always so cold,' she said. 'Barty should never have cleared the spinney.'

'Indeed, Miss.' Mason stepped purposefully up to the front door and reopened it, standing to one side to allow Bunch to enter, and then closing the double leaves smartly to cut out the draught. 'You will find the mistress in the morning room,' he said. 'I believe the younger Mrs Tinsley is in her rooms. Shall I serve tea?'

'Bunch, hello.' Dodo appeared in the lobby like a rabbit from its burrow.

'Morning, Dodo.' Bunch lowered her voice, glancing at Mason and gauging how much the man should hear. 'I say, are you sure about this? Sure either way, I mean,' she said as Dodo hustled her toward the stairs. 'Certain you want to move out and if so, are you sure you want to do it today?'

'Yes and yes. I have some stuff I want to take; I'll need your help to carry it all.'

'Like what? Not furniture and things?'

'Oh, don't be flippant, Bunch, you do make me so cross sometimes.' Dodo glanced at the drawing room door. 'Stuff, things I need to take,' she whispered. 'Come with me.'

'You surely don't believe people are trying to steal from you?'

Dodo frowned. 'I doubt they would see it that way,' she said. 'There are things that were Georgie's but Olivia thinks are hers.'

'Family jewels, you mean?'

'Photos, documents. Those sorts of things.' Dodo didn't wait for a reply and bolted straight up the staircase.

Bunch followed at a more leisurely pace. 'Not going to say cheerio to dear Olivia?' she murmured.

'Not unless I have to,' Dodo replied. 'She has a ... a bad *habit*. Did you know?'

'What do you... Oh, you mean drugs?'

'Yes, yes I do.'

'Oh, Dodo, you hinted at something of the sort before. Are you certain? That must be terrible for you to cope with. Why did you never tell me about it?'

'How could I? George kept it quiet, obviously. After he was gone, well, it never seemed that important in the scheme of things.' She motioned Bunch's hand away. 'No don't, I shall just start blarting.'

'How simply awful. Is that why Barty was so eager to get you home?'

Dodo shrugged. 'Partly.'

'It explains much. I know Olivia mixed with the fast crowd in the old days but I didn't know she was on that muck. I am so sorry, I hadn't realised things had become so difficult here. You really should have said something.'

'It wasn't too bad until George – you know.' Dodo opened the door to her bedroom and closed it quietly behind them. 'She has been getting worse and so unpredictable. I hardly dare to open my mouth. She threw a tureen at Mason at dinner last night. Upended it all over the dining table.'

'Hence the hurry to leave?' Bunch said. 'Has she ever been violent toward you?'

Dodo looked awkward. 'No, not as such. Aggressive. I put it down to her drug-taking for the longest while, but she is starting to give me the heebie-jeebies. It never occurred to me until you mentioned George leaving me Banyard Manor as an inheritance.'

'Then why did you return here at all?'

'Granny said I should collect some items before Olivia got her hands on them.'

'You should have that maid – Willis, is it? – you should have her pack for you and send it on.'

'I shall for the bulk, but Granny said to get the important things, in case... In case.' She crossed to the dressing room and unlocked a door tucked away at the side of the wardrobe. 'There's tons of George's papers and stuff here. I keep meaning to sort through it. Olivia even offered to store it all in the attics but that seems rather beastly, like tucking his memory away, out of sight.'

A voice was raised from somewhere along the corridor and Dodo lifted a hand to her mouth. When nobody knocked she relaxed by a fraction.

'Are you all right? Really?' Bunch asked.

Dodo pulled Bunch into a small, windowless dressing room. Along one wall was a row of cupboard doors. She raised her keys to a lock but her fingers trembled around the brass catch and fell away. 'I haven't opened these since the funeral,' she whispered. 'I wasn't ready to deal with George's things.'

'Let me.' Bunch stepped around her, unlocking and flinging the first set of doors open revealing serried rows of boxes and files, all neatly organised by colour. It was plainly George's storage because Bunch knew her sister could never be so organised. 'Now then, what are we looking for?'

Dodo knelt to haul out a large cabin trunk from the darkest recesses. Flipping open the lid, she burrowed amongst tissue-wrapped shirts, dragging armfuls of paper and fine cloth out onto the floor until she reached the bottom of the trunk. She felt along one edge for a cloth tab, which she tweaked upwards, lifting a false base to reveal a jumble of trinkets and gee-gaws. She dug deeper still and yanked out a binder full of papers. 'Here it is. Thank goodness nobody decided to start sorting without me. I was worried they might have begun before I got back.' She waved the folder over her head. 'I was afraid the vultures would sniff these out.'

'What are they?'

'George's private papers. Mine now, I suppose. Some stocks. Details of safety deposits where the bulk of his personal money was kept – Georgie never trusted his mother, you know – and most importantly, a copy of both his and his grandfather's will. He had them sent down from the bank during his last week's pass. Just a few days before—' Dodo uttered a sharp sound, somewhere between curse and cry, and reached up to pick a leather satchel from a lower shelf. She rammed the bundle of papers into it with all the finesse of a child digging in a Christmas bran tub.

'Why would he do that?' Bunch asked her.

Dodo shrugged. 'His squadron had lost so many pilots. Half the people he trained with were gone.' She selected a few other items from the base of the trunk, stuffing them into the satchel before fumbling the buckles closed with shaking fingers. 'I can't imagine what it must have been like for him.'

'Struck by his own mortality?'

'Something of the sort.' Dodo froze, looking at the door, before looping the bag's strap over her shoulder.

'Why are you so nervous?' Bunch demanded. 'These were George's and you were his wife and this is your room, so everything here is yours now.'

'It didn't matter while George was alive and then it all changed, and I was the only one who didn't realise how much. I am so stupid! They would be furious if they knew these documents had been here all this time.' She began cramming the clothes back into the trunk and slammed it shut.

Bunch relocked the door and returned the keys to Dodo's pocket. 'We should go down and see the gorgon,' she said. 'For form's sake.'

'I would rather not.'

'We shall keep it brief,' said Bunch, 'tell her I have estate business to get back for.'

Dodo clutched the satchel to her side and gazed at her sister in near reverence. 'You are a brick, Bunch. I can't tell you how this has been playing on my mind.'

'You are a blockhead,' Bunch replied. 'You know you could have told me.'

'I was going to, the day we found Jonathan. Afterwards, it seemed not to be quite so important.'

'What changed your mind this time?'

'Something Barty mentioned when he came to the Dower. He said Olivia had unearthed some papers that I needed to sign for the estate, but the solicitors had already been through the paperwork with me in the week after the funeral. He said Olivia found papers that had been misplaced, but I am absolutely certain she's lying. She hasn't shown me any of them as yet. Barty is clueless, as always. As far as I can tell, the only important papers none of them have seen are in this bag. Nevertheless, I am convinced somebody has been searching my rooms whenever I'm away. Not overtly, but things have obviously been moved around.'

'That could be staff just clearing up.'

'No. George always kept this dressing room locked and he made me promise to do the same. We didn't think anyone else had a key but it seems we were mistaken. It's a miracle no one found these.'

'Dodo darling, you really should have told me.'

'You could not have done anything so there was no point. I didn't want your Chief Inspector involved. Just in case…'

Bunch gaped at her. 'What on earth has Wright to do with it? And, in case of what?'

'Just in case.' Dodo shrugged. 'It made sense to me at the time. Come on, the quicker I am out of here the better I shall be pleased.'

~~~

Olivia Tinsley was as tall and lean as her husband was stocky. Her body, as she rose to greet them, was sculpted by a regime of abstinence rather than exercise, and her black day dress only served to enhance the effect. She had been a beauty in her day and was still a striking woman. Her naturally blonde hair, lightened by age, was pinned intricately off an elegant neck. When she smiled it accentuated sharp lines around her darkly shadowed eyes. Her scooped neckline exposed the deep hollows of her clavicles.

Bunch looked at her with a fresh eye. The woman seemed both ill and ill at ease, though skilful make-up disguised the former and her affected air the latter.

Olivia seemed amused at Bunch's blatant stare. 'Rose, how lovely to see you. I rather thought you might have to come to visit before now. I know you have been rather busy, of course, what with your parents away, and so hard to get petrol now.'

'I don't have much time for social calls, Olivia,' Bunch replied, 'except to see Dodo when she needs me.'

'That's good of you but a little rest was just what she needed. Gird her loins for going through George's things,' Olivia said. 'I was quite willing to help all I could, and we do have good staff, although I can understand she'd want her sister to assist her. I only thought you would come and say hello first. Catch up on all the news. Poor Jonathan. My goodness, that family has had some bad luck. Now Willis tells me there are two more bodies on Perringham land. Policemen everywhere.' She shook her head. 'You do realise people will start to avoid you. Nothing the county hates more than that kind of attention. I will do what I can to keep it to a minimum, although you've both been avoiding society these past weeks.' She spread her hands and smiled with little humour. 'What can I say?'

'The murders are hardly your concern,' Bunch replied, 'and isn't staying away from parties exactly how you'd expected a grieving widow to behave?'

Olivia looked Bunch up and down and sighed. 'We are all grieving, Rose. Daphne lost her husband, I lost my son. It is impossible for you to imagine what that is like. You have no children nor ever will, one supposes.' Olivia looked down at the carpet as if to compose herself. When she looked up once more she had regained her icy calm; only a suspicion of water in her eyes hinted at her pain as she added, 'If I was sharp with Daphne it was for her own good.' She smiled, showing even white teeth through the thin, red gash of lipstick. 'Your sister is unexpectedly fragile. We thought all of you Courtney women were Amazons.'

'All? There are only four of us,' Bunch growled.

'So there are.' Olivia held out her hand for the satchel. 'What have you got there Daphne, dear? I remember George buying that bag when he went up to Oxford. Can I see it?'

'It's private and nothing to do with you.'

'If it's George's then it is all our business,' Olivia replied. 'So many things to sort out.' She sighed. 'It has been so hard on us all.'

'We've all had a demanding few months,' said Bunch. 'Which is why Dodo has decided to stay with Granny for a while. She wants to come home to her family. Would you have her things packed and ferried over, please?'

'She lives here. Dammit all, she's a Tinsley.'

'Dodo will always be a Courtney.' Bunch smiled sweetly. 'And Granny needs her for war work, which rather trumps your social whirl.'

'Beatrice has you.'

'You'd think so but no, I am up to my ears in WLA work. Granny is very keen to make the Dower the WVS headquarters.' She signalled to Dodo and made as if to stand. 'Speaking of which, I need to get back, so if you can get some of Dodo's stuff sent over that would be splendid.'

Olivia worked her face into a smile. 'You can stay for tea, surely? I had Cook to prepare something special when Dodo said you were coming over. I told Mason to serve tea the moment you came down. Ah, right on cue. Leave the tray, Mason, I shall pour. Milk for both of you? Sugar?'

'No sugar,' Bunch said. 'Doing our bit by going without.'

'How terribly patriotic. I'm afraid I'm already finding this rationing nonsense rather tedious. It's so hard to come by the essentials, according to Cook.'

Bunch suppressed a snort. She assumed that Olivia Tinsley had not consumed anything in any quantity since 1916. *One doesn't get a figure like that by indulging in cake.* 'Of course,' she murmured, 'we all have to tighten up.'

'It's such a shame not to have the odd treat now and then. I know Daphne simply adores cake.' Olivia lifted the cover from the dessert stand to reveal a sponge covered in a thick layer of butter cream, and a second slathering between the layers. She cut two generous slices. 'Cook does wonders.'

Dodo took up a fork and dug in. Bunch was more cautious. She had tasted some fairly awful mock creams and frostings over the past month, experiments in new austerity cuisine. The first taste told her this was the real thing, made of butter and sugar. She knew their households were more privileged than many, and money could and did ensure a better supply than most, but sugar was scarce and this cake alone had to contain the month's ration for the entire household. 'How are you all coping here?' Bunch asked with faux shine. 'Granny is organising a Knitting for Victory campaign. It's very laudable but we can't move for hanks of yarn. I hope she can count on your support?'

'Your grandmother has always been such an organiser,' Olivia replied. 'Perhaps it's fortunate you moved in with her, Rose. You are quite alike in so many ways.'

'Perhaps we are. Granny is not a well woman, though she'll have you believe otherwise, and with Daddy away I have so much to do. The Land Girls are fine enough but I could really use an extra pair of hands, one that know how the estate works.'

Olivia set her cup down sharply enough to send her spoon tumbling to the floor. 'This is where Daphne belongs. People will *expect* it. *I* expect it.' She pursed her lips, bringing her emotions to heel once more. 'This is so unjust. I lose my son and I feel I am being punished for it. Would it hurt you so very much to stay, Daphne?'

'Dodo would only have been able to remain for a little while, anyway,' Bunch said. 'I have it on good authority that the Ministry of Labour will require all women over eighteen to register for work in the next few months, and conscription for all young women will be in place before the year is out. If she doesn't want to join up then I think WVS and WI duties, at least, place her on reserve within the county for a little while longer. If she gets conscripted for the WAFs or WACs she could be sent anywhere.'

'Conscripting women? Is that proper?'

Bunch chuckled. 'Proper? Most of the girls Dodo came out with have already volunteered. We all had to change our ideas about what is proper, Olivia. I suspect polite niceties will change beyond our wildest imaginings by the end of all this.' She prodded at the half eaten cake and shook her head. 'We shall adapt. Look at sugar. I thought I liked sweet things but this confection has defeated me.' She pushed her plate away. 'Time we departed. You will have to excuse a rapid exit but I do have a mountain of reports to write this afternoon. Come along, Dodo. Chop, chop.'

'Stay where you are Daphne. Wait until Barty gets home. You can't run away from life, you know.' Olivia stood rapidly and placed herself between Dodo and the door. 'This is wrong. I forbid it.'

'Forbid?' said Bunch. 'You can't forbid a grown woman from doing what she pleases. Dodo is over twenty-one.'

'Barely,' Olivia said. 'She was far too interested in parties and gallivanting around the county to be responsible for herself.'

'Two trips up to Town before Christmas is hardly gallivanting,' said Dodo. 'There are some things you simply can't get elsewhere. I am leaving now so don't try to stop me.' She grabbed her satchel tightly and swept out of the room as fast as was possible without breaking into a run.

~ ~ ~

Safe within the shooting brake Dodo allowed the tears to fall. 'She is such a horrible, horrible, woman,' she sobbed. 'I never realised how awful until I moved back into Banyards.'

'There's nothing like living under the same roof for knowing what people are really like.' Bunch took her gaze from the road for a moment. 'You look a bit green.'

'It was that cake,' Dodo said.

'Butter icing will do that. Not seen that much on one cake for quite a while. She doesn't exactly stint herself, does she?'

'Olivia would never do without.' Dodo rummaged in her pocket for a handkerchief and dabbed at her eyes before pressing it against her nose and taking several breaths of lavender cologne. 'She claims she barters for her luxuries. Heaven knows with what. Cook is forever complaining about ration cards and short deliveries.'

'Not to mention with whom,' said Bunch. 'I can't think of anyone who would have that much sugar. Except the spivs, obviously.' She glanced at Dodo again and frowned. 'Do you want me to stop?'

'I'll be all right if you don't take the corners too quickly.'

'Sing out if you feel upsy. Daddy will never forgive us if you vomit all over the upholstery.'

Bunch eased her foot off the accelerator even though she was already driving at a crawl due to the ice. *Any slower would be walking pace,* she thought.

They were half way along the High Street when she saw a figure she thought she recognised: a tall man, broad shouldered beneath his winter coat, waiting to cross the road as she passed. He stood out not just because of his height and build. He stood out because he was a young fit man not in uniform. Bunch tried hard not to judge in such circumstances without knowing the facts; she knew there were a hundred reasons why a man might be in civvies. Quite logically he might be on leave or in a reserved occupation. Whatever the situation, the fact remained: he had attracted her attention. Which, from her point of view, was fortunate: he turned to stare at a short queue of people waiting outside the butcher's, giving her a perfect view of his features – and she *knew* that face.

The frozen moment when she had stared at him across the woodland clearing was not unlike the view one had of people from the confines of a slow-moving car. She was in no doubt this was one of the men who ran away from her the day Roger had been shot. The day that she had come so close to being shot herself.

'Quick pit stop.' Bunch swung off the road outside the Post Office, pulling on the hand brake and peering in the rear-view mirror for any sign of the man, scanning the street with rising impatience.

'What's going on?' Dodo asked.

'I have to check something. Shan't be long.' Bunch scrambled out and took a few steps back down the High Street. The cold weather ensured there were not sufficient people walking the pavements for the tall man to be easily obscured. *Though,* she thought, *a man who has to be well over six foot is not going to hide easily in any crowd.* Past the line of women at the butcher's, close to the pub, a couple of airmen huddled, deep in their blue overcoats, waiting for opening time. Beyond that, no one. *He's vanished. He's ducked into a shop, perhaps, or down one of the alleys between them.* 'Dammit,' she grunted. 'Damn and blast!'

'What's wrong?' Dodo called from the car.

'Nothing. I thought I saw— Oh, damn it.' Bunch glanced back at Dodo and smiled. 'Sit tight whilst I get you some stomach powders. All right?' She crossed the street and walked rapidly toward the pharmacy near where she had last seen her suspect; she slowed and peered down an alley in the hopes of another glimpse. There was no one to be seen. Mistaken identity was always a possibility but her gut told her not. Being shot at had sharpened her recall and she was now positive she could recognise all three men.

The alley led to the backs of the shops and offered a short cut to Church Row which, as the name implied, branched off from the bottom of the High Street toward the parish church, and beyond that a row of tiny terraced houses. The shoppers waiting to collect their meat ration were watching her so she dared not linger in anticipation he would reappear, nor could she justify walking down the alley to investigate further after they had all seen her get out of a perfectly good car, and patently not in need of a short cut to anywhere.

She nodded and issued a general 'good morning' and was answered with varying degrees of enthusiasm. She noted, with some asperity, asides were being whispered behind hands, with knowing nods and glances. Olivia's comment about reputation came back to her. Bunch doubted it was the village folk Olivia had in mind but it made her somewhat uneasy to think herself the butt of common gossip from either county or village sets. She had done plenty of things in her younger years to have earned a reputation for wildness, and so it now seemed perverse to attract further attention for something out of her control. Bunch took one last glance along the alley before she plunged into the pharmacy.

'Miss Courtney, what a pleasure.' Mr Brice waddled out from his dispensary to greet her, his dimpled hand thrust forward to extravagantly shake Bunch's. 'How's your mother? And father? Goin' to foreign parts, so I 'eard. There's nice.' The dumpy Welshman beamed at her, twitching his ample greying moustache like an enthusiastic walrus.

'Yes,' she replied. 'They left a few days ago.'

'I hope they have a good trip. Lot of storms this time of year, though.'

'Indeed.' She smiled blandly whilst scouring her mind for some way of asking about the tall man.

'What can I get for you today, Miss?'

Bunch looked at the shelves behind him for inspiration. 'I'm not sure. Dodo's been a bit under the weather. Gippy tummy. Nothing serious, I don't think. Something she ate, I'm certain. It has been such a stressful few months for her.'

Brice adopted a suitably mournful look. 'I 'eard about that young Mr Tinsley. Sad, that is. So many young men. After the last war you'd think people would have had enough. And it's so close to home. Duw, Duw. Mrs Brice and I were only sayin' this week, first her 'usband and then young Mr Frampton. Those lads were always close, right from babbies. Now that poor child – Mary was it? And right there on your own estate.' He shook his head, maintaining his doleful expression.

Bunch was used to the pharmacist gabbling on – he was renowned for it – and she waited patiently for him to finish. A pair of young women chattered as they walked past the window and ducked into the entrance to the passageway; she glanced at them by instinct. There was her opening. 'It seems that lots of people use that shortcut,' she said. 'Doesn't it bother you?'

'No, you get used to it. It's like trains, see. You don't 'ear them after a bit. Even in this weather we get people up and down at all hours. Can't blame them. It cuts that much of the walk up the terraces.'

'I can imagine.' She picked up a packet of cotton wool from the counter and examined it. 'I saw a young chap going down there just before I came in. Tall chap.' She indicated a height just above her head. 'Skinny lad. Farm worker, maybe?'

'Oh, that would be Arnold Crisp,' Mr Brice said. 'He's a nice enough lad, I suppose. His mother had German measles when she was expectin' and he came out a bit twp.'

'Is that why he isn't in uniform?'

'Doesn't 'elp, I imagine, but no. I think it was his bad ears that kept him out.'

'He's the deaf chap our cook was talking about? She said he called at the kitchen a few weeks ago looking for work.'

'Yes, that would be Arnold, I expect. Strictly speakin', he's more 'ard of 'earing than deaf. He does well enough if you've got the patience, but people don't take to him because he can come over a bit surly.' He pursed his lips and glanced around. 'He's got into a bit of bother a few times down the pub. Nothin' serious. People take the rise out of him an' he gets mad. He can't 'elp being the way he is, can he?'

'No, no, of course not.' She had never regarded herself as a nurturing, motherly sort of person, but the idea of people objecting to such a boy because of those problems had other connotations, and she shuffled uncomfortably. The notion made Bunch feel a little guilty. 'I wondered why Cook sent him away? We could have done with some extra help. Where does he work now?'

'Nowhere much. He used to do odd jobs for the vicar round the church and some labouring up at Banyards. His mam was a maid up there. Started when she was a little thing and worked there right up till she died. Ooh...' He looked up as though searching for thoughts above his head. 'It must be almost six month ago now. Influenza. Poor woman. His da was taken way back. I heard Arnold was living with his mother's family down near Storrington.'

'I wonder what brings him back? Does he have relatives here-abouts?' She smiled, hoping to encourage further details. 'Or perhaps he found some work.'

'I doubt that. He has no references, see. He started an apprenticeship at Beckenham's last year.' Brice leaned forward and dropped his voice several notches. 'But I 'eard he was sacked for thievin'. That was only a rumour, mind. More likely, didn't catch on to the job fast enough. Not enough work for the shop lads to do these days, and there'll be less still with all the rationing. Old Beckenham expects a lot for his money. But folks talk and people wouldn't give him any work. That's why he moved to his nan's, I expect.'

'Seems a shame,' Bunch murmured. She struggled to keep her face calm. The information fitted too precisely for coincidence. This Arnold Crisp was the man, or rather the boy, who had stood in gory shirt sleeves butchering her stock. She was minded to rush out of the shop and catch up with him, but knew with legs that length he would be long gone by now. 'Poor lad can't help being the way he is,' she agreed.

'War's hard on us all, and harder still for people like him. You know his old dad was killed in a riding accident?'

'I think I remember that.'

'The family's never had any luck. I remember Mrs Brice sayin' Arnold's nan Hurst had three sons out of four taken on the Somme. And he falls off a horse just 'arf a mile from 'ome. There's bad luck for you. Which reminds me—'

'Yes, how awful.' Bunch interrupted and smiled sweetly, knowing she should pursue the issue of Arnold but not sure she could take one of Mr Brice's long wanders down his Great War's memory lane. Once started he could witter on for hours. 'Why would he be here?'

'To see his auntie, Jean Crisp. Her that runs the stores. She told me 'ow she gives him money now and then, just to tide him over,' he replied. 'She's got a kind heart, though. Always been good to the boy.'

'Just not enough to take him in?'

'I gather she told him he'd be better movin' away for a bit.' Mr Brice shrugged. 'Jeanie Crisp knows the village. Knows how they get.'

'He was walking away from the shop just now.'

'Going to the bus stop up on the crossroads, I expect,' Brice replied. 'The Worthing bus doesn't come down this end of the High Street.'

'No, of course not.' The doorbell jangled abruptly to admit a new customer and Bunch knew her window of opportunity had closed. She pasted on a bright smile and pointed at the shelves behind Brice. 'Would Rennies do the trick? For Dodo I mean.'

'Oh, yes, sorry. You came in for your sister's tummy, didn't you?' He took down a packet of chalk tablets and a tin of bicarbonate. 'If these don't 'elp she will have to come in and see me herself,' he said. 'Or better send for Doctor Lewis.' He set the items on the glass-topped counter. 'No bags, I'm afraid. We're out. Terrible shortage of paper bags, there is.'

She laughed and swept them up in one hand. 'There's going to be a terrible of shortage of everything, Mr Brice. Put these on account please and send it to the Dower. We aren't at Perringham now.'

'Moved out by the Army now, is it?'

'Absolutely.' She shrugged. 'My regards to Mrs Brice, but I must dash. I left Dodo in the brake and she will be absolutely freezing.'

Had she been alone Bunch would have considered driving around to Church Street to see if Arnold was still at the bus stop but that was an action she was forced to abandon. As she emerged from the shop she saw Dodo standing on the far side of the car, head bowed, and the unmistakable sounds of retching drifted across to her.

&EIGHTEEN&

Bunch eyed the open door to the sitting room and could almost feel elderly ears straining in her direction the moment the handset jangled. She did not doubt it would be weeks, possibly months, before the new line was installed, and it could not come soon enough. It was just too inconvenient to trek down to the hall every time she needed to speak with anyone over the telephone. It was also very obvious that private conversations simply would not happen. She hadn't anything especially sensitive to convey to the police that wouldn't be common knowledge at some point. Nevertheless, she believed that her grandmother would be more than happy to listen in with alacrity on her private life, for the sheer fun of it

She then rushed up the stairs and reached the top floor slightly out of breath and, as she had on each landing, waited for Roger to catch up before entering her new study. She had been allocated a sizable section of the lumber room, which had been partitioned off with a bizarre collection of bedroom screens borrowed or purloined from where Bunch dared not to think. *Perhaps they had been here all the while. Bentwood relics of the Raj, side by side with Chinese lacquered and French ormolu screens.* It made for an interesting backdrop but at least they cut some of the raging drafts from howling across the space, though it remained an icehouse despite the fire burning in a meagre grate.

Knapp had done her best to have it all arranged as alike her old office as was possible. The same battered desk and chair and personal items were artfully placed around the dusty loft, and that was what it was: a grubby attic space. Located on the corner of the house, natural light filtered through a series of round windows set on two sides, though they all were that bit too high to see anything more than sky when sitting at her desk. If she did stand to gaze through them she had a reasonable view of both the front drive and the stables, and beyond that a section of the farmyard and its barns. The room was also far enough along the corridor from the occupied servant rooms to feel cut off. She supposed the old lady had assumed this was a prerequisite for work, but Bunch found its isolation disturbing. She made a mental note to find a wireless set to break the silence.

Two form-filling hours later she threw her pen down and stretched forcefully, standing up to peer through the window. She felt her joints snap and click. Roger yawned and struggled to his feet, waiting expectantly by the door. He had been barely more than three steps from her side since she arrived back indoors, determined she should not leave the house without him. She reached down to scratch his ears before staring up at the small round window, squinting at the pool of sunlight. For the first time in days there were stretches of blue sky with a promise of frost to solidify the melt.

The sound of a car drawing up at the front attracted her attention. She moved close to the glass and peered down to the drive, at the black Wolseley that had parked close to the doors. A uniformed constable climbed out to open the rear doors for the Chief Inspector to unfold his long body into the cold afternoon air.

'Wright?' she muttered. 'With a driver?' She wondered why he was not alone, as seemed to be his habit, and she wondered why he was here at all. She looked at the desk, at the pile of record cards still awaiting her attention. She didn't doubt he was here to speak with her but she was loathe to rush down to greet him like some giddy debutante. Better to allow the mountain to come to her. She sat down and selected the next bundle of papers, took up her pen, and waited for a tap on the door.

'That inspector is back, Miss Rose.' Sheila sidled in, staring around her in awe at seeing Family in traditional servant territory. 'Mrs Knapp has shown him into the sitting room.'

'Has she really? Well I have work to finish. Where's Granny?'

'Morning room, Miss. Mrs Courtney is with her WVS people. Knitting,' Sheila replied, a little gloomily. 'Wool lint all over carpet. Awful stuff to sweep up. Not that it's my concern, of course.'

'Never mind, Sheila. I hear they are trying to commandeer the church hall, if that's any help,' said Bunch. 'If they can keep a corner free from the ARP then all of your lint worries will be over.'

'I shall believe that when I see it. My old dad's a warden,' she replied. 'There's a right old battle going on over it. Only one village hall an' the world and their uncle's claiming the space for themselves.'

'Fortunately not my concern,' said Bunch. 'Have you served tea yet?'

'Yes, Miss.'

'Good. Is Mrs Tinsley well this morning?'

'I took her tea but Mrs Tinsley's stayed in her room'

'Probably just as well. Show the Chief Inspector up and fetch us some coffee, would you? Tea won't quite cut it today.'

'Yes, Miss.'

Bunch detected a hint of frost in the girl's tone but chose to ignore it. Annoying as it was, she gained a slight satisfaction in knowing the girl had finally developed enough backbone to be capable of taking umbrage. 'See that the driver gets something to drink as well, and tell Knapp I shall want the blue silk for dinner tonight.'

~~~

'Chief Inspector. How good to see you.' She put down her pen and rose to greet Wright as he appeared in the doorway. 'You must excuse me but Ministry paperwork waits for no man. Dead or alive. My superiors do not consider murder a good enough reason to fall behind.'

'That sounds a great deal like the police,' he said.

'Bureaucracy,' she replied, 'I was raised on it. Please do sit down. It's nice to see you, if something of a surprise. I only spoke to your station sergeant a couple of hours ago.' She sat near the tray and began to pour, an automatic action to avoid looking him in the eye. 'I didn't expect you to come all this way personally.'

'I was out here to see Colonel Kravitz,' he replied. 'I finally have permission from the War Department to enter the premises and speak with base personnel.' He offered a dry smile. 'Of course, now it's arrived the man I needed to speak to is dead so the warrant is as good as useless. Kravitz is all hail fellow, well met, and how eager he is to help with enquiries but at the same time making sure I don't actually talk to anyone.' He shrugged. 'That is a very strange place. Hush-hush stuff, I imagine.'

'I have drawn the same conclusion. What did you discover?'

'Very little. I asked him if he had any information linked to the deaths of Mary Tucker or Johansson – or Jonathan Frampton. He said no, so I left.'

'Is that why you have a driver today? Reinforcements?'

'We have a lot of house to house enquiries on going. It's very time consuming and something we rather not do alone. Visiting you is a welcome break from the routine calls.'

'Any luck so far?'

'Not as yet. I hear you drove over to Banyard Manor this morning.'

'Dodo wanted to come home, for personal reasons. It wasn't a terribly pleasant trip. I had not realised what a bad time she'd been having over there.'

'Where is she now?'

'Resting.' Bunch poured coffee and handed over a cup to Wright. 'She's not at all well.'

'I hope it's nothing too severe?'

'So do I. I rather think all this death has taken its toll on her'

Wright sat back in his chair and watched her intensely. 'What was it you wanted to tell me?'

'I have a possible name for one of the chaps who was butchering sheep up in the woods the other day.' She jutted her chin, enjoying a little triumph.

'Do you indeed?' He leaned forward, attention piqued. 'You didn't think to tell the station sergeant?'

'It's all hearsay and the more I go over it in my mind the less sense it makes,' she replied. 'Although I am almost certain I saw one of the men I caught rustling. Oh heavens, I can't think who started using that word. Rustling sounds as if it came straight out of Hollywood.'

'General theft,' said Wright. 'That is the legal term.'

'Theft it is then.' She related the conversation with Mr Brice and ended with: 'I would have gone after him but Dodo was in such a state.'

'Perhaps just as well you didn't,' he replied. 'You really shouldn't be tackling these people on your own.'

'I was told he's a simple boy who has had a hard life. He's half deaf and an orphan. That does not make him Al Capone.'

'He is a young man with nothing to lose,' Wright said, 'one who can butcher a sheep in minutes. And he has friends with guns.' Wright tucked in his chin and glowered at her from under his eyebrows, a move of his, she suspected, developed to intimidate the junior ranks.

'At least you have a name now.' She bent down to smooth Roger's head. The dog moaned quietly and thumped his tail against the desk.

'I shall call the station, see if the Worthing lads can pick him up. Now what about the butcher? The name fits with what was seen on the vehicle in question.'

'Beckenham? That name was never confirmed. Lieutenant Johansson said he thought it ended with *ham* and so we just made assumptions. Besides, I can't see Mr Beckenham being involved. He's a lay preacher. He's not a particularly warm sort of man, unless you count all that hell fire and brimstone.' She shook her head. 'No, I would really doubt it. The Ten Commandments are sacrosanct. I can't see that he'd be involved.'

'A man of conviction,' Wright said. 'He's not one to bend to need?'

'He's a Cokeler,' Bunch replied.

'A what?'

'Cokeler. They call themselves the Society of Dependants. There used to be a lot more of them around these parts before the Great War,' Bunch replied. 'A very strict, abstemious kind of Wesleyan chapel. They are objectors for the most part, which has caused a few family rifts when sons have opted not to object.'

'Family or duty, that's not an easy decision...' He trailed off, gazing out into the distance. 'Despite the van?' he said at last.

She shook her head. 'I am certain he would not do anything like that. If he had, would he use his own sign-written vehicle in local thefts?

'People don't always think logically,' said Wright.

'It could be a decoy. Or one of his apprentices...' She thought for a moment. 'Jenner was quite emphatic about their being not local. You do know that Beckenham sacked Crisp? Not seen the other one for a while. Harry Haynes, I think it was, and he – oh, good heavens, I am so dense! Frank Haynes, our stockman, has gone missing.'

'Frank? Are he and Harry related? Brothers?'

'Not brothers but cousins, of sorts. There are not that many families around here that you have those with the same name and yet have no connection beyond coincidence. On this occasion yes, they are related. Harry is a few years younger than Frank.'

'Where does this Harry Haynes live?'

'His name is actually Henry, but people just call him Harry. His parents live on Church Terrace.' Bunch slapped the heel of her hand against her forehead. 'God, you must think me so unbelievably stupid. Of course, that was where Arnold Crisp must have been going.'

'What about the other sheep thief?'

'I've already given Botting a description. The third man was short, wiry and definitely not local. A Londoner, I wouldn't be surprised.' She raised her eyes to gaze at a cobweb that the admirable Knapp had missed. It wafted in a draft, appearing and vanishing as it caught the lamp light. 'That doesn't mean too much, does it? I had the impression he was almost laughing at me, not flapped at all. Damned cool, in fact.' She looked back at Wright. 'Harry Haynes is a big man. I thought he joined up the same time as Frank. I could be wrong.'

'All good information, thank you. I shall have Botting make enquiries.'

Bunch rolled her eyes. 'After all that,' she asked, 'do we know who the chap with the gun was?'

'We may well know him, as it happens. I am aware you don't have a very high opinion of Constable Botting but he is a good man. Tenacious. He has already discovered some of what you have told me; he was following up on reports of your lad Haynes going missing. His parents reported a contact with a navy pal, who seems to be involved with a gang operating out of Mitchum.' Wright's mouth tweaked at her puzzled expression. 'It's a south London district. Not one you would know, I suspect. There's a little rhyme about it: *Sutton for good mutton, Cheam for juicy beef, Croydon for a pretty girl, and a Mitcham for a thief.*'

'Sounds delightful.'

'Right now it's a villain's paradise. Nobody knows who or

what is where. Total mess. There's a munition factory in the area, as well.'

'Why would anyone build a munitions factory in a place like that?'

Wright shrugged. 'It used to be a fireworks establishment. They were geared up for explosives so I suppose it seemed logical at the time. The Metropolitan Police are on to the Mitcham lead.' He leaned back in his seat and looked around him. 'You seem to be settling in.' He crossed his legs and stared at his right knee, crooked up a little higher than desk level, and picked an imaginary speck from the ill-pressed crease in his trouser leg. 'We were very interested in some other items,' he said carefully. 'Crisp was already on our watch list because he has form.' He flicked another speck from his trouser leg and looked toward Bunch. 'Which way would your suspicions run? Banyard Manor? Or Hascombe?'

'What do you mean?'

'You know these people,' he said. 'Leaving your sister to one side, you must have some good idea of what they are likely to do. What they are capable of.' Wright uncrossed his legs and leaned forward, resting his forearms on the desk, hands clasped, as he looked Bunch straight in the eye. 'Come on, surely you have an opinion?'

'Perhaps I do.' She stood up, crossing to one of the windows to look out. The past few days had been frenetic, following clues with no clear idea of what they meant or how they connected. The goal she had kept in mind all this time was to prove Jonny was not the sort of person to take his own life. She had not in her wildest imaginings believed it would go any further, that the body count would rise, as it had, even to being shot at herself, however wildly the aim. It had started as the kind of mystery she read about in books, and yes, she imagined herself being that amateur sleuth. Wright's bald-faced demand that she should verbalise her deepest suspicions took her by surprise. 'I don't know,' she said. 'I can't believe that any of them would do these awful things. I've known these people all my life and it defies belief that they would be involved with such hideous activities.' Wright gazed at her with clear-eyed expectation. He meant it. He wanted her to make a judgement beyond her immediate thoughts. 'You have far more experience than me in these things,' she said.

'I do,' he agreed. 'Being able to draw conclusions is all about assessing the facts, laced with a good pinch of instinct. Imagine you have never met these people before this week. Look at all the evidence and base your thoughts on how they have acted.'

Bunch paced the length of the makeshift room divides, running a finger nail along the screens, staring at the patterns in the frayed rug beneath her feet. Wright turned in his seat to track her progress, expectant yet silent. It felt momentous. She had not been this nervous since being presented at Court. 'Saul Frampton could be seen to have the most to lose and the most to gain,' she said at last. 'He loses control of Hascombe with Jonny's death, but he could have some hand in whatever racket was going on. His steward was in those woods the night Jonny was shot.

'On the other hand, I gather that the two men involved in the rustling had once worked for the Tinsleys. When the van left the wood I gather it took a back road around the village, which would pass Banyards. It's quite clear that rationing is not biting as hard there as it should be for Olivia. But Barty Tinsley is a magistrate; I cannot see him being involved. He is a pompous ass but I do not believe him capable of deliberate dishonesty.' She spread her hands. 'I don't know what to think.'

'There was also one of your employees, don't forget, and he may be involved,' he reminded her. 'You could apportion guilt to your own estate, on that score. However, at this stage we don't have enough real proof.'

'What do we do now?'

Wright smoothed his hair and exhaled loudly. 'I am being given the hairy eyeball by all kinds of people,' he said. 'Avenues of questioning cut off from all directions. Over my head, in the eye, below the knee – in fact at about every sort of level you can imagine.'

'Everyone's pulling rank?'

'Bluntly? Yes, but closing ranks might be closer to the truth. That Tinsley woman, in particular, is being difficult.'

'Oh, don't take that personally. Olivia Tinsley thinks she can stare down the Medusa,' Bunch replied, 'and I'm not sure she might not succeed.'

'Doubtless, although if I could take them down to the station, questioning would be easier, but there is not enough evidence as yet for that. I should not do this but I would appreciate your helping me batter down the barricades.'

'That has a somewhat revolutionary ring to it,' she drawled. 'Are you sure the descendant of a peer of the realm is the right person?'

'The descendants of peers of the realm are far more likely to kick over the traces.' Wright looked at his watch. 'I should go. Lot's to do.'

'You are very welcome to stay for dinner.' She hoped she didn't smile too brightly. 'Cook always has some amazing trick to spread out the food for the odd unexpected guest.'

'I would love to but I have a meeting with my superintendent. He wants my report on these deaths – in full.' He slid his perennial black notebook into an inside pocket and patted his jacket. 'Thanks to the additional information you've provided I may have something to tell him. It more than makes up for Kravitz. Now, if you will excuse me. I shall be back tomorrow, bright and early. If that is convenient?' He nodded. 'Good afternoon, Miss Courtney.'

❧NINETEEN❧

Perringham House was being slowly and inexorably transformed. Bunch was not entirely sure into what but the change was rapid. Pill boxes had been added to the main gates and more permanent looking barriers erected, and she would never get used to being passed fit to enter her own family home by a gun-wielding sentry. Changes to the inside were even more striking. The foyer could barely be seen behind rows of notice boards fixed over the panelling. Flags and banners covered the intricately carved balustrades and finials in the gallery. It made the once imposing foyer seem far less open which, Bunch supposed, was the idea. She was pleased to note the oak panelling surviving behind the new adornments, but she was not sure she wanted to know what would happen when the main body of troops, or whatever they were, arrived in the next month or two.

Bunch felt another lurch in the pit of her stomach as she and Chief Inspector Wright entered the study. Her father's belongings had been placed in storage, and though it was a logical choice for Colonel Kravitz to take as his own office she had never envisaged anybody else using the study. It was, she had once thought, an inviolate sanctum. For a stranger to take over so comprehensively the heart of Perringham quite made the invasion complete. She had been gone from the house for just a few days and Kravitz had turned the entire building into a military cave. Gone were the artworks and bookcases to be replaced by military paraphenalia. The only items Kravitz seemed to have retained were the vast desk and its chairs. The Colonel looked up and half-rose from his chair to proffer his hand to them. 'Chief Inspector. And Miss Courtney. Good morning, sit down, please.'

'Thank you, Colonel.' Wright took the chair nearest to the desk. 'I have some more questions for you after yesterday.'

'I don't doubt it. Fire away.' He smiled icily. 'Coffee?' he added. 'It is coffee, not that God-awful bottled crap you people pass off.'

'No thank you,' Wright replied. 'We shan't keep you long. Just a few minutes.'

'How may I assist the constabulary this time? I'm here to help.'

'Thank you,' said Wright. 'Johansson talked to Miss Courtney about seeing vehicles parked on the road the night before Mary Tucker was murdered. Since your officer did not return to base that night, and as we don't yet have a coroner's report, we assume Johansson was shot the same day as Miss Tucker.'

'I see.' Kravitz picked up a pen, twirled it between his fingers. 'If you're saying he talked to Miss Courtney because Miss Tucker was fretting, then he did. I didn't hear him report anything at all on that subject.'

'Who said Mary Tucker was fretting?' Bunch grumbled. The sharp pain to her foot came from Wright's adept kick. She managed not to cry out.

'It's an educated guess.' Kravitz watched his pen, turning it end over end against the desk top with a steady tap-tap-tap. 'I know the lieutenant was very close to Mary Tucker. I shall try to see it does not happen again.' He shrugged, raising his gaze to stare directly at Wright. 'In normal circumstances these romances would not blossom so quickly. But in times if war?' He shook his head. 'I think you know what I'm saying.'

'Including this?' Wright withdrew two tattered slips of paper from his pocket. 'We found these at the cottage, in Miss Tucker's room. From tinned ham and chocolate candy.' He smoothed the paper out and smiled.

'Mary's room?' Bunch asked.

Wright flushed a little. 'One of our officers found it in Miss Tucker's lingerie drawer.'

'Oh, gosh, I never suspected.' She stopped herself saying too much that might smack of excuses. She was shocked to see evidence of contraband on her own property, and angry at the Chief Inspector for not telling her before performing this stage magician act of producing the crumpled-paper bouquets That the paper flowers were a sheet of plain white paper speckled with black print did not lessen what could only be viewed as a lack of trust. 'Lingerie drawer?' she said. 'Why would any woman keep them there?'

'Why does any woman, or man sometimes, keep these things?' Wright pointed at a scrawl in blue pen on each slip, reading *Food of love, SJ xxx.* 'Gifts from a lover are precious.' He looked at Colonel Kravitz. 'Can you explain how they got to her?'

'Are you serious? Candy bars and a can of ham?' Kravitz laughed. 'Ham's a weird kind of gift. And American.'

'Plenty of American goods coming in with the Canadians,' Bunch replied. 'Parcels from home.'

'Except that Johansson was Norwegian,' Kravitz said. 'Though he had family in the States, I believe. If he stayed for supper at Miss Tucker's it stands to reason a boy brought up properly would pitch in with his share. There is nothing to prove it was anything other than a few simple gifts. It means nothing.'

'It means a lot to people in this country.' Wright sighed. 'A few luxuries meant to impress his lady and her friends. Your quartermaster sergeant, on the other hand, seems to have been a little more organised. He is French, I understand. Quite the League of Nations you have here.'

Kravitz regarded him stonily but said nothing.

'We already have reports of quite large amounts of goods entering the black market,' Wright continued. 'Police officers had seized a vehicle full of contraband in the village just two nights ago. Sugar and tea in wholesale quantities. I will need to question your sergeant about it later but for now we have a murder to solve.'

Kravitz leaned back in his chair, hands together, steepling his fingers against his lower lip. 'I will deal with it, Chief Inspector,' he drawled after a long moment. 'We don't need to start an incident over one case of supplies.'

They stared at each other, like scrap-yard dogs circling for fight.

'If it were the odd tin we would not have a problem,' Wright said at last. 'It could be overlooked. What we are seeing here is wholesale theft and black marketeering is a prisonable offence. We know these goods are being passed on from here to person or persons unknown in the immediate vicinity. I will need to speak with all personnel who have access to stores.'

'I said *I* will deal with it.' The Colonel's tone dropped to a crackling ice.

'If I don't get some sort of solution you can certainly expect a call from the Ministry of Food. I can't do anything about that.' Wright scooped up the labels and slid them back into his pocket. 'It would be much easier if you let me talk with your chaps. One chap in fact. Your quartermaster sergeant has already been implicated by various witnesses, so I have narrowed it down for you. Unless you have more than one?'

'Discipline in these cases is a military matter.' Kravitz picked up the pen and again began tapping it end-over-end on the antique rosewood veneer. Bunch winced at each blow and made a mental note to demand the desk be removed to the Dower for her own use, and for the sake of the desk's salvation.

'I would not dream of interfering with the chain of command.' Wright smiled dryly. 'Right now I only want the name of the British civilian your man's been selling Army property to. What you do with your sergeant then becomes your concern. View it as an exercise in allied forces cooperation.'

The pen tapping and turning continued for a few revolutions. Kravitz looked from Wright to Bunch, plainly considering various possibilities. 'Wait here,' he said and launched himself out of the chair and the room.

'Well that was odd,' Bunch observed. 'That man likes being in charge just a little too much.'

'The Colonel is hiding behind the rule book.' Wright rose and wandered around the desk to poke at a few files on the table top before moving on to peer at the maps.

Bunch glanced nervously toward the door. 'You don't suspect Kravitz of being involved?'

'No. Just like to know what's happening on my patch.' A few paces and he was back in his seat as the Colonel returned.

'I believe it would help if you knew the name of your hoodlum,' Kravitz said, handing Wright a folded note. 'You have to understand that I can't allow any of this trailing back to the men under my command. Bad enough Johansson being shot. You have no idea the amount of waves that sent up the line. The War Office staffers are having all kinds of fits.'

'As are mine. Now if that is all?' Wright reached into his

pocket for the can labels and they swapped evidence. 'Thank you, Colonel Kravitz. Very civil.' He glanced at the slip of paper and grunted before he placed it in his notebook. 'Meanwhile, if you could ask your men about anything Johansson may have said about commercial vehicles, or sheep thieves, please contact me.'

'I will.' Kravitz rose and shook Wright's hand. 'You have our total cooperation on that. Miss Courtney.' He saluted Bunch. 'I hope we won't be here for too long.'

~ ~ ~

'What does it say?' Bunch demanded. 'Who is it?' The inside of the car was only a little warmer than the outside, save it being out of the wind. She rubbed at her arms and felt a little sorry for the driver, SPC Dyer, who had waited for them in the Wolseley.

'Interesting. Our black marketeer appears to be your old friend Harry Haynes,' said Wright. 'No great surprise there.'

'He's in the Navy. I asked the maid, Sheila, when you mentioned him before. He definitely joined up.'

'Was. He deserted.' Wright turned away to gaze out of the window and Bunch could not avoid noting the hunch of his shoulders even in the semi-dark of dusk. She stayed quiet, knowing instinctively that he was not open to idle chatter at that particular moment. She empathised; she was not a chit-chatterer on her own account. 'Was he always such a bad lot?' he finally murmured. Chief Inspector Wright's question seemed so casual yet the edge to his voice could not be ignored.

Bunch wondered if this was why she'd been asked along, as an oracle on local people and places. *He'll be disappointed,* she thought. *Knapp knows far more than me. Or indeed Botting.* 'I gather he was not best liked by various employers. I also gather he had rather a lot of them.'

'Such as?'

'I can't say I knew him well enough to list them all,' Bunch replied. 'Beckenham, the butcher, for one, though we can't hold a chap to account for leaving that post. Amos Beckenham is a bit of a tartar. Gets through apprentices like an entire ladle of salts.'

'Expects a lot of them?'

'More than most could possibly live up to. He sacked his own son Joseph'

'What for?'

Bunch shook her head. 'Would you believe blasphemy? I don't recall all the village gossip but I do remember that, if only because it was so very bizarre. I did tell you he's a lay preacher?'

'You did. And the son? Where would he be?'

'Joseph? Not a clue.' She spread her hands. 'Joe left the village in high dudgeon after one particularly public altercation. That would have been in 1936? Or was it thirty-seven? Before the war began, I do remember. There was a rumour he left for Australia but I have no idea if that's true or not. You know how it can be in a small community. What the doorstep matriarchs don't know they make up.'

He nodded. 'It's useful background information which we'll follow up.'

'Wouldn't Botting be a better person for you to ask?' she said. 'He knows more about people in the village than I do.'

'Possibly, but he's a lot less fun to be with.' Wright grinned at her; the clouds that had gathered in his eyes cleared in a moment. 'You are a lot quicker to catch on. Our PC Botting is a good man but turns out to be rather quick at marrying up the apparently unconnected. He's a reliable sort, otherwise.'

'He knows his patch.'

'He does. Ah, here we are.'

They alighted into the early evening with the dusk well advanced, to stand in front of the row of unlit shops. The street was deserted, as far as they could tell in the near-night. Wright took a torch from the depths of his overcoat pocket and shone it briefly along the parade. 'Quiet,' he observed.

'Wednesday,' Bunch replied. 'Early closing day. They would all have shut at midday and be long closed, whether they had people queuing or not.'

'Of course. Foolish of me.' He flicked the torch on again to pick out the shop doorways. 'Does our evangelist butcher live over the shop?'

'Yes he does. I rather think he's the sort of person who would see owning two premises as wanton profligacy, or greed, or some such.'

'You disapprove of his views? A lot of people find comfort in churches and chapels.'

'Not at all. I'm a church goer myself. I just find myself

uncomfortable with his particular brand of evangelism. It is a little oppressive.' She looked down and shuffled her feet in the slush. *Father always said never discuss politics or religion. It will never win you any friends. As always he was right.* 'I think the door to the house is down the side,' she mumbled.

'It would be. Coming?' He strode off toward the side of the shop. His torch shed a thin inadequate beam and Bunch had to hurry to catch up in order to benefit from it, and found herself walking closer to him than she felt was polite. Their shoulders brushed every other step; she took a wider track, deciding she would rather risk falling flat on her face than give him the wrong impression about such casual contact.

The domestic door to Beckenham's had been painted white some years ago and, even flaked and scarred and in need of fresh paint, retained a vestigial luminescence, glimmering faintly in the darkness. Wright leaned forward and rapped sharply.

It was a full minute before the door opened a crack revealing a hallway beyond which was almost total darkness.

'Yes?' The woman's voice was quiet, almost soft were it not for a dry rasp burring her country vowels.

'Mrs Beckenham? It's Rose Courtney and Chief Inspector Wright. We need to ask your husband a few questions. Is he at home?'

'Come in and be quick. That ARP warden is the very devil himself.' She opened the door just wide enough for them to sidle in and promptly closed it again, pausing to pull a heavy curtain over the doorway before she flicked on the light, all done in the prescribed-Blackout fashion. 'This way, Miss Rose.' She trotted ahead of them, her plaited grey hair, normally pinned in a tight bun, bouncing between her shoulder blades and almost down to her waist. She was old beyond her years, her bones jutting through an inadequate black cardigan, but she possessed a straight-backed severity.

As though, Rose thought, *she feels like the weight of the world is draped around that long-suffering neck of hers.*

The woman ushered the two into her husband's presence and then retreated from the room, which was as ferociously clean as it was threadbare, with evidence of more fiscal prudence than months of war and the Ministry's *Make-do and Mend* could ever account for. Beckenham was seated in a large armchair before a paltry fire, wearing his habitual black suit. He looked up and rose only when he recognised Bunch. 'Miss Courtney – and you must be Chief Inspector Wright?' He nodded, not offering a hand to shake. 'Gladys, tea!' he called. He sat again and folded the newspaper he had been reading, taking painful care, and placed it on the floor beneath his chair. He crossed his hands over his stomach and stared at his constantly twitching fingers.

He was an average man in every respect: of average height and build, and average brown hair that was thinning at the crown and greying back from the temples. The grease that held its razor-sharp parting in check was entirely natural. 'Please do sit down. How I may help the constabulary?'

'Thank you, Mr Beckenham.' Wright unbuttoned his coat and sat, placing his hat on his knee, brushing off imagined dust in a show of pernickety care to match his host's.

His mimicry gave Bunch cause for thought. *Does he intentionally mirror his interviewee's mannerisms or is it something he does by instinct? Is it a habit cultivated to disarm and confound? Does he fool me the same way?* Wrapped up in that train of thought she almost missed Wright ghosting past the niceties and into polite interrogation.

'I think you may be able to help us with details of two lads who, I understand, were apprenticed to you.' Wright made a show of wielding his opened notebook ready for any pearls that Beckenham might drop. 'One Harry Haynes,' he read, 'plus an Arnold Crisp?'

The master butcher sat back in his chair with folded arms. 'They don't work for me,' he replied. 'Neither has worked here for a while. Haynes received his call up some months past. As for Crisp, I had to let him go.'

'For what reason?'

'He proved unsatisfactory.' Beckenham glowered down the length of his nose at Wright. 'It is not my duty to speak ill of any man.'

Wright nodded, jotting down a few words and murmuring a casual, 'I'd heard he was a thief. Is that the case?' He raised his cool gaze to meet Beckenham's.

Beckenham in turn raised his chin another defiant notch, which gave Bunch a startling view of the old man's flaring nostrils. 'Crisp needs all of the help God can provide,' he said. 'I cannot condone gossip.'

'Was there any truth in those rumours?'

There was a moment's hesitation, the quiet broken only by the muffled clatter of pans coming from the kitchen. The butcher shrugged. 'It was not something I would like to confirm.'

'You didn't report it, though?' Wright tilted his head like an expectant spaniel.

Beckenham held still for a moment, his eyebrows drawn together in patent disapproval, and then transferred his attention to the teacup that had already been at his elbow on their arrival. He was apparently confused that the detective was not affected by his ire. 'It did not seem a very Christian act, what with Crisp having so many problems,' he said at last. 'The boy needed clear instruction on the true path to salvation. I would not be true to my calling if I allowed myself to walk away from an act of charity.'

'*Thou shalt not steal* is clear enough for most.' Wright pencilled a few glyphs in his notebook and Bunch shuffled in her seat to catch a glimpse of them. She had taken a secretarial course before accepting her post with the WLA, but his jottings looked like nothing she had learned and wondered if it were his own form of shorthand, or merely bluff. 'So what was is that you suspected Mr Crisp stole from you, Mr Beckenham?' Wright added. 'Just for the record.'

'Knives,' Beckenham replied after a long pause. He looked down at his teacup. 'Good forged steel, passed down from my own father. I could not be absolutely sure it was Crisp. Perhaps I should have spoken to PC Botting on the matter, but the boy was the logical suspect. He was the last lad working at the bench.'

'That would seem a fairly major theft,' Bunch said. 'Tools of the trade and all that.'

'Good knives yes, but old tools,' Beckenham said. 'I would not have missed them but Daniel Coffey was coming through the village and I like to keep all my steel ready for use. We sharpen our own knives as a rule, but with this rationing a keener edge goes a long way to stretching out what we have. Coffey does a good job for a fair price. A Papist, it's true, like many of his tribe, but a Godly man. I can't fault him for all of that.'

'Did you find the knives after Crisp left?'

Beckenham shook his head, obviously deep in thought. 'Arnold Crisp harbours sin. He lies and steals and drinks and blasphemes. Even if the knives had not gone I should have had to dismiss him. I took him on as a favour to his aunt. A poor orphan boy. It was my duty as a pastor to offer him assistance into the Lord's house and not the road to Perdition. It was a matter of Christian charity.'

Why, he's suddenly changed his tune, Bunch thought.

'Harry Haynes: was he also reliable?' Wright asked.

'Far from it. That whole family are Godless scaddles. I wonder any would employ them.'

'I'm slowly gaining that impression,' Wright replied. 'One more question, Mr Beckenham. Have you had wind of any black market activity in the area?'

Beckenham started visibly. It was a measured reaction, Bunch realised. *Is he so shocked by the very notion? He's a pious old hypocrite. The malicious gossiping old maggot!*

'Greed is rife,' Beckenham growled. 'Greed and avarice. You hear it – see it – everywhere. Was young Crisp a part of that?'

'We're looking into the possibility.' Wright turned to look toward the kitchen, for no reason that Bunch could fathom. *Except that it's gone very quiet in there.*

'If he is it would most likely be at a very menial level.' Wright leaned forward, his hat dangling from clasped fingers, his elbows resting on knees. 'We want the far bigger fish than Arnold Crisp. Black market traders will be causing huge problems for all the legitimate businessmen such as yourself. That's not to mention the terrible affect it will have on morale when the law-abiding public are denied rations that are syphoned off by these villains.'

'Evil exists in many forms, Chief Inspector.' Beckenham replied. 'If any man working for me was involved in anything of that nature he would be dismissed immediately. Harry Haynes was not a man of conscience and Arnold Crisp may merely have followed where he was led.' He glanced at Bunch. 'I heard his cousin has walked away from your employ, Miss Courtney.'

Where's his Christian charity now? Bunch wondered. 'Vanished,' she agreed, 'although Frank's parents had worked for Daddy for decades and they never caused a moment's concern.'

'Nor would they. You know that Simeon Haynes is a senior stalwart at our meeting house?' Beckenham smiled mechanically. *'The fathers shall not be put to death for the children, neither shall the children be put to death for the fathers: every man shall be put to death for his own sin,'* he said. 'Deuteronomy, 24:16.'

'Unless they happen to be called Haynes?' Wright said.

'Hardly a time for levity,' Beckenham muttered. 'Some might even call that blasphemous.'

'No offence was intended.' Wright smiled encouragement. 'I appreciate your honesty about young Crisp. We knew he had some connection with the Haynes family. We had hoped to learn from you the identity of another associated party. Someone has to be buying from them, possibly someone else in the butchery or slaughtering trades. We have witnesses who saw vehicles moving around at night, out in the woods. One was a sign-written commercial van. Would you happen to know whom that might belong?'

'No, I'm sorry, Chief Inspector, I do not.'

'Not a hint?'

'Smithfield Market.' Beckenham glanced at the silent kitchen and lowered his voice. 'We all deal with that place because we must, though London is an iniquitous hellhole.'

'I know it well and not all of its inhabitants are bad people, Mr Beckenham, and finding a butcher in Smithfield would not be wholly unexpected. Could you be more specific?'

Beckenham's dour demeanour turned positively sour. 'I saw someone. Perhaps I should say *seen* because he's been through the village a few times in recent months.' He pursed his lips, looking around the room. Bunch could see the turmoil going through his mind. 'It is not easy for me to cast aspersions,' he said. 'Once said, it cannot be unsaid.'

Being pompous once again!

'A name, Mr Beckenham. This is a multiple murder enquiry. The manners of polite society will hardly count.'

'Yes, of course, of course. The name on the lips of village worthies is Percy Guest. Those who take note of such things will tell you he has been seen skulking around the area for some weeks now.' He assumed a pose of pious satisfaction. 'Major Tinsley would not have that one on his premises, and rightly so.

He was prohibited from Banyard Manor several years ago. I'm lead to understand he never normally leaves London but if you are looking for a bad apple he would be the one to taint the barrel any week you care to choose.'

'Percy Guest you say?' Wright made a careful note. 'Why was this Guest person barred from Banyard Manor?'

Beckenham looked to Bunch and for the first time a smile twitched at his mouth. 'Miss Courtney is better placed to talk about him than me.'

'Really?' Wright turned to Bunch, left eyebrow quirked.

She shook her head abruptly. *This man is such an appalling old hypocrite,* she thought. *There are many things to say about Percy Guest but not within Beckenham's hearing.*

'Would Guest have anything connection with the commercial vehicle that people have mentioned?' Wright persisted.

'I could not possibly say whether he has anything to do with it,' the butcher replied. 'But if it's stray vehicles you are looking for, perhaps you should wander up to the terraces. Several villagers mentioned seeing a van along that way for a few days. It's gone now.'

'Did these people say who owns it?'

'No, but Percy Guest is nothing more than a common thief.'

'Fascinating. There appears to be quite a crime wave,' Wright replied. 'I remain constantly amazed at how sleepy hamlets and villages can be so rife with crime.' He smiled disarmingly at Beckenham. 'But I shouldn't be. After all, people are people, in town or country. Did Guest have dealings with Haynes or Crisp?'

'I have no idea, Chief Inspector. I do not move in their circles.' Beckenham unfolded himself from his chair. 'If I can help you at all in the future please do call me. Now I must prepare for the chapel meeting. Only one a week now, for our sins. Travelling in the dark is so much harder but as a stalwart I must attend.'

Bunch recognised the signs of impending oratory and stood up, followed reluctantly by Wright. 'Thank you Mr Beckenham,' she proffered her hand. 'That is most helpful. We can see ourselves out.'

❧TWENTY❧

'I know only a little about Percy Guest.' Bunch adjusted her hat in the scant reflection offered by rear-view mirror, using the gesture to gather her thoughts. 'I met him once or twice. Hideous man. We had assumed he was some weekend barnacle who turned out to be a bit harder to dislodge than most. I mean, Barty Tinsley can be a terrible prig, but if half the stories I've heard are true one can't blame him for giving Guest the old bum's rush. If you want my opinion, Guest was something of a slime.'

'I can't work with that. Can you give me some facts.'

'Guest first appeared at Banyards several years ago. It was obvious from the start that he was not the kind of person Olivia or Barty would entertain in the normal sort of way. In point of fact, he was probably not the type they would even allow through the tradesmen's entrance let alone sit at their dinner table and eating off their good flatware.'

'He didn't fit?'

'He didn't *belong*. I have absolutely no doubt that *he* felt completely at home. He strutted around positively revelling in the whole affair and treated Banyards like some members' club, like a home from home, whenever he felt like it. Whether he fitted in or not absolutely did not bother him.' She eyed Wright from the edges of her vision. 'I even harboured some sympathy with Olivia. Guest was a dreadful creature. Manners of a rat.' She shrugged. 'Oddly, though, she seemed rather *embarrassed* by him, seemed to accept him, that he was just how he was. He stayed over at Banyards for weeks and then he vanished as fast as he'd arrived. I'm told he reappeared later in the year, and then again around New Year of thirty-nine, but I didn't see him myself then. Dodo and I thought it was all terribly peculiar. George positively loathed him and went up to Town when the wretch turned up. Which is probably why I never ran into Guest all that often. I had the distinct impression he rather enjoyed the effect he had on the household *and* the other visitors there.'

'Would you say he had something over the Tinsleys?'

She nodded. 'I would say so, yes. Barty was angry, but then he often is. I was more surprised by Olivia since she's not the sort to tolerate *oiks* – not without a damned good reason, anyway. As it turns out, though, I am not sure why, given her—' She came to a halt. *How much should I tell him? It's not my business but all of Dodo's and she has enough already. On the other hand...* 'Olivia, she has a drug problem,' she said at last.

Wright nodded. 'We know about that. It would seem your Mrs Tinsley has a somewhat chequered background from before she married into the Tinsley family, and for some while afterwards.'

'You know? I only just found out myself.'

'I do have many more resources to draw on,' he replied. 'What we don't have is information about her habits after her stay in the sanatorium. Would your sister know more, do you think? She lived in Banyard Manor, after all.'

Bunch shook her head. 'I doubt Dodo knows anything much. She didn't visit Banyards much more than I did before she married George, and that was well after Guest was thrown out. She did say there were *secrets in wardrobes*. I thought it an odd sort of comment at the time. I'm sure Dodo never felt part of the Tinsley herd.'

'Then let's go straight to the stable and talk to the horse.' Wright leaned forward, opened the privacy window and tapped the driver on the shoulder. 'Banyard Manor, Dyer.'

'No, not yet.' Bunch laid her hand on Dyer's shoulder. 'Back to the Dower House please.'

Dyer turned to look at his superior officer. 'Sir?' he said.

'One moment, Dyer,' Wright murmured and then to Bunch, 'I thought you wanted to be in on the kill.' He hesitated. 'Are you all right, Miss Courtney? Not gone down with the same illness as your sister?'

'I am fine. But the Tinsley's dine early and if you go now you will probably arrive as they are sitting down to dinner. Olivia hates people turning up unannounced at meal times so she'll draw out the courses for as long as she can and have us kicking our heels for an hour or more.'

'She might try,' Wright growled.

'She will do more than try, believe me.' Bunch tapped Wright's arm. 'We do need to ask Dodo a few questions before we blunder around alerting the whole of Banyards. I don't expect the Tinsleys *are* involved, not directly, but there's no point giving them a heads up. Dodo may not know much about Guest but something has changed at Banyards in the past few months. I thought it was strange for her to want to come charging back over to stay with me when she knew Perringham was in chaos. The more I think about it the more I know there is something, or someone, making that decision for her.'

'You believe Guest may be there?'

Bunch was not sure what she thought, though gut instinct was pulling her toward Dodo having a lot more to say. 'Knowing what you've told me now, I think he may have been around and about. If he has I doubt Olivia will admit anything willingly. Yes, I think you are correct: Guest has something over her. He is obviously a shady sort. Dodo may know more than she realises about all kinds of things, including Guest.'

'I have a report on him,' said Wright, 'but the Yard hasn't been able to collar him for anything specific. Yes, he's very much known to us. His entire family are villains.'

'You didn't think you should have mentioned this before?' Bunch felt slighted by his withholding information, and angry that he had dragged her along under what she now saw as false pretences. The fact that she had come willingly, even eagerly, was in her opinion quite beside the point. 'Pardon me,' she added, 'I had thought we had a deal on sharing information.'

The Chief Inspector sighed heavily. 'Initially I had no idea he was involved in this case, and you were no more willing to tell me things just now.'

'I did not want to say anything in front of the Beckenhams. What is your excuse?'

'I am an officer of the law.' He leaned forward and slid the glass privacy screen shut. 'Sorry. I apologise. That was pompous and it wasn't meant to be, but all this is very delicate. My Superintendent has got wind of your digging around in this crime and then he got a tip-off from Frampton's more – shall we say – elevated relatives, and he's not happy about it. Yes, you are a *very* well connected lady and you have helped me a great deal with this case, for which I am extremely grateful, but you are not a police officer. The less you know about a man like Guest the better. He is not the sort you want to draw attention to yourself.'

'That is utter nonsense, man. The more I know the better I'm able to deal with it.'

'It is not the sort of thing any girl should be mixed up in.'

'Don't you dare!'

Wright started, staring at her in bug-eyed confusion. 'Pardon?' he said.

'Granny campaigned for Suffrage,' Bunch said and prodded him sharply in the shoulder and carried on prodding as she leaned in close, her nose almost touching his. 'I am not some scatter-brained debutante. Well alright, I was a deb but I do not need protecting. So don't you dare say it's not suitable for a *girl*. Good God man, we have women building bombs and airplanes. I send girls out to plough fields and I'm recruiting women to cut down damned trees! Don't insult me and say I am *just* a woman!'

'Miss Courtney – Bunch – this is no reflection on womankind, most especially on you, because you will never be *just* anything. But you have to see that this is a not just a touch of poaching by some local farmer's lad. This is dangerous, by any yardstick you care to use.' His reply was measured as he counted off on his fingers. 'Mary Tucker, a tough girl from a tough East End family. She suffered more beatings in her life than you've had ball gowns: slaughtered. Johansson, a trained military officer: shot dead. Jonathan Frampton, in special military services and as it turns out up to his neck in things that even I'm not senior enough to know about, yet still managed to get himself murdered.' He placed a hand over hers. 'I don't doubt your abilities, you know that. I do doubt the wisdom of bringing any civilian into this case. I regret letting you indulge your passion for sleuthing like some Lady Peter Wimsey. It is getting bloody dangerous and I would never forgive myself if you ended up lying on a mortuary slab with the rest of them.'

The cover of darkness was a blessing as she felt herself turn a delicate fuchsia. 'I began this Wimseying, if you recall, because the police would not,' she replied. 'Please do me the courtesy of allowing me to finish it.'

He nodded. 'I doubt I could stop you. We can speak with your sister by all means, if you think it will help.'

~~~

'This is getting to be something of a habit, Chief Inspector.' Beatrice Courtney settled beside Dodo on the sofa and turned her best smile on the Chief Inspector. She accepted coffee from the maid and set it on the occasional table at her right hand. 'You were fishing for details on Olivia and Barty Tinsley over dinner. What exactly are you after?'

Bunch stared at her grandmother. The old lady's metaphorical gloves were seldom removed when it came to protocol. Nor was she prone to displays of perspicacity, or in voicing it.

'Oh, don't look like that, Rose dear,' she said. 'I may be old and I may forget things now and then, but I'm not completely stupid.' She turned back to Wright. 'You are interested in any connections they might have?'

'I am, Mrs Courtney.'

'Anything in mind?'

He shrugged. 'What do you know?'

Beatrice smiled, or smirked as Bunch saw it. 'Barty is an open book. He blusters a lot and his war record is a lot shorter than he'd have you believe, but he was a regular. He is the second son, you know; supposed to be the spare but then his elder brother was killed in the Dardanelles.'

'And Mrs Tinsley?'

Beatrice glanced at Dodo. 'I am sure my youngest granddaughter can tell you more of what goes on at Banyards.'

'I am more interested in Mrs Tinsley's background, specifically her family connections.'

'Oh,' Beatrice said, 'he wants the gossip, Rose. It was all a long time ago, Chief Inspector.'

'Why, Granny? Apart from being an actress what did she do?' Dodo breathed.

'It's not so much what she *did*. I knew Olivia's father back then. He was what used to be called a rake, a regular stage-door Johnny – and don't look so shocked.' She smiled at Wright. 'It seems my granddaughters find it difficult to imagine I had a youth. Or that I understand anything about that kind of thing. It is a perpetual joke that youngsters never imagine old people could ever know about sex.'

'Very true, Ma'am.' He coughed. 'I understand from Miss Courtney that you were quite political at one time,' said Wright.

'I was.' She smiled sadly. 'That fire went out a long time ago. My darling Charles took it with him when he passed away.'

'You have my sympathies,' he muttered.

Beatrice gazed at him for a moment. 'You have mine, Mr Wright. I can see you've had losses of your own. But we are not discussing *our* pasts are we? Forgive me, it's a habit of the old. Where were we?'

'Olivia's father?' Bunch said.

'Richard Mead. He liked the ladies rather too much, if one could honour most of the women he chased with such dignity. The Meads were a terribly old family. Nothing left of them now, of course, largely due to Richard's excesses.'

'Really?' said Dodo. 'I had the impression Olivia was still well connected.'

'Olivia Tinsley will do all she can to give that impression. She is a Mead by blood, but some of us still remember how she had to earn her living before she married Barty. She was an actress,' Beatrice said, smiling grimly. 'Just like her mother although, perhaps, chorus girl is closer to the truth. Barty first met her in France.'

'What has that to do with what is going on now, Granny?' Bunch asked.

'About what dear?'

'About Olivia's family.'

'Your Chief Inspector asked about Olivia and Barty.' Beatrice frowned as she picked up her coffee. 'Richard Mead had two legitimate sons. Neither of them survived the trenches. The rest of his many progeny were bastards. Including the self-righteous Mrs Tinsley.'

This revelation left a stunned silence in its wake as the sisters avoided looking at each other. Beatrice saved them the trouble. 'I think that is what the good Inspector wants to hear. Is that not so?'

Wright nodded. 'It is, thank you, and you are only confirming my suspicions.'

'That Olivia Tinsley has dubious connections? Yes, she has

them. Quite a number of them, I understand.'

'One of those being Percival Guest?' Bunch asked.

'I'm not familiar with *all* of her feral relatives.' Beatrice shook her head. 'I'm sorry, my dear, I can't recall all the details.' Her voice faltered as her spike of confidence faded. 'I have an early start tomorrow so if you'll excuse me, Chief Inspector, I shall retire.'

'Of course, Mrs Courtney.' He rose and crossed to open the door. 'If you do remember anything else please let Miss Courtney know.'

'I shall. Please, make sure Mrs Tinsley does not stay up late. In her condition she needs her rest. Good evening.'

'Good evening.'

'Condition?' Bunch demanded after the door closed firmly on her grandmother.

Dodo flushed. 'It's only a suspicion, but well, you know.'

'Congra—'

'No!' Dodo held up a hand and turned her face away. 'Not yet. Don't say anything until I know for certain. It's not to go beyond these walls. Please.'

'All right, of course.' Bunch raised one eyebrow at Wright who shrugged. 'It explains a great many questions, and if it is confirmed then it changes a great many things.'

'Exactly why I want it kept quiet.'

'Understood, darling. Is that why you wanted to be away from Olivia?'

Dodo nodded. 'It's one reason.'

'Did you know about her dubious relatives?'

'Yes, but only a little of it. Barty would drag it all up when they rowed, which was often, especially since George died. Not the full details though, only veiled comments. When I say *veiled* I mean that he usually stopped just short of naming names.'

'But Percy Guest was one of those names?' said Wright. 'Did he visit often?'

There was a moment's hesitation before Dodo shook her head. 'I'm not sure. He came a few times before I moved to Banyards but only once since then. It was just before George was killed. I remember that he unexpectedly turned up before dinner, and you know how Olivia could be about unexpected guests.' She smiled weakly. 'Queer thing was, I thought it was Barty who was going to have a seizure.' She faltered. 'Georgie wasn't even there that night and I remember he was furious when he found out latter. I think he disliked Percy more than Barty did.'

'Do you remember anything that was said? Anything at all?'

'Oh God, no. Mason was trying to drag Percy out the door after he had just barged in unannounced and Barty was screaming himself blue in the face. I had never seen him so angry. It was Olivia who finally hustled Percy out and I heard her saying something like, *Not here. I've told you before. Not here.*'

'You're sure about that?'

'Maybe not those exact words but something along those lines. I was too shocked to pay close attention at the time. I mean, people don't usually get turned out of the house, do they?'

'Probably not.'

'Excuse me, Chief Inspector, a telephone call for you.' Knapp entered the room and gestured toward the hall, withdrawing as silently as she had arrived. Wright followed her out.

'Pregnant? Why didn't you tell me?'

Bunch's stage whisper made her sister roll her eyes. 'A: because I still don't know for sure. I'm going up to Harley Street soon to see Mummy's doctor. And B: I've barely seen you, and when I do its all murder, murder, murder.' She shuddered. 'I know you started all this for all the best reasons but... Ach, it's positively ghoulish.'

'Perhaps it is,' said Bunch. She knew Dodo had a point. It was hardly a pastime to be listed in Debrett's. She could not really admit that she had gained a sense of achievement in the unearthing of lurid facts, and she could now appreciate why a person such as Wright spent so many years pursing a Scotland Yard career and, not for the first time, wished she had been accorded the same opportunities as a man. 'Are you all right, Dodo?' she said. 'Shouldn't you be resting or something?'

'I'm not exactly dancing a Paso Doble,' her sister replied. 'Don't fuss. It doesn't suit you.'

'Yes, but—'

'Do not fuss, Bunch.'

'We have a lead.' Wright strode into the room, shrugging on his coat. 'Not far away.'

'Oh,' said Bunch, 'so you are off then?'

'I will, yes. My driver is bringing the car round.' He looked her up and down. 'You might want to change. It's a cold evening.'

❧TWENTY-ONE❧

'Where are we going?' Bunch asked as the Chief Inspector slid into the Wolseley beside her. SPC Dyer sat behind the wheel.

'We've received information that concerns an old disused church. Does that mean anything to you?' Wright replied.

Bunch grinned at the brief temptation to lighten his sombre mood. 'Yes,' she said, 'you want Old Church Lane.'

'That's what I thought. I'm expecting reinforcements to meet us there.' He grinned back and gestured at the road. 'Botting is bringing them and I shall have to rely on you and Dyer to show me the way.'

'With pleasure.' Bunch leaned forward. 'Dyer, take the road running from the village toward Hascombe Wood. I'll tell you where to turn.'

'Yes, Ma'am.'

'You said you called for back-up? Are you expecting trouble?' she asked.

'Not necessarily. Our information is that the church had been used as some sort of depot. Apparently it's a place where nobody is likely to go, especially in this weather. We've received a report of activity going on some weeks ago, but nothing since the snow. I fully expect it to be deserted but we do need to check it out.'

'If anyone was there it might not have been too obvious,' she said. 'Old Church Lane is a dead end.'

'I gather someone had put about a rumour that it's used as a Ministry listening post,' he said. 'Botting tells me there were even warning signs set up. It's brazen but effective; no one was likely to question it when so many places are being commandeered. '

'Isn't it a bit far inland for a listening post?' She frowned. 'I don't go that way often, haven't since before it snowed, but it is on our estate so I would have thought Daddy might have said something about it to me.'

Wright sighed, taking off his hat and running a hand through his hair. 'Well, there's the thing: it hasn't been claimed by anyone. Not the RAF, Army nor WD.'

Bunch was aware from his tone that such an apparent contradiction had to be significant, but she was jiggered if she knew why or what. She supposed she should feel flattered that he assumed her au-fait with such things, but all it did was make her feel vaguely annoyed because she had to prompt explanations like some dim-witted child. 'Well?' she demanded.

'Well what?'

'You obvious have a codicil. You say it's been logged as a site without official ownership. What does that mean? Are we going to discover that it has been commandeered by some top secret government department?'

'If it belongs to any of *those* chaps they would have been sending men in black hats to warn us off.'

'They do that?'

'Oh yes.' He laughed without humour. 'Oh yes. They're very protective. You wonder sometimes whose side they're on. In this case, it probably means someone has altered records somewhere in Whitehall.'

'Oh.' She looked away, peering out of the window into a darkness barely dented by the Blackout headlamps, as she digested the possibilities. 'Spies?' she said at last.

'Villains,' Wright replied.

'Surely the ministries would know better than… I mean, times are hard but would they employ someone with a criminal record?'

He shook his head. 'No they wouldn't and they don't, officially. But I've seen it all before. Some young lass in an office has a beau walking on the shadier side of legal. She's persuaded to *just add this place onto the list. It won't hurt anyone.* And Bob's your uncle. It seems the bigger London gangs are better organised than any ministry department. It's mostly because they bend to contingency, you see, and romancing some unthinking young secretary is one of their ways. '

'You're very sure it's a woman,' she said.

He shrugged. 'Only because most of the clerks these days are woman and most of the villains are chaps.'

'I suppose you're right.' Bunch nodded uncertainly. The moon was hiding beyond a thick cloud layer, and even the remains of the snow, which had shrunk to greying banks and shoals, gave off scant reflected light. She peered out, trying to identify where they were. After a few moments she said, 'Old Church Lane is just a bit further. Ah … stop. Here we are, just here.'

Dyer slewed to a halt at what was little more than a gap in the hedge. The lane could barely have been given the dignity of being termed a cart track. Skeleton branches hung over it forming a dark cave-like entrance into a tunnel of dense trees. A few yards in, a glimmer of a torch flickered toward them.

'Sir?' Stan Botting loomed out of the darkness, followed by two more constables. He stopped by the car and bent to speak through the window that Wright had wound down. 'Somethin'' had driven up there. A van,' he said, 'and a car.'

'Still up there?' Wright asked.

'The van is, sir. The car came back out yesterday morning, we 'eard. The tyre marks are all over the snow, but tis pelled off a mite.'

Wright glanced at Bunch. She could not see his expression in the shadows but the spread of his hands said it all. 'Washed away,' she said.

'I shall get the hang of the local lingo eventually. All right, Botting.' He looked at the other constables waiting in the lane. One was an elderly war-reserve constable, older than Wright by more than decade or more. 'Just three of you?' Wright demanded.

'Yes, sir. Fer now.'

'Are you armed?'

'No, sir.' Botting shifted uncomfortably. 'We haven't been issued any weapons as yet.'

'Of course you haven't.' He sighed. 'You know, if Hitler ever does invade we are doomed.'

'We can send for the guard unit at the air field,' said Botting. 'It'd take a while, though.'

Wright shook his head. 'Time is running out. Guest must know we are looking for him by now. Is there any other way up to this church?'

'Across the fields obviously, but no other roads,' Bunch said.

'Then we have only one plan of action. Move in on this church and see what we can see.' He drew a revolver from his pocket and checked it over. 'Come on, men.' He grasped Bunch's arm. 'I will leave you here with Dyer. It will be warmer in the car.'

'You'll do no such thing.'

'These men are dangerous, if they are still here.' He tapped the gun. 'I'm not going to be able to watch over you.'

'Did I ask you to?' She got out of the car before he could stop her and took a few steps into the wooded tunnel. 'This is my land. You can't really stop me.'

Wright hesitated for a moment, aware that all eyes were on him. 'In that case keep to the rear,' he grunted. 'There have been enough deaths in this neighbourhood. I don't want to find myself explaining yours to the Commissioner.'

With much of the ground now free of semi-melted snow banks, the track was thick with red Sussex clay that dragged and sucked noisily at their boots. Bunch hurried in Wright's wake, taking in gulps of frozen air that smelled of cold and damp earth, and trying not to stumble too often on ruts and roots hiding in the dark. The few short minutes it took them to reach the low square stone chapel felt far longer.

Wright stood back amongst the trees and watched the site for a full minute. Deep in the woodland the wind was light and little was moving. A fox barked some distance off. Closer in, a tawny owl called its mate and was answered with high *kee-wik's*. Otherwise all was quiet.

Bunch listened and felt the hair on her scalp prickle in nervous anticipation. The sounds of war had been an almost a nightly lullaby since before the New Year, that depressingly regular *crump, crump* away toward the coast. Its absence disturbed her.

She had not been to this place for a long while but it was still familiar enough that she could fill in from memory the details masked by the deep night. The deconsecrated ruin of the ancient church would be half-obscured by the huge darker mass of obligatory yew trees. She recalled that a few grave markers and sarcophagi emerged at intervals from the tangle of brambles and scrub, and the whole site was encircled by the remains of a boundary wall. The church building itself was smaller than that which currently served the village, and far older. It was a low build of pale-yellow sandstone and granite, with arched windows that punctuated the longest wall.

Just visible in the feeble light of her torch were tyre tracks leading through a gap in the graveyard wall where a lych gate had once stood. Even the moonless night could not hide the fact that the church porch was no longer there, or that the doorway was hacked and scarred into a gaping black hole some ten feet wide and about twice as high.

'Seems like a lot of new damage,' Bunch whispered. 'Not bombs, I'm certain. We've had no strays this close to Perringham. It looks to be recent demolition. I know people need building materials for repairs and such like but who would do this to a church?' She tutted a little more loudly than she intended and the echoes rattled louder than a cracking branch. They all froze but nothing stirred amongst the ruins.

'It may not be what you think,' said Wright. 'It's possible that builders had paid the parish for repair materials. That happens a lot up around the docks.'

'I doubt it. I would have heard,' she whispered. 'The church was relatively intact when I was last here. It's deconsecrated, I know, but I still can't imagine anyone stealing stone from it. Nevertheless, there are all these wheel tracks yet I can't see signs of any vehicles.'

Wright nodded, glancing back at the waiting constables. 'We may have been led on a wild goose chase, after all. I doubt our targets would stay here for long, not now we're on to them, and not in this weather. However, we shall proceed carefully and hope for the best.' He raised his voice enough to carry to the officers behind him. 'All right, let's move in.' He waved Botting and the older officer through to the left of the building.

'What about us?' said Bunch.

'I, not we,' he corrected. 'Stay here until we know the building is as empty as it looks. Stay right here. That is an order.'

She could not make out his expression but imagined it being pretty grim. She did not reply. Bunch felt he was being impossible and she was not going to waste breath on pointing out that she was not some junior clerk he could order around. Wright had already moved forward with Dyer and the third constable and, leaving a gap of a few yards, she could do nothing but seethe silently and follow.

The dark within the abandoned church was shadowless.

Bunch paused at the entrance to allow her eyes to adjust. A strong smell of diesel oil, dampness and decay emanated through the open frontage, all the stronger for being an harsh odour after the fragrance of tree and root.

It quickly became apparent why the wall and doors had been demolished. Inside, taking up the space normally occupied by pews, was a large van. Wright signalled PC Dyer to go left whilst he and the other constable stepped to the right of the vehicle. Bunch padded along behind, sliding her feet cautiously to avoid misstepping amongst the debris, and almost collided with Wright when he stopped suddenly by the cab. He frowned at her and touched a finger to his lips then placed his hand on the vehicle's bonnet. Bunch did not need to ask why. The air was redolent with the van's hot-oil stink that spoke of recent use. Yet there was no sign of whoever might have driven it.

Even derelict and devoid of all the trappings that inspired devotional awe, the church's interior still possessed an air of reverence. Standing close to the police inspector Bunch could hear his breaths, drawn deep and slow as he reached up to grasp the van's door handle; she heard the scrape of a constable's boot on the stone flags; heard the flat click and metallic whine of the cooling engine. She looked up at the van's window, somehow anticipating the engine's howl of protest before it burst into life.

The vehicle lurched forward yanking the Chief Inspector off his feet and brushing Bunch aside as easily as a horse's tail flicking away bothersome insects. She sprawled backwards, arms flailing, finding nothing to prevent her hitting the stone floor, shoulder first. Her head struck the cold damp surface and she lay for a moment struggling to regain the breath so forcibly expelled. Men were shouting; a deafening roar rattled in her skull, then a gun-shot and a second.

Bunch hauled herself to her feet by sheer instinct and stared after the van's fast vanishing tail lights. The vague outlines of policemen rushing after it faltered and came to a halt. She heard muffled voices; and then she realised, as her senses came back into focus, that Wright was standing just a few feet away, exhorting his men to *keep after it!* Then he was speaking to her in angry tones but to Bunch it seemed as if from afar, despite his taking her by the shoulders and staring into her face. Sound gradually crystallised, the powdery noise reforming into words.

'Bunch? Rose? Are you hurt?'

She felt the back of her head and grimaced at the sizeable egg already rising there. 'Yes, I think—' There was a crashing outside the church followed by whistles being blown. Wright looked toward the exposed frontage. 'Go,' Bunch said, 'they are getting away. Go after them.'

'I shall send someone back for you.' He gave her shoulders a squeeze. 'Wait here.' He loped off, leaving her standing in an empty space.

It took Bunch several moments to fully gather herself. It was her second brush with danger recently. She felt shaky. Since whoever had been hiding here now knew for certain that the police were aware of the hideout, he was probably on the road heading to London, Bunch decided a little light would not go amiss. She fumbled for her torch and played the small beam around the space. The pews, screens and other accoutrements of worship had been removed to the new parish church after the congregation had moved on, and the empty shell of the building had been a place fit for children's games by day and lovers' trysts by night, at least before the war. Shapes near the church walls were little more than piles of rubble and detritus. She looked over them and saw nothing beyond evidence of loading and unloading: discarded boxes and a pile of bloody muslin. There was nothing of a personal nature, not a sign that anyone had been here for more than a few hours at a time.

Bunch carefully worked her way around the interior until she came to the vestry door. She shouldered open the half-rotten wood, shining her torch all around the space before daring to step inside. The thing that struck her first was warmth. Not the heat of spring but it was substantially warmer than the church itself. A small unlit paraffin heater stood in the centre of the room, with a desk to one side of it and to the other a small camp bed made up in military style. She saw no personal items, suggesting it was only infrequently occupied.

In the corner of the room she noticed a tall cupboard with a large hasp locked firmly across the door's opening edge. She grabbed the padlock and gave it a quick jerk, more in hope than expectation, and allowed it to fall back, still firmly locked. There had to be a way to break it open. She yanked open one of the lower drawers and stirred amongst the junk with a reluctant hand before coming up with a long, paint-spattered screwdriver. *Perfect.* Bunch put the torch on top of the desk and rammed the blade of the tool behind the hasp, shifted her grip to get the best purchase, and yanked sharply. She adjusted the screwdriver and levered again. The wood, weakened with age that held little substance to resist, released its hold.

Inside the wardrobe, away from scavenging rodents, was a small camping stove along with a kettle, soiled mugs and plates, tins of MOD-issue meat and condensed milk, a pack of tea – and a decidedly civilian BSA .22 rifle along with a box of cartridges. She picked up one of the shells and examined it in the torch light, recognising the make from ten days and a lifetime ago, found lying close to her friend's corpse.

'Go ahead and pick it up. The rifle. Yer dabs on there will go down a treat.' The voice was steady, matter of fact. Bunch had not heard him enter the room, nor realised she was reaching for the weapon. She let her hand drop to her side.

'Mr Guest. I would say it's a pleasure but that would be an obvious lie.' She tightened her jaw and pulled her fists close against her thighs. She was struggling to control a head-swimming sensation of sheer panic that was gripping at her skull, and to keep all of that from showing to the killer standing a few paces away. The pressure behind her eyes relented and she risked nodding at the revolver in his gloved hand. 'Is that entirely necessary, Mr Guest?' she said, and wondered at how her voice sounded so normal.

'Yeah, it is.' He drew his lips back wide enough to reveal several gold teeth glittering in the feeble torch light.

She jerked her head toward the open cupboard. 'Was that the gun used to murder Jonathan Frampton?' She might have been talking about the weather, or feeding the horses, for all the emotion she permitted herself – a complete contradiction to the trembling sensations she felt in her clenched hands and watery knees.

'Now then, Miss Courtney ... Rose, we 'ave met before, you know. You've bin a regular Mrs Bradley pokin' about in stuff, but yer no good at it. Should leave it to the cops, cos we all know that

Frampton bloke shot 'imself,' said Guest. 'The good Major saw that posh gun down in the woods, 'isself.'

'How do you know that?'

'Common knowledge,' he drawled.

'I wouldn't think the villagers would talk to you,' she said. 'You being an outsider.'

'What? Me? I heard it from Livvy—' He smirked. 'That's Olivia to you.'

Bunch shrugged. 'Of course, except—' She clamped her lips closed to stop her instinctive need to put this man down. *What does he think I don't know? That he's related to that ghastly woman? Stupid thing to say. He knows Jonny was already dead from a .22, and that the shotgun was used to ... it took out the back of his head.* She swallowed hard as the murder scene flashed through her memory. *He knows it better than anyone. Probably his finger on those triggers, perhaps...* 'What now?'

'You know the way to Tinsley's gaff from here?'

'Yes.'

'Then we walk.'

'It's a fair distance.'

'All the more reason to get goin' straightaway.' He opened a drawer in the desk and produced a pair of handcuffs. 'Put 'em on.'

Bunch snapped one piece around her right wrist and the other around her left, not taking her gaze from the man's face. 'The police won't be long,' she said. 'Hadn't you better run instead of wasting time with me?'

'An' 'ave you yellin' yer 'ead off?' Guest grabbed a length of rope and expertly fashioned it into a noose, slinging it over her head. He motioned her to step away from the cupboard. Jerking on the rope to stop Bunch walking off too far, he grabbed the box of cartridges, stuffing them in a pocket, and slung the tattered webbing strap of the rifle over his shoulder. 'No sense leavin' the cops with a get out.' He gestured to the door 'Ladies first.'

Bunch stepped forward, slowly at first, in the hope that Wright would return quickly.

'Don't 'ang about,' said Guest. 'Out through the back. It ain't locked in case you're wonderin'. No point when arf the front's missin'.' He flicked the rope like a ploughman urging his team forward. 'Hop to it now, Rosie, and keep that torch of yours on your feet. No flashing it all over the shop for your mates to see.'

They slipped out of the rear door and crossed the churchyard, following the glow-worm beam of her pocket torch. Bunch could hear raised voices in the distance, perhaps as far away as the road. It was difficult to tell; sounds carried differently at night, she had always thought. She slowed again hoping that Wright or Botting, or one of the other constables, or even the green recruit, Dyer, would come back for her. Another flick of the rope against her back made her pick up her pace. She wondered if she could double back and lead her captor toward the police officers, and veered right as she reached the wall, tripping over the straggles of bramble snaking out across the track.

Guest hauled on the tether choking off her throat so that she gagged, struggling for air, eyes watering. 'Straight on,' Guest snarled. 'I ain't daft.'

'I was looking for a break in the wall,' Bunch croaked.

'Don't bovver. Climb over.'

'All right.' It was not a high wall but taxing to traverse with her hands linked together. She sat on the top and swung her legs over. The rough stones caught at her Land Army fatigues that she wore from habit. *Or I'd be scratched to pieces*, she thought. She jumped down into deeper remnants of snow on the far side and waited for Guest to repeat the manoeuvre, keeping the torch shining on her own feet rather than his; she saw no point in helping him out.

'I thought you was a lady,' he said. 'But 'avin' no light's not goin' to 'old me up. I spend half me life in the dark. Been eatin' me carrots, I 'ave. How far is it, do you reckon?'

'A mile or so. Over half an hour's walk in the dark, at least.'

He glanced back at the church. 'Move. Quickest route. I've bin around here enough to know if you start playin' silly buggers.'

Bunch nodded and started off through the wood. It was easy terrain to traverse despite the dark, compared with overgrown headlands. She paused twice to gain her bearings and earned a reprimand from the gunman. It took ten minutes of trudging to reach the fields on the far side of the wood. Faint light from the now thinning cloud showed a snowy blanket, more-or-less unsullied despite the rain, with only the tips of plough ridges poking through here and there.

'Keep to the hedges,' Guest muttered.

'It will take longer,' she replied.

'Better cover and less tracks. Now shift yourself.'

Bunch started around the edge of the field, heading for the gate on the further side. The wind blew cold but it was more than chill that had her shivering. They soon reached the small coppice that surrounded a dew pond below the next rise. From there it was a almost a straight route following the line of hedges to Banyard Manor in one direction – and to the Jenners' cottages in the other. She paused, wondering if she should risk misleading him. Her blind fear had passed and logic returned, which she felt was a mixed blessing, and the flow of adrenaline was a cushion against the situation. She began to turn to the cottages.

Guest grabbed her arm and gave her a shove toward the manor. 'Move that way,' he growled. 'Don't get smart.'

With that clear-headed logic she knew that the man walking behind her was a multiple killer; he was a man who had killed three people in the past two weeks, or had ordered those killings to be carried out. She had no reason to believe he would not kill her also once they reached the manor. *Why am I still alive?* she wondered. 'Why do you need me?' she eventually asked. 'You must know where we are.'

'Insurance,' he said. 'In case the cops're waitin' for me. But you're still dispensable, in case yer wonderin'. So shut yer mouth and walk.'

~TWENTY-TWO~

Bunch and her captor approached Banyard Manor from the west, crossing old sheep meadows, now ordered under the plough by the Ministry, to where the ground suddenly fell away to the ha-ha. The gulley was filled with driven snow, hiding the barrier's flint wall. To the right was an iron kiss-gate guarding the steps leading to the uninterrupted lawns at the rear of the Manor. In normal times it would have been impossible to cross unseen. Blackout changed all of that; nobody would dream of pulling the curtains aside before dawn.

Bunch limped across the veranda with Guest close on her heels. They stood in the shelter of the building for a long moment listening to the faint jingle of dance music filtering through closed windows and doors and their thick curtains. She could not hear voices. Dinner would be over by now and Bunch could imagine Barty and Olivia seated close to the fireside, sipping coffee, reading perhaps, with neither of them willing to make conversation for its own sake. They were not her favourite people but she would welcome standing in front of them there and then if it meant getting rid of her captor.

She wondered if she could shout loud enough, or long enough, to attract their attention before the rope in Guest's hand was yanked back hard against her larynx. She glanced sidelong and saw a glitter in those shadowed eyes that told her he was watching her intently. *Reptile,* she thought. *He'd shoot me in a trice if he didn't think he has a use for me. I'd be dead already. Big question is, when does that value run out?* She licked at her lips, dry with fear and cracked with cold.

'I gotta talk to me big sis,' said Guest, 'and yer goin' to stay quiet. Not a bleedin' word.'

Sis? 'Sister?' She pleaded her ignorance once again, hoping to knock him off balance with idle chatter.

'Yeah.' He grinned. 'Nice to get t'visit her now an' then. She's got a nice gaff. Now shut yer mouth.' He tugged the rope for silence and examined the windows though narrowed eyes.

'Why not let me go?' she whispered. 'You can find your own way now.'

'And have yer copper mate creepin' up on me? Like I said, a drop of insurance.' He regarded her with some amusement and came close, tugging the rope tighter still and bringing the barrel of the pistol up under her chin. 'Be glad of it, sweetheart. You wouldn't like the alternative.' His moist sour breath trickled across her cheeks and into her nostrils. Bunch nodded, forcing herself to stay calm, not to give in to the shiver wavering deep in her chest. He turned her toward a door that led into the house. 'Remember, keep yer mouth shut an' do what yer told.' She fumbled the door open, pushed past the drapes, and they entered the large drawing room. The music was barely louder, drifting in from the another room.

The Tinsleys, like everyone else, saved fuel by heating smaller rooms for their daily use, though the fire blazing in the hearth was hardly stinted. Barty dropped his newspaper at their sudden entry, looking as if to rise until he spotted the pistol. Olivia seemed no less surprised although there was no hint of fear in her features, only annoyance.

'Allo, sis.' Guest said.

Bunch felt a hand push on her back and she sprawled across the Turkish rug to fall at Olivia's feet. Air was punched from her lungs and the noose tightened just that little more making it difficult to suck in breath.

'What in hell—' Tinsley used the flurry of movement to finally get to his feet and take a single stride. Bunch heard the click of the gun readying for use, but she dared not move her hands to her neck to slacken the rope. She could only gasp for air and wait, staring at Tinsley's soft patent pumps a yard from her face.

'Sit down,' said Guest. 'No. That one.' He waved the weapon at the upright chair. 'Livvy. Tie him up.'

'I beg your pardon?'

'You 'eard. Tie 'im up!'

'What with?'

Guest pitched the end Bunch's tether onto the rug. 'Plenty o' stuff there, you daft bint.'

'You are impossible, Perc.' Olivia knelt to ease the tightened noose and slipped the rope free.

With the sudden unfettering Bunch's head dropped back to the rug with a thump. She suppressed a heartfelt ouch, and resisted the temptation for more than a brief rub at the sores developing around her neck. She eased herself up to where she could see most of the room; otherwise she kept as quiet and static as she was able, waiting and watching for an opportunity to run.

'What in hell are you doing, woman?' Tinsley barked as Olivia attempted to lasso the noose around his wrists. 'And what is this lout doing here?'

'Sit still, *Bar-thol-ee-mew*.' Guest swung the rifle round and rested it on his forearm, barrel snouting in the general direction of Tinsley's stomach. He cocked it, the slow deliberate click louder than the longcase clock clunking away in the corner. Tinsley froze, his face leached of all colour. 'That's better, me old mate. Hands round the back an' keep quiet, an' I'll be gone in no time.'

Tinsley sat heavily in the straight-backed chair glowering whilst his wife pulled the rope tight around his wrists and bound him firmly in place. 'When I told you never to come back I bloody well meant it,' he snarled. 'Up to no good, I see. You should stay in the docks with the rest of the scum. Not fair on Olivia, you turning up like this.'

'Our Livvy ain't worried, are you, pet? Never been one to look a gift 'orse.'

'More like bloody Greeks bearing gifts,' Tinsley replied sourly.

'Oh, for gawd's sake. Find something to stuff in that gob of his, Livvy. That regimental rag'll do for starters.' He turned away as Olivia did as she was told, removing Tinsley's tie to gag him.

'You've done it now, Perc,' said Olivia. 'Police will be all over this place when they realise she's missing.'

'Police are goin' to be all over it now, anyway,' he replied. 'A blind cat could follow the tracks we made gettin' here.'

'The police will have road blocks set up,' said Bunch without thinking. 'You won't even reach Billingshurst.' Guest snarled an unintelligible reply and kicked out at her, the soles of his Blakey-tipped boots impacting on her ribs. Pain blossomed through her chest, radiating to head and limbs as an aftershock. She drew a sharp breath and regretted it in the same instant. She recognised the signs from riding falls: a broken rib? Or perhaps two? She clenched her teeth against the pain, stopping the impulse to curse him. *Damned upstart, get back under whatever stone you crawled from.*

'Then why did you bring her here?' Olivia's voice rose to a screech. 'You're a bloody idiot!'

'Not idiot enough not to make sure the evidence don't lead to me,' he snarled. 'Not like you an' yer 'abits.'

Olivia stared at him for a moment. 'What are you saying?'

Guest tapped his nose, a malicious grin slicing his lean face in two. 'Buying stuff locally. Not a good plan.'

'I needed a lift,' she whined. 'I lost my son!'

'So did... What was his name? Frampton?'

'Shut your mouth.' Olivia moved near to him so that the gun tip was close to her own nose. 'I have stuff on you as well.'

'Like this one?' He lifted the rifle by a fraction. 'Hearsay. Never touched this thing without gloves, meself. But you did.'

Slow dawning crept across Olivia's features as she digested the implication. 'Bastard,' she muttered. 'You little bastard.'

'Ain't we all, sis,' he replied cheerfully. 'At least you knows who yer dad was. Rest of us 'ad to guess.'

Olivia raised her hand as if to slap him.

Guest rapped her wrist with the rifle barrel, and she staggered back a few steps. 'Won't change nuffink,' said Guest. 'Still got yer dabs. You was there, so yer an *ack-ses-ery* as well, so to speak. Not to mention yer hoarding.' He grinned at Tinsley. 'His nibs's got some explainin' to do with all that stuff in yer cellar.'

Olivia rubbed at her wrist and glared at her sibling. 'What am I meant to do now?'

'Scarper,' he replied. 'Sharpish.'

'What about these two?' She waved at her husband. 'He won't say a lot. Too much to lose, but her...' She looked down at Bunch. 'She's never anything but trouble, just like the rest of her insufferable family. I don't need her dragging me through the mire. I wish I'd never let you stay that weekend. George knew you were up to no good, and so did the Frampton boy. God knows what George told that stupid wife of his.'

'Keep yer hair on. I ain't stayin' and nor is she. All we needs is yer motor and we'll both be out of 'ere.'

'And me?' Olivia asked.

Guest grinned, glancing around the room with an exaggerated thoughtfulness. 'Wot about you?'

'I'm coming with you. I've had it with this place. Besides, I'll be arrested, for sure. Never mind murder, they'll be hanging black marketeers next. Did you know that?'

'I did. You never knows what's down the road do ya, Livvy? Now: keys. I'll take that shooting brake. The Bentley's nice but she's 'eavy on the old juice.'

'All right, all right.' Olivia tugged at the ropes holding her husband and grunted in satisfaction. 'What about her?'

'She's insurance.' He gave Bunch another kick. 'On yer feet, sweetheart. We've got a long drive in the dark an' I wanna be gone before yer rozzer mate turns up.'

Bunch rose slowly and awkwardly due to handcuffed wrists and the aching in her side. She glanced at Guest, rifle now rested over his arm, the pistol back in his right hand. The same pistol that had been pointed at her once before, and had injured Roger. She pressed down a surge of anger. This man was the brute who had shot her lovely dog just because he could. A lunatic. A dangerous man. One responsible for three bodies – bodies which she had seen with her own eyes. That tally kept coming back to her, whichever way she steered her thoughts. *God knows how many people this monster has done away with. Three at least and I'll be the fourth. He won't bat an eye over me.*

He noticed her staring and chuckled, a throaty rattle of cigarettes and whisky. He waggled the pistol and winked. 'No good long distance, but it works better than a rifle close up. An' we're gonna be real close and comfy for a few hours. Now move yer selves, ladies. Yer lookin' at a man in a hurry.'

The three of them hurried through to the rear vestibule and Olivia collected a coat and boots before grabbing the keys to the Ford. She threw the keys to her brother before rushing to open the garage's double doors.

Guest opened the rear passenger door. 'In,' he said and gave Bunch a shove forward. 'Livvy?' He handed his sister a small key. 'Cuff her to the dog grille.'

Olivia crammed into the back seat and fumbled to unlock the

cuff from Bunch's right wrist. Close to, Bunch could see Olivia's eyes struggling to focus; her hands trembled as she slotted the restraints through the metal grille dividing rear seat from the space at the back of the vehicle, a space normally reserved for hunting dogs. *Drink*, Bunch wondered, *or drugs? Or both?*

Bunch glanced at Guest, who was making himself comfortable behind the wheel. He still had the guns but now his back was to her. That could be her chance as Olivia was clearly not quite in control of herself.

Olivia dug her in the side, sneering at Bunch's grunt of pain. 'You and your dreary little sister should have gone with your precious father,' she said. 'You'd be half way to Singapore and none the wiser.' She snapped the handcuff shut and her smile widened. She stepped back and shut the door with a bang. Too late for Bunch to make her escape.

'Fer fuck's sake,' Guest hissed. 'Let the whole 'ouse know yer takin' the car, won't cha.' He gently tossed the rifle onto the passenger seat. 'Well, get in if yer comin',' he said to Olivia. 'Be quick. If I get caught yer in deep shit, too, cos I won't go down on me own. Shtumm it sis, if you don't want the Old Bill t'know about that tart.'

Olivia slid into the passenger seat and closed the door, moving the rifle to the foot-well. 'We should go,' she said. 'Not the time for raking over old news.'

'You didn't kill three people,' Bunch murmured. 'You needn't be arrested for his crimes.'

Guest looked over his shoulder at her and laughed sharply. 'No? She only shot one of them. 'Ow else d'ya think she got her mitts on that .22?'

The horrible truth that she had been pushing away ever since they left the church finally sank in and Bunch felt her head swim little as her adrenalin level rose. 'Oh, Olivia, it was you that shot Jonny.'

'Bingo.' Guest gurgled a throaty laugh.

Bunch leaned forward as far as her shackle would allow and shouted, 'Why Jonny? He was George's best friend!'

'He was a nothing.' Olivia twisted back toward Bunch, almost nose to nose. 'He seduced my boy. He was a monster!'

Staring at Olivia's face, at that malignant glimmer of malice, made Bunch realise how much the woman had hated Jonathan Frampton. 'He did no such thing,' she replied.

'No?' Olivia grabbed the rifle and struggled to bring it around toward Bunch.

Guest was quicker. He pulled it from her grasp, laughing still. 'Now then, I don't wanna get plugged just cos yer posh lads were fruits.' He slid out of his seat, with both weapons now in his grasp. 'I suggest you both be quiet. I don't want to have to settle you fer good, if you get me meanin'. Livvy, out. Yer drivin'.'

'Me?' The woman glanced at the steering wheel as if it were totally alien.

'You can't be trusted with this. I ain't 'avin a repeat of last time. Pluggin' Frampton was what got us all in this bleedin' mess.'

'You shot him,' Bunch shouted 'You shot Jonny—'

'Shut yer fuckin' cake 'ole.' Guest retorted. 'And you, behind the bloody wheel. Now! Cos if I leave you behind you ain't gonna be breathin'.'

His was not an idle threat, Bunch had no doubt on that score. Olivia might have taken a life through hate – and insanity – but Percy Guest was a cold-blooded killer born of a hard life and the wrong paths chosen. Olivia tottered around to the driver's side, and slipped in behind the wheel. Guest nodded at her compliance and took his seat on the passenger side.

'Go,' he snapped.

Olivia started the engine, eased the car into the driveway and headed to the road. The dirty-pale snow-drifts lining the road should have been as plain as airfield lights now the clouds had thinned, but the meagre beams slanting from cowled headlights barely stretched the width of the vehicle and little more than a car's length ahead of them. Bunch knew it was not far to the road, even driving at Blackout speeds.

Bunch stared at the top of Olivia's head visible over the back of the driver's seat. That woman had killed Jonathan Frampton. Bunch wished she had known that before she was cuffed to the grille, when Olivia was close enough to touch, gun or no gun. She would have scratched the woman's eyes out. She wished she could as easily tear the smile from Guest's smirking face. He sat half-turned in his seat to watch her, the pistol resting on the leather ridge between them, its muzzle aimed directly at her head.

Bunch stared down at her lap. She rather not antagonise her captor; she saw no point doing so until some sort of plan of escape presented itself.

Without warning Bunch was jolted forward, the weight of her body tearing at her fettered arm. Olivia screamed; Guest uttered a string of oaths. Bunch glanced up to see a car, the word POLICE printed along its side in white lettering, coming toward them at speed.

The heavy Ford brake slid across the freezing slush, through the main gate, slewing out into the road that headed north. The vehicle was a solid machine, built for rough terrain. Bunch held on to the grille as tightly as the handcuffs would permit.

Olivia braced her foot solidly against the accelerator, judging by the screeching revs, her hands clutching the wheel, as if seeking solidity where there was none, as the car gathered speed.

Bunch peered at the road ahead, seeing nothing but dim glimpses of tarmac and dirty snow verges. Above it all she heard a final desperate howling.

'Livvyyyy!'

Olivia hauled at the steering wheel, stamping on the pedals, sending the car into a sideways skid, engine and driver screaming in unison. Bunch had a glimpse of glimmering lights and dark shapes – the other car; then more men, and then blackness.

❧TWENTY-THREE❧

The sitting room was warm with a small inferno roaring at one end. A day bed had been moved in for Bunch. Her left wrist, weighted down by a cast stretching up to her elbow, rested on a bolster. Her right arm was also swathed in bandages, as were her cut head and cracked ribs.

All in all, she reflected, *I'm a bit of a mess. And bored witless, but still breathing.*

The matron had not wanted her to leave the hospital on the same day her arm had been set but the family's nanny had arrived, conjured from retirement like a black-clad genii, and unexpectedly presenting Bunch with a much needed get-out-of-hospital free card by impressing the doctors with an impeccable Great War nursing record.

Bunch turned to see who was at the door and her head swam with the sudden movement. The painkillers she took every four hours were strong enough to combat the pain of multiple fractures but scrambled her brain. Dodo bustled in with comb, mirror and compact. 'We need to spruce you up, darling girl,' she cooed.

Nanny swept the things from Dodo's hand. 'Daphne, you should not be rushing around, not after all the shocks you have had. Now, sit down, Knapp will be bringing us tea shortly.' The tone was one both sisters recognised, and one obeyed without thinking, though Dodo raised exasperated hands. She flounced across to the chesterfield and plumped down next to her grandmother.

'Bunch is the invalid, not me,' Dodo whined. 'A powder compact is hardly heavy lifting.'

Beatrice reached over to pat her knee. 'Listen to Nanny, dearest. She knows what is best. You have had a stressful few days. You should be resting.'

'But—'

Beatrice tapped her knee a little harder with her forefinger. 'Listen to Nanny.'

'Still can't get over this sprog of yours,' said Bunch. 'What does Barty think about it?'

'Difficult to tell.' Dodo ran a hand over her belly and smiled a little sadly. 'He's still in shock over Olivia's death. The police have been all over him, poor chap. I don't think they quite believe he didn't know what she and Guest were up to. However, I think he's pleased about the baby. It gives him a little bright spot to concentrate on.'

'I can imagine,' Bunch remarked. 'He must feel perfectly dim, not seeing what his wife was up to, right under his nose.'

'Do give him some slack, Bunchy.' Dodo scowled at her. 'I was living there as well and I had no idea.'

'True. Steady on Nanny, I've got a cracked skull, you know.'

Nanny slapped her hand down and carried on tidying Bunch's hair. 'You have a concussion. Not the same thing at all. Now sit still.'

'How are you feeling?' Dodo asked her sister.

'Not wonderful. Bloody frustrated. I still can't remember a damned thing. We hit something,' she whispered. 'Then I was at the hospital. I remember that, but there are more things I should remember and...' She slapped her fist on the coverlet. 'I do so hate not knowing.'

'You may find out quite soon. We are expecting a visitor.'

Nanny set down the brush and started tugging at the pillows, propping Bunch up with an experienced arm.

'I can manage' Bunch muttered, and tried to hoist herself up and hissed at the pain shooting up from her ribs. Dodo leaped forward to help her sit, placing her arm around Bunch's back and brushing her ribcage, making Bunch squeak through gritted teeth. 'Stop fussing,' Bunch growled. 'Both of you. It's only making it worse. I need to move around a bit or I shall seize solid. It's my arm that's broken, for heaven's sake. Nothing at all wrong with my legs.'

'Not forgetting your ribs,' said Dodo.

'That sounds more like the Rose we know,' Beatrice observed.

Bunch touched at the bandage on her head. 'There was a

crash,' she said. 'Olivia and that Guest.' She sat up, and gasped at the agony in her chest. Nanny clasped her gently and rearranged the bolsters before gently lowering her back again. 'Probably shouldn't do that,' said Bunch. 'Just a bit sore.'

'With cracked ribs and the most ghastly bruises?' Nanny tutted. 'You will be all kinds of colours in a few days. The concussion doesn't help with recollections but I'm sure it will all come back eventually.'

'Not a lot wrong then. I thought for a moment I deserved to be in bed.'

'You are very lucky to be alive.'

'You are,' Dodo agreed. 'Botting told Cook that the whole left side of car was a mangled wreck.'

The hint of memory that had been playing through her mind on a loop made Bunch sigh. The grinding of metal, Olivia's scream abruptly ending, the metallic stickiness of blood spraying back over the seat. She said: 'I need some answers if I am going to rest. What happened to Guest?'

'You will have to ask William about that,' Dodo replied. 'He's out in the yard talking to Old Haynes. He'll be here in a minute. Been here on and off since dawn. Shall I go and call him?'

Dodo's face was eager, puppyish, and more animated than Bunch had seen for a long while, which she thought a rather trenchant emotion given that the young woman's mother-in-law had apparently met an ugly end. She took another look at Dodo's face and decided there was obviously a lot more to be told. Her sister was never good at concealing her thoughts and she was fairly humming with something or other.

'William? How very chummy.' Bunch adjusted the bolster beneath her cast to avoid looking at her sister. It had taken her a moment to even register who Dodo had meant, and using the Chief Inspector's Christian name was a surprise. Dodo barely knew him, as far as Bunch was aware, but then she had always got on better with people than did Bunch. *This apparent intimacy is the very devil when...* She stopped herself from following that line. She knew she could be waspish and Dodo did not deserve it. It was hardly going to matter, anyway. Once the case was a closed they would not be seeing Wright at all. 'I suppose we had better see if he has any news.' She tried to sound offhand but looking up she could see concern in Dodo's eyes; and was that a hint of guilt?

'He's nice,' Dodo said, carefully, 'and very helpful.' She was now on the defensive.

It seemed churlish to nip this new vigour in the bud but Bunch was really not feeling up to making nice. All of a sudden the only thing she really wanted to do was sleep. Her eyelids felt heavy in sympathy with the rest of her body. 'I must look an awful drudge,' she mumbled. 'Not fit for anyone to see.'

'Which is why I am trying to make you presentable,' said Nanny.

Bunch dodged away from the brush Nanny was again attempting to pull through the hair, the brush held awkwardly in crooked and arthritic hands. She seemed to be pulling out more hair than she smoothed. 'Leave it, Nanny. Please.'

Her nemesis sighed and carried on plumping and straightening the pillows.

'He won't mind. He saw you at your worst, when you were unconscious. He was terribly worried. He insisted on getting you to hospital himself. I'll go and get him, shall I?' Dodo gave the fire in the grate a quick prod, added a log for good measure, and left, closing the door softly.

The room was warm and sleep still beckoned but Bunch wanted details. She eased herself a little higher on the daybed and pulled the shawl awkwardly around her shoulders.

Voices outside in the corridor made her look toward the door expectantly.

Dodo strolled in, tipping Bunch a saucy wink. 'Someone to see you, darling.'

Wright sidled in behind her, looking awkward. 'Miss Courtney, are you feeling all right?' he said.

That question again. Bunch had a feeling it was one she would be hearing often in the next few days, or even weeks. 'Yes. I'm fine. Come and sit down, Chief Inspector.'

'I'm glad to hear it. You gave us such a fright – and I have told you before, it's William.'

'William. It sounds awfully formal. What do people usually call you? Bill?' Wright shrugged which gave Bunch the idea he was not pleased with the sobriquet.

'Wilbur,' he muttered after a pause. 'My friends call me

Wilbur, after the plane chap.'

'Wilbur,' she said. 'In that case I shall call you Will, if that is permitted?' Wright nodded

She returned his smile and wondered at the stilted mode of conversation. Somehow their easy acquaintance had changed and she didn't like it. 'Olivia was killed in the accident, I guessed that. It's perfectly terrible but I don't remember much else—' Bunch indicated the chair by the bed. 'Come and tell me all the ghoulish details.'

'Are you sure you are up to hearing all this?'

'Of course I am. Not knowing will simply keep me awake. How did you know where to find Guest? Was it a guess?'

'Partly,' Wright said. 'We knew you'd been taken across the countryside but we didn't have the men to pursue you directly. Botting thought the only place you could be going was Banyard Manor. We had just set up a road block when Guest made a run for it. We thought he'd be alone. We never imagined that he'd take you and Mrs Tinsley.'

Bunch snorted. 'Olivia was *not* taken. I think she'd have done for Guest herself if he'd tried to leave without her.'

'So we gathered from the Major. He seems at a loss. Never knew what was going on. We knew Olivia was such a sly creature.'

'That I can believe. He loathed Percy Guest. Olivia would have done her best to hide her brother's presence. Brother,' she grunted. 'Who'd have thought?'

'Guest has gone,' Wright replied. 'Out the moment his vehicle ploughed into our squad car, then he was off into the dark running like the weasel he is. Two of our lads gave chase but they lost him within fifty yards. That man has a charmed life.'

'More like a snake charmer,' said Bunch.

Wright shrugged. 'We shall have his picture up as a fugitive but he'll be in London by now and, once he's back on his home territory, we don't stand much chance of apprehending him. The whole of London is in turmoil and it will only get worse.'

Dodo stared. 'He's getting away with it? After all he did? Not just to me or even poor Olivia, and I really never thought that was something I would ever say. He's a murderer. Surely there will be a manhunt?'

'In peace time, yes there would be. But as I said, once a villain like Guest plunges into that labyrinth he is as good as invisible.' He sighed. 'Oh, we'll have his face on every Post Office notice board in every London borough. Nonetheless, I would be very surprised if we get so much as a sniff of him.'

'How very inconvenient.' Bunch waved her fingers a little feebly. Wright glanced at her, his brows knitted. 'Was it really all about the black market?'

'It was. The local boys somehow connected with Guest when he was here last year.'

'The Hayneses?' Bunch said.

'Yes. Among others.'

'How sad for his parents. They're good honest people.'

'With a shed full of contraband.'

'Really? Oh my.' Bunch gazed at the coverlet over her legs. A wave of fatigue washed through her. 'Did they know?'

'They must have suspected but I doubt they were deeply involved, beyond turning a blind eye to their son's doings. We shall question them officially, of course, but I can't see a prosecution coming out of it. The same will apply to Major Tinsley. He has been a fool, but an innocent one, we believe. He'll lose his place on the Magistrate's Bench, naturally, and that will be punishment enough.'

'Are you any closer to knowing what happened to the... I mean, how people were killed?'

'We've rounded up Crisp and a few others. The boy especially has been very helpful. Spilled the beans right and left.'

'Such as?'

'Such as Mary and her lieutenant being in the wrong place once too often. They were hunted down. They had seen the van and could maybe identify the men with it.'

'Including the one in the church?'

He nodded. 'Probably recognise Guest, as well. He was the driver, they say, that night. Guest tracked them down and executed them.'

'Good God.' She put her good hand to her mouth, swallowing hard. The thought of bright chipper Mary staring down the barrel of Guest's gun, as she had done herself, made her feel physically sick. She closed her eyes and waited for the room to stop shimmering.

'Are you feeling okay, Bunch?' Dodo turned to Wright. 'You shouldn't be bothering Bunch with all this. She's been through a perfectly beastly time.'

'What about Jonny? I know some of it…' Bunch whispered. 'Then perhaps I can sleep.'

'That we know less about.' Wright replied. 'We know he had evidence of stock thefts. More than half the flock had gone off the books in six months. He thought it was his father.'

'Did he, by Jove? Was he right? Is that why they were arguing in the wood that night?'

'It would appear that young Frampton had followed his father into the wood that evening and yes, they did argue.'

'Which was heard by Jenner?'

'By Jenner, and also by the people Saul Frampton had gone out to find. Saul Frampton is a difficult man but he's not a crook. If he was I think he would have been living a lot better than he has been. He had realised something was wrong and tried to discover what was happening because he also realised his name was on the paperwork.'

'It had to be someone dealing with the estate. Oh.' Bunch nodded slowly as realisation dawned. 'Pole?' she breathed. 'Len Pole? I never gave him a thought. He is a sly one.'

'Exactly. He's been taken into custody for fraud, amongst other things.'

'Who did kill Jonathan Frampton?' Beatrice demanded. 'I have heard several versions.'

'Most evidence pointed to Percival Guest but…' He paused, looking at Bunch. 'It was—'

'Olivia Tinsley.' Bunch frowned. She still found it strange to believe that Olivia had pulled the trigger. *Not Saul,* she thought. *Heaven forgive me, I thought the man capable of shooting his own son. But then who would have suspected Olivia?* 'I don't understand why she was in Hascombe Wood at that time of night,' she said finally.

'She wasn't. According to the Crisp lad, young Frampton tracked them back to the old church and confronted them there, and was shot through the head with a .22. at point-blank range. The post mortem results confirmed that.'

'But I found the cartridge with his body. In the wood.'

'Sheer coincidence. It's a common make. Probably poachers. I found some more cartridges there, myself, and they are not from the .22 that killed our three.'

'You are certain?' she said. 'Surely…'

'Crisp said he was outside when the shot came. The only people inside the church were Guest and Olivia Tinsley. Crisp maintains Mrs Tinsley was angry with Frampton. That she was screaming about something other than missing sheep. She kept calling the Frampton a tramp. Crisp didn't know what she meant.'

'But we do,' said Dodo. 'She blamed Jonathan for starting the relationship with George. Ridiculous of course.' She sighed. 'She was so strung up on appearances. In many ways it's not surprising she shot Jonathan.'

Bunch leaned back closing her eyes. 'It takes a pretty cold fish to cart him up to the woods and then go through the rigmarole of staging a suicide. You would think they'd have just buried him near the church. A lot less dangerous. Why take that risk?'

'Guest knew people would look for young Frampton so he hid the murder in plain sight, so to speak. In the unlikely event that we did suspect your friend had not committed suicide then the most likely murder suspect would be his father Saul. They did not reckon on you being the one to find him. Nor that you would go to quite such lengths to prove it was murder.

Bunch pulled her head back and gazed at him. 'You should not sound so surprised. I said I would prove it by the time the snow began to melt and thanks to you, I have.'

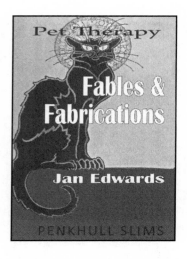

Fables & Fabrications

Fourteen tales of mystery, mirth and the macabre.

From the arctic wastes of Norway to a fun-laden evening at the fair, Jan Edwards leads us through a world where nothing is as it seems. Shape changers, ancient spirits that roam, and cats all play a crucial part in stories that unsettle and disturb the reader's perception.

Chosen from her back catalogue of horror and dark fantasy these stories are leavened by a sprinkle of verse, and have been collected for the first time in one volume.

Also from Penkhull Press by Jan Edwards

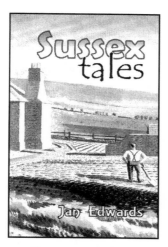

Sussex Tales

Winner of the Winchester Conference Slim Volume prize.

Jan Edwards' prize-winning *Sussex Tales* runs a witty and thought-provoking gamut of village events and of its more curious characters. From fanged ferrets to bulls in lead masks; ancient hand grenades to exploding ginger beer; cricketing dogs to wassailing orchards, *Sussex Tales* weaves traditional country wines and recipes, folklore and local dialect, into stories of a farming childhood in the vanished world of 1950s and 60s rural life.

'Superbly crafted … creating sub-plots as it unfolds with purpose and fluidity… Whether you're from Sussex or not, this is an appealing and often amusing collection of tales from a bygone age. I defy you not to like them.'
— Barry Lillie